She lifted up the blanket and gasped.

"What the hell?" She was in only her underwear and an oversized T-shirt, not her own. No bra. No dress. No stockings.

"You bastard! What did you do to me? Where are my clothes?"

He slowly pulled a chair up to the bedside and she scrambled to the farthest corner away from him, wrapping the sheet around her. His dark brown eyes invited confidences, but she wasn't in the mood for sharing.

"I'm not going to hurt you—believe me. If I'd wanted to hurt you, you wouldn't be talking to me now." He patted the pillow where her head had been. "Please, relax. Come back and we can talk."

"I'll stay right here, thank you." Jenna edged a leg over the side and eyed the door. If he made one move toward her, she'd drop the sheet and run like hell. She didn't care if she was half-naked; it would be better than being raped.

"Start talking," she said. "What happened after you hit me on the head?"

"I didn't hit you on the head."

"Right, and you didn't kill Tanya, and you didn't take her baby." She stared at him, her teeth clenched. She could bite him too, if she had to.

"Who's Tanya?"

"As if you didn't know, you murdering bastard."

Praise for Maggie Jaimeson

"Maggie Jaimeson's debut provides a page-turning, complex, suspense-filled story with passion and characters who will stay with you long after you finish the book."

~Roxanne St. Claire, New York Times bestselling author

~*~

"Beautifully flawed characters come to life in Maggie Jaimeson's thrilling debut."

~Jenna Bayley-Burke, Amazon bestselling author

~*~

"Against the backdrop of the magnificent Columbia Gorge, fall in love with Reed Adler—a true-blue ex-Marine, tough yet tender, willing to take on a truly chilling villain to save a little boy and a woman he's only just met. This one is going on my keeper list."

~Cathryn Cade, futuristic romance author

~*~

"*EXPENDABLE* is a heart-pounding thrill ride wrapped in a heartfelt romance that is guaranteed to keep you on the edge of your seat. A fantastic debut offering that has Maggie Jaimeson on my must-read list! Romantic suspense at its best!"

~Gemma Halliday, mystery and romantic suspense author

~*~

"Gripping and sexy as hell, *EXPENDABLE* is everything you want out of a book...only more. I loved it and am breathlessly waiting to see what Maggie Jaimeson will come up with next."

~Delilah Marvelle, historical romance author

Expendable

by

Maggie Jaimeson

This is a work of fiction. Names, characters, places, and incidents are either the product of the author's imagination or are used fictitiously, and any resemblance to actual persons living or dead, business establishments, events, or locales, is entirely coincidental.

Expendable

Contact Information: info@thewildrosepress.com

Cover Art by *Kim Mendoza*

The Wild Rose Press
PO Box 706
Adams Basin, NY 14410-0706
Visit us at www.thewildrosepress.com

Publishing History
First Crimson Rose Edition, 2011
Print ISBN 1-60154-961-X

Published in the United States of America

Dedication

To Jim—
my support, my confidant, my love.

Chapter One

Reed Adler lifted the mug of coffee to his lips and inhaled the earthy, robust aroma. This was his favorite time of day, early morning, sitting outside his cabin looking across the small meadow and into the trees. Filled with purple lupine and the first bursts of crimson Indian paintbrush, the meadow shimmered like an image in a kaleidoscope. A slender trail emerged from the forest into the clearing and then plunged back into the trees. Reed often enjoyed hiking the steep trail, which wound for several miles along the Sandy River. As the last vestiges of winter faded and soft flowers erupted along the trails, it was easy to forget the dangers present when hiking in the late spring and early summer. On his first mountain rescue last year, Reed had learned that rain and ice were still a very real danger. The deceivingly clear skies and bright sunshine tended to fool hikers into thinking it was warm outside.

He pulled up the collar on his Pendleton. "Protect yourself," he mumbled into his coffee. He took a sip and sighed as the crisp air of early summer mixed with the invigorating taste of a strong, powerful dark roast. This was the life he wanted—one without the guns of war, the heat of the desert, or having to say "Yes sir" to yet one more idiot.

Boom!

Coffee sprayed across the deck. Reed's training kicked in as he took cover behind his chair. All senses alerted as he built a wall against the shrapnel of fear strafing his chest. The meadow blurred and he tightened his focus on the mountain trail, his gaze cataloging every rock, every tree as he prepared for an enemy attack.

Nothing.

Reed peered into the stand of trees. Something wasn't right. Afghanistan didn't have redwood trees. *Where are the rocky, desert mountains?* Reed glanced over his shoulder. *Where is the rest of his unit?* They never went on a mission alone in broad daylight. They must be hiding in the trees. He scanned left and right for the enemy. Seeing none, he jumped off the deck, crouching low as he ran toward the tree line.

A boy burst from the trees running as fast as his short legs would carry him, the sun glinting off something metal.

Reed shouted to his unit. "Down! Gun! Down!" He hit the dirt and covered his head, waiting for the boy to start shooting.

Nothing.

He turned his head slightly. The kid had stopped dead in his tracks, as if not moving a muscle would make him invisible.

Why wasn't his unit responding? Shit. He must be the only one left. The bastards must have killed them. He reached beneath him for his backup weapon in an ankle holster.

Fuck! Where's my gun? No uniform? No flak jacket? What the hell is going on here? Have I been drugged? Escaped? Why can't I remember?

Flat in the dirt, Reed raised one knee to his side and placed both hands beneath his chest so he could push up quickly. He would spring forward when the boy made a move. He'd have to kill him with his bare hands. Reed would have to kill him before being shot—before joining the rest of his unit in hell.

The kid did nothing. The gun. Why hadn't he drawn it? The boys always had a gun. Usually a rifle, but sometimes a handgun. Was the kid the pawn? Were there others hidden behind the trees?

Dammit! He should have been prepared. He knew that young Afghan boys were often sent on suicide missions. How did he let himself get in this situation?

The boy's eyes were wide and frightened. It was as if he was paralyzed by Reed's deadly stare. When no one else fired, Reed looked up the trail again, trying to find where the others were hiding. He frowned in confusion.

Conifers. Heavily treed. What the hell?

Where were the brown hills, the scrawny, sparse trees barely hanging on to the white peaks above him?

Oh, God. No. Please God. Not again.

He closed his eyes and let out a breath. He wasn't in Afghanistan. He was home. Mt. Hood. His own backyard. The adrenaline still pumping through him, he took a shaky deep breath and let it out slowly.

Reed took his time getting up to one knee, then pushed carefully off the ground. The boy flinched. Reed stood motionless. He worked on slowing his breathing, stopping the automatic kill reflex.

"Sorry, kid." His voice was rough, dry from eating dirt when he hit the ground. "You okay? You lost?"

The boy screamed, turned, and took off back the way he'd come.

Fuck! It was a lost kid and he probably just scared the shit out of him.

Reed pursued. It wasn't safe for a young kid to be climbing around these mountains alone—especially at six in the morning. If he stepped off the wrong side of the trail, the boy would be dead.

"Hey, kid. Hold up. I'm not going to hurt you."

The kid stepped off the trail on the up slope and started climbing cross-country, then scampered further south again. Reed closed the gap. Only a few more strides and he'd have him. The boy slipped and screamed, tumbling down the slope. Reed braced himself, scooped his arms down and caught the boy, bringing him up against his chest.

The boy flailed at him, kicking and crying.

"Hold on," Reed said. "Just a minute. I'm not going to hurt you. What's wrong? What's going on?"

The boy kicked again, and Reed let out an "oof" as the boy's foot connected with Reed's kidney. He set the kid on the ground, tightly pressing down on his shoulders. The kid kicked his shin.

"F…if you do that again, I'm going to sit on you." Reed said. The kid twisted in his grasp and Reed applied more pressure, forcing the kid to bend lower to keep his balance. "Now tell me what's going on. Maybe I can help."

For a moment, the boy quieted, tears streaming down his face. For the first time, Reed had a chance to actually look at him. Red marks encircled the kid's wrists, as if they'd been tied for a long time. A large purple bruise on his left cheek looked as if he'd been hit hard by someone strong. His shirt was ripped at the collar with what looked like dried blood along his shoulder.

Reed loosened his grip a little. "What's happened here?"

The boy's shoulders slumped and he looked down at the ground. Reed let go completely and the kid took off again, running up the trail.

Shit! Whatever had scared this kid was way beyond Reed's stupid flashback.

The boy turned suddenly, jumping over a large boulder, and then veered sharply to the left. Reed tried to adjust, but he stumbled and landed flat on his chest and face-to-face with a woman on the ground. Obviously dead. Reed scrambled back to a sitting position and scanned the woods for the kid.

Nowhere.

Had the boy been part of this? Maybe escaped from the assailant?

The woman wore a nice suit—skirt and jacket—but she was bent in an unnatural way. One leg splayed out to the right crossing over the other, putting her almost completely face down, with one arm pinned beneath her. Her long blonde hair, matted with blood and needles from the conifers, looked sticky and stiff. She'd probably died several hours ago. He'd seen people bleed out in Afghanistan; he knew that look of resigned horror.

His training kept him close to the ground, though he doubted whoever did this was still around. If they had been, the boy would be dead too. He listened for a moment, unmoving, just in case.

Nothing.

Slowly, he turned the woman onto her back. Her clothes were intact except for an open shirt that showed some type of wound beneath her bra. Her hand compressed fabric against the wound, a torn yellow piece of paper clutched in her fingers with dried blood acting like a type of glue to keep the note there.

Based on the amount of blood, he guessed it had been a gunshot wound. Shit. No wonder the kid was running. He probably didn't know the good guys from the bad.

Reed didn't want to move her any more. The police would need to see her exactly as he'd found her. They'd want the kid, too. It's likely the boy was a witness, and probably also a victim. He braced his hand against the ground and pushed himself up. To his surprise, the kid stood just ten feet off the trail. There were no tears now, no trembling, just him standing still as a statue with a tortured look in his eyes.

Reed didn't move. He didn't want to scare him into running again. "I'm sorry, kid. She's dead."

The boy stiffened and refused to look Reed in the eye.

"I guess you already knew that."

The boy dropped his eyes to the ground and let out a big breath. His shoulders slumped.

"Do you know who did this?"

Again, the boy said nothing. He stared at Reed, his eyes wide, unblinking, as vacant as a sacrificial lamb. His lips trembled, but he didn't cry out. Suddenly, he folded to the ground and curled into a fetal position.

Reed took a step forward, then another. When there was no flight reaction, he hurried to the kid and scooped him into his lap. Small arms went around his neck and held tight. Reed rocked him, hugging him to his chest.

"I don't know what happened here, kid. But I'll keep you safe. You hear? I won't let anyone hurt you."

The boy didn't cry, didn't say anything, but he held on as if his fingers had a death grip on a hand grenade.

Reed stood, shielding the boy in his arms, and started down the path to home. He'd have to call the police and get them out here. And he knew he'd have to tell them about the boy. He didn't like the idea that some social service person would come and take the kid away, but that wasn't his call.

At his cabin, he laid the boy on the sofa in front of the wood stove, covered him with a blanket, and just watched him for a while. He was waiting for the kid to say something or do something. Cry. Talk. Whatever.

After several minutes of silence, it struck him.

The kid was like Reed. He couldn't talk. He couldn't think. He was just trying to put whatever happened as far back in his mind as he could. Trying to go on without thinking, without feeling, hoping he would wake up tomorrow and it would all be just a bad nightmare.

Reed perched on the edge of the sofa, within inches of the boy in case he reached out. He wanted to say, "I understand. It's okay. Do what you gotta do to get through this." But he didn't. He couldn't get close. He couldn't get involved. As soon as he called this in, someone would come take this kid away.

He dialed 911.

He'd barely gotten out the basic details about the body and the location when the operator began asking questions about Reed.

"Yeah, I found her on the trail. She's been shot."

"Look, I'm a Marine. I've been back from the Middle East for a year. I know when someone's been shot."

"Yeah, my name is Reed Adler, my address is..."

The boy grabbed the phone and ran out of the cabin.

Shit! Reed took off after him. He'd thought he had everything under control. He'd thought the boy had calmed down and wanted help. He scanned up and down the trail. The kid was nowhere.

It was going to be one of those FUBAR days.

Chapter Two

Murder?

Jenna sat quietly in the gloom of the chapel where the detective said they could meet. She hunched forward, her head resting in her arms on the pew in front of her. She couldn't face a busy cop station again. Here the light was too dim for anyone to see her. She didn't have to pretend to hold herself together.

The image of her sister's torn body hadn't left her mind since she'd identified it in the morgue three days ago. The black and blue swollen face marred Tanya's flawless skin. Her legs and arms strafed with random knife cuts as if the killer enjoyed torturing. Under her professional clothing, her sister's distorted and slender body was hardly recognizable. But there was no doubt it was Tanya. There were signs of multiple rapes, but no semen. The police conjectured she'd been held for up to a week and assaulted.

The fatal blow had been a gunshot wound to her side. The coroner said Tanya had tried to stop the bleeding with compresses from her clothes, but it didn't matter because the internal bleeding from the beating would have caused her death within a few hours. At least this way, she was probably only alive for ten or fifteen minutes after she was dumped.

They'd said Tanya had been found by a man who lived on the western slopes of Mt. Hood just below the Timberline Ski area, within only yards of a hiking trail near the man's home. She'd barely been covered by dirt and a few rocks.

When the police had given her Tanya's purse, her wallet was missing. She'd had no identification. No driver's license. No credit card. The bottom of her purse had contained a business card with the name of Sheila Lancaster, a fertility specialist at Vienoy, Inc., and a faded newspaper clipping of Jenna's restaurant. Tanya had saved the article about the Chat Précieux grand opening seven years ago. Scrawled across the picture, she'd written, "You go, girl. Love you, Sis."

How had Jenna let so many years go by without trying to find her sister? Their last fight was burned into her memory. It was the first and only time she didn't give in to Tanya. Jenna closed her eyes and sobbed. If only she'd gone after her. The memories of that day ripped through her like a fire in a dry forest, quickly and without mercy.

Tanya had shown up pregnant, again. She'd already had a fifteen-year-old daughter who lived with the father, and then three years ago, she'd had an abortion. But this time she had an offer that would haunt Jenna the rest of her life.

****

Tanya reached for Jenna's hand and squeezed. Her lips trembled with a hesitant smile. "I'd like to give the baby to you and Aaron. I know you can't have children and you want them so badly. You'd make a great mom, Jenna. This will be my present to you."

Jenna's heart clenched like a vice as her lungs emptied of all air. She shook her head. The timing couldn't have been worse. She couldn't take a child now. Not the day after Aaron had served her with divorce papers and moved out to live with his pregnant secretary.

She looked up, steeling herself to give up her only chance to ever raise a child. "It's just that I—"

"Oh, I get it." Tanya paced in front of the counter, her arms flailing. "You don't want it, right? Because it's mine. Because my baby isn't good enough for you. Is it because I don't know who the father is? You only want a baby from a perfect man with a high IQ and the right background—someone like Aaron. Right? Well, I can guarantee it was one of three graduate students—all very smart."

"One of three? Have you ever heard of birth control? You're in law school, for God's sake. You'd think you'd be smarter than this." Why was it Tanya could conceive by just sharing the same air as a man? It was so unfair.

"Sex isn't always planned, you know. Some of us just go with the flow—go for the moment." Then she laughed. "Maybe sex is always planned for someone as perfect as you. Do you schedule it in your calendar, Jenna? Does Aaron have to ask permission?"

Jenna reached out and slapped her sister across the face. "How dare you."

****

The memory shook Jenna's shoulders and tears spilled to the pew railing. She'd never slapped her sister before and now that would be the last memory they shared. The fight had ended with Tanya leaving to get an abortion, and Jenna doing nothing to stop her. If only she'd gone after Tanya. Jenna never thought her sister wouldn't talk to her again. She'd always expected Tanya to show up at her door one day with another problem to solve. But then one year turned into ten and now her sister was dead—murdered.

In hindsight, Jenna could have taken the baby. She *should* have. Jenna had no family now that Tanya was gone—no husband, no children, nothing but her work.

How could Tanya have been in Portland all this

time, and they'd never crossed paths? Tanya had lived in Gresham, only twenty-five miles from Jenna in the Pearl District of Portland. They could have gotten together. Obviously, Tanya knew what was going on in Jenna's life but Jenna had no idea what her younger sister had been doing. Worse, she had never tried to find out.

The police said her sister had been an attorney for Vienoy for the past two years. Her work had something to do with patents and intellectual property protection for research the lab did.

Jenna wiped a fist across her eyes. Now she'd never again have the chance to hug her sister...to tell her she loved her...to tell her she was sorry...to finally get to share in Tanya's successes.

Utter silence blanketed the chapel. Deep black shadows filled the corners of the church and crept down the aisle. Soon she was swallowed up in them. A patch of moonlight filtered through the tall stained-glass window—a beautiful window of lilies in a field with a meandering stream. She was sure it was designed to give worshippers a feeling of peace, but it didn't feel that way to her. It only added to her pain, her guilt.

The door to the sanctuary creaked open. She turned to see a hooded man look in and then close the door again. A rush of cold air moved in and covered her for a long moment before it moved on. She pulled her jacket tighter and turned toward the front of the church. Candlelight cast the small pulpit in sharp relief, blurring the edges around the choir loft. The shadows crept forward and back as the light flickered. She squeezed her eyes shut and prayed for relief from the pain. The pain of death. The pain of guilt. The pain of being alone.

A hand tapped her shoulder and she lurched forward, hitting her head on the pew in front of her. The hand reached out again. She screamed.

"Ms. Mosier? It's okay. It's me, Detective Novak. Sorry to startle you."

She leaned on the pew to regain her balance, her breath coming in short, shallow bursts. "Oh…silly of me. I just—"

"Slow, deep breaths, Ms. Mosier. I'll wait."

Jenna concentrated on her breathing. "Thank you, Detective. I'm better now."

"The funeral must have been hard on you. So many people you didn't know, so much to take in. I'm sorry to have to talk to you again. I know you've already answered a lot of questions."

"Yes, well… On the phone, you said you found something important. Something I might understand which could help with the investigation."

The detective pulled a plastic bag out of a manila envelope. Jenna could see a scrap of paper with something scrawled on it. He held it out to her and she gasped. It was her sister's handwriting, smeared with blood. She would know it anywhere, the printed curve of the letter "e" in the middle of a word, the half unfinished loop in the "y."

Jenna gulped. The crumpled note said *please save my baby*.

"It's been verified as her writing," the detective said.

"Yes." Jenna barely choked out her response.

"We found it clutched in her hand."

"But how? When did she write it?" The police had told Jenna her sister had been raped repeatedly, tortured. Did she write the note knowing she would die and then keep it with her?

"The man who found her said it was under her shirt near the bullet wound." The detective pointed to a spot on his chest near the left lower ribs. "Perhaps it was secreted in her bra. After the killer shot her and left her to die, she somehow found the strength to retrieve it. It seems clear she wanted to make sure anyone who found her would see it."

Jenna looked away from the note and swallowed. "But it doesn't make sense. She doesn't have a baby. She has a daughter, Amber, who must be...sixteen now. In fact, I saw a picture of her in the paper recently as the homecoming queen for her high school."

"We didn't know she had a daughter." The detective looked at his notebook and flipped pages, as if verifying everything they'd learned about Tanya.

Jenna sought the candlelight once more for comfort. Their lives had always been messy. "They didn't really see each other much. Tanya gave full custody to the father when my niece was only three years old. It's hard to explain, but Tanya really wasn't the motherly type. She loved her daughter, in her own way, but...well...they only saw each other once or twice a year."

"Uh huh, what's the father's name?"

"Miguel Sanchez."

"Address?"

Jenna fumbled in her bag for her address book. She held it open at the page with Amber's address while the detective scratched out the information in his notebook.

"Is it possible your niece is in danger? Maybe the father isn't all that good? Maybe your sister found out something and this Miguel Sanchez killed her?"

"No, he isn't like that." Jenna wasn't fond of Miguel, but he was a good father. A little overprotective of his daughter, but certainly not dangerous. "He's a good man. He'd do anything for Amber. She's his only child and he dotes on her."

"Is he remarried? The stepmother, maybe?"

"He is, but his new wife loves Amber, too." The detective looked skeptical as Jenna continued. "In many ways, I think their family is the normal one.

My niece really lucked out with them."

"It sounds like you and your sister didn't do too well with relationships in general. She rarely saw her only child. You see your niece maybe once a year. You haven't talked to your sister since your divorce ten years ago." The detective checked his notes. "From our background check on you, it also appears you never date and, outside of the people who work for you, there are no close friends. Do I have all that right?"

She nodded again. She did not want to get into the miserable excuse she had for a social life. She long ago decided it was easier—safer—to devote all her waking hours to Chat Précieux.

Jenna sighed. "Tanya had nothing to do with my divorce. It's just a coincidence that the timing matches."

"Are you sure?" The detective raised a brow, challenging her. "Maybe you found your sister and your husband in a compromising position. You might as well tell me everything now, 'cause I'll find it out anyway."

Jenna's stomach spasmed and she wrapped her arms in front of her. "No, my husband and sister were not lovers. We divorced because he was sleeping with his secretary."

"So, what was it that caused your break with your sister?"

"It's…complicated," Jenna whispered. "My divorce was over my inability to have a child. It has nothing to do with Tanya's murder."

"Interesting then that she worked for Vienoy—a company specializing in infertility research. She was a patent attorney there."

Oh God, Jenna hadn't even taken the time to look up Tanya's company. Was it possible that working there was Tanya's way of trying to help Jenna? The tears began again. Why didn't Tanya call? Why didn't she make contact? She obviously knew where Jenna lived and worked.

"So, you haven't heard anything from your sister, even once, in the past ten years?"

Jenna swallowed and choked out a response. "That's right."

"And what about her daughter…Amber, was it? Did your niece mention talking to her mother in the last couple of years?"

Jenna looked away and whispered, "Oh my God, what have I done?"

When she turned back, she found the detective's dark eyes staring straight into hers. "What was that, Ms. Mosier? What *have* you done?"

She closed her eyes and rubbed her forehead. The guilt just kept building. At every turn another realization of where she could have, should have, made a different choice.

"Ms. Mosier?" He tapped on his notebook.

She looked up again. "I just realized…I don't know when I stopped asking my niece about Tanya. It's like I'd given up on seeing her again…or maybe I just refused to think about it. Oh God, do you think she told my niece something that would have made a difference? Do you think I missed a chance to save her?"

"I don't know." The detective wrote something in his notebook. "I'll check into it." He snapped his notebook shut. "You are absolutely certain she doesn't have any other children? The note mentions a baby. Perhaps she recently had a baby you don't know about."

"I don't really know." She swallowed again and wiped more tears from her eyes. "I guess I really didn't know my sister. When I last saw her, she was going to have an abortion and get her tubes tied. She didn't want any more children."

"It's possible she was hallucinating when she

wrote the note," the detective offered. "It's not unheard of in torture cases. Maybe she didn't remember how old her daughter was."

Jenna couldn't answer. She couldn't think straight. All she could do was wonder if there was another abandoned child out there. A baby that Tanya only thought of as she was dying. She was convinced her sister was not hallucinating or getting her daughter confused. Even with all her dramatics, Tanya was never confused. She'd written that note purposefully, her writing strong. There was someone else out there. The question was where and how old? Did the killer take him or her?

Detective Novak stood. "I'm sorry for your loss, Ms. Mosier." He paused. "If you think of anything…"

"Yes, detective, I'll call you."

She waited and watched until he was all the way out the door before she slumped back in the pew. She hadn't been in a church for a long time, but if she ever needed divine help this was it. She bowed her head and searched for something to say. She couldn't really think of anything to pray for. She didn't even know how to start anymore.

She may not have been able to save her sister this time, but she'd make sure she found that baby and saved it. She didn't know how, but she would do it. She'd failed miserably with Tanya, but now she would make it up by putting her family above everything else.

Determined, she stood and focused on the stained glass windows. The shadows seemed to have steadied. Resolute, she walked out of the chapel and turned right to walk up the street where her car was parked beneath a beautiful oak. As she unlocked her car door, she looked up at the night sky. It seemed as if millions of stars beckoned her toward the path she'd chosen. With a sigh of relief, she slid into the seat and closed her eyes. It was the first time in days she'd felt any sort of peace.

Something hard and heavy hit the back of her head. An iron-hard arm locked around her throat and forced her head back in a painful arch.

"Move or make a sound and I'll snap your neck."

The man's voice was cold and menacing, the words spoken low and with an accent—Russian maybe. She could barely hear his voice, but she understood his intent perfectly. The arm cutting off her oxygen was clear enough on its own.

Her vision blurred and she managed a small gasp.

"You said you weren't going to kill her," a woman's voice sounded behind her.

"This is for Marya," the man said.

"Just scare her, then," the woman pleaded. "You don't have to kill her."

The arm around her throat loosened just enough for her to drag in some air. Her back ached from her neck being so roughly handled.

The man's face pressed to the side of her head. She couldn't see him, but she could feel the stubble of whiskers.

"Forget your sister. She's dead and buried, as is her baby. If you keep looking, you'll be joining them." He locked his arm tighter and said, "Now, go to sleep."

She gasped for air and her world went black.

Chapter Three

Reed stretched and caught a glimpse of an osprey flying low, searching for prey. He pulled off his denim work shirt and raised the axe again. It didn't take him long to work up a sweat and pull off his T-shirt as well. His rhythm sped as he split each log into four pieces. The sun warmed his skin and seeped into his muscles, renewing his energy with each stroke of the ax.

He paused to mop sweat off his face with the T-shirt he'd thrown on the pile. He stacked ten more logs upright next to his stump to make it easier to put each one to the axe, then dispatched each one, keeping to that hard, smooth motion, feeling his muscles flex and loosen, grow tight with power and release.

Out of the corner of his eye, Reed saw the boy open the front door. Two large scratches on his face still blazed bright red. The bruises on his wrists were fading a little. The boy limped out the door and then stopped, his eyes wide. Reed froze in mid-swing.

Holding perfectly still, Reed let the silence speak for them both. A faint breeze stirred the hair on his head and he lowered the axe slowly. The last thing he wanted was for the boy to run again. He hadn't expected to see him up this early. Wandering around on his own could be dangerous, for both of them.

The boy continued to stand at the door, his face leached of color, the fear so palpable Reed could sense it crawling inside the boy's skin.

Reed put the axe on the ground and said very slowly, not moving. “It’s all right. It’s me...Reed. Remember? I took care of you. I made your arms and face feel better. I won’t hurt you.”

The boy didn’t move. He just stared up at him. Then, very slowly, he put a hand on his stomach.

“Are you hungry?” Reed asked without moving. “Ready for some breakfast?”

The boy nodded, but didn’t move. Though he appeared frozen in place, his eyes darted around the yard as if he were waiting for a chance to run, to escape.

Reed made no move toward the boy, giving him a chance to settle. He didn’t need a repeat of last week when the boy ran off with Reed’s cell phone. Even with the police helping Reed search, it was obvious the kid didn’t want to be found. It was over two hours after the sheriff gave up the search that the boy returned to the cabin. They’d silently shared dinner and then Reed had tucked the boy into bed.

After the kid was sound asleep, Reed had let the police know the boy turned up, and on a recommendation from the local fire chief, Social Services had agreed the kid could stay with Reed, at least for now.

The product of an absent father and a drug addict mother, Reed had grown up in the foster system. Though he guessed it was better than living at home most of the time, it certainly wasn’t a fate he’d wish on any kid. The boy needed love and protection. Reed wasn’t so good on the love part, but he sure as hell knew about protection.

Reed set down the axe and straightened, making sure he smiled at the boy. “How about we get some breakfast then?” Taking long slow strides toward the door, he kept his body loose, non-threatening, “I’m going to fry you up some eggs and pancakes now. Okay? Just like we did yesterday.”

The boy tensed as he got closer, but he didn't run. Reed made a wide circle to get past him and go in the door. He left the door open so he could watch and make sure the boy came back inside for breakfast. He removed the frying pan from the cupboard, turned on the gas stove, sprayed a little olive oil for flavor, and then cracked two eggs into the non-stick pan. Just like yesterday, the boy slowly edged back into the cabin.

Reed smiled. "I guess you still like eggs then."

The boy took a seat at the table and reached deep into his pants pocket. As if hiding a treasure, he cupped his hands around something.

"What's that you have there?"

The boy drew his hands toward his stomach and turned to one side, bending forward.

Reed looked back to the pan. "No worries, kid. I'm not going to take it. Just curious."

The kid's cupped hands moved back to the table. He lifted the side of the top hand just enough to reveal a matchbox car. Reed couldn't quite make out which one, but it looked like a red, two-door sports car of some type.

"Cool. You like cars?"

The boy nodded and covered the car again.

Reed fished the leftover batter out of the fridge and started warming another pan on the stove. He turned back to the boy. "Want to help with the pancakes?"

The boy turned away from the window but he didn't move from the table. He looked everywhere except at Reed.

The eggs finished cooking and Reed immediately got them onto two plates. He turned toward the kid. "I could really use a little help."

The boy's eyes widened.

Reed opened the oven. "Can you put these two plates in here to keep them warm while I finish with the pancakes?" He smiled; warm ovens were the savior of unorganized cooks.

The boy returned the car to his pocket and stepped up to the stove, but stayed as far away from Reed as he could and still reach the plates. Reed stepped aside to give the boy even more room. The boy took one plate at a time and placed it in the oven.

"Thanks. Now close the door and we'll be all set."

The boy closed the door then backed away until he was at the other end of the kitchen.

"Another couple minutes and the pancakes will be ready. I hope you're as hungry as I am." Reed poured himself another cup of coffee and then put a tall glass on the counter next to it, about a foot away from his own cup. "You want to pour your own milk today?"

He'd asked the kid the same thing every day this week and so far no go. Now he understood the kid just didn't want get too close, didn't want Reed to have any chance to snatch him. He'd read somewhere that repetition was a good thing when recovering from trauma, something the kid could count on. To his surprise, the boy moved to the fridge and got the milk out. Then he slowly poured it into the glass, not spilling a single drop.

The boy took his glass of milk and Reed's coffee cup and placed them on the table opposite each other. Reed smiled. There was hope after all.

Reed put the breakfast on the table and the boy dove in without speaking, eating as fast as possible—as if this might be his last meal. Reed ate more slowly. Thinking. Watching.

He took a bite of eggs and then a good gulp of coffee. "I'd sure like to know your name." The boy glanced up. "I could make one up I guess, like Wolf or Raccoon. But that wouldn't really be fair. It just helps to have something to call you."

The boy continued to stare, unmoving.

"I know you don't wanna talk. What if I gave you a pen and paper and you could write it. Would that be okay? You don't have to say anything."

The boy visibly shrank back in the chair.

"Okay, that's not gonna work. Look, you should know by now I'm not here to hurt you. I don't know what happened to you before, but whatever it was, I can see it was bad."

He paused and they ate in silence awhile.

"Look, I'll make you a promise." The kid looked up. "If anyone comes near here and I don't know them, I'll beat the crap out of them. Okay? If that doesn't work, I'll shoot them."

The boy's eyes opened wide, but he leaned forward.

"Well, maybe I won't shoot them. Killing's not a good thing to do, unless you absolutely have to in order to save someone."

The kid didn't move. He stared straight at Reed.

"I don't mean to scare you, kid. I'm just not used to being around anyone younger than twenty-five or so. I don't have any brothers or sisters, so I don't have any nieces or nephews to learn on."

The smallest bit of lip upturned. *Is that the beginning of a smile?* Reed took that as a good sign.

"You gotta help me here, kid—help me learn how to be around someone your age." He squinted. "So, I figure every kid likes a birthday party, and I figured I'd make a cake for you today. The thing is I don't know how old you are. If I knew that, I'd know what to do with the cake. Do you know how old you are?"

The boy shook his head slowly from side to side.

Ah shit! What had happened to this poor kid that he didn't even know his age? Did no one celebrate birthdays with him?

"Okay, we're going to guess then." He took another gulp of coffee and leaned back in his chair. "Stand up and let me get a good look at you."

The boy stood, his head canted to one side, his brow furrowed.

Reed stayed seated but made a show of sizing up the kid. "I'm guessing by your size you're nine or ten." He paused. "Hmmm. Ten is a pretty easy number to remember, so for now let's say you're ten. How's that sound?"

The boy shrugged again. This was good. Two shrugs in one day and an almost smile.

"It's official then. I'll put ten candles on your birthday cake. Okay?"

The kid sat down and worked on eating his pancakes. It seemed as if his face was a little lighter, a little less worried.

****

That evening, after they'd roasted hot dogs over a fire, Reed strummed and finger-picked tunes on his guitar, the same as he did every night. His repertoire consisted of some bluegrass tunes, a few blues melodies, lots of 70s rock and the occasional McCartney song—after he started Wings. Playing helped soothe Reed's demons and it seemed that the kid relaxed a little, in spite of Reed's bad singing.

As the embers died down, Reed said, "It's time for your birthday cake. You want to wait here or come with me?" As usual the boy didn't answer, but he stayed put. "Okay, I'll be right back."

Reed brought out the chocolate cake, topped with white frosting, he'd put together while the boy took an afternoon nap. He'd only been able to find two candles, so he'd used M&Ms to form the number ten and then lit one candle in the middle of the number one, and one in the middle of the zero.

The boy looked at the cake, his eyes wide in wonder, but he didn't seem to have a clue what to do with it. Reed said, "You make a wish now, but don't tell me what it is. It's a magic wish. Whatever you wish for will come true sometime in the future if you blow out all the candles."

The boy squeezed his eyes closed and Reed hoped that meant he was making a wish. Did the boy even know what a wish was? Then he saw him open his eyes, take a deep breath and blow hard. Both candles went out immediately.

Reed laughed heartily. "Wow! You practically blew those candles right off there. I'd say your wish is certain to come true now."

For the first time, he saw an actual full smile from the boy. Reed felt a tug on his heart. It was strange, but it felt real good.

They ate cake in silence, then threw their paper plates into the fire. Together they watched the embers die.

"David," the boy whispered.

Reed's mouth dropped open. Then he consciously closed it and cleared his throat. "So...that's your name? David?"

The boy nodded.

"That's good." He paused, holding his breath, hoping for more.

Nothing. "I guess Wolf wasn't a good idea then," Reed teased.

The boy smiled and shook his head.

Reed guessed that was going to be the extent of speaking tonight. Getting David's name was a huge step. Satisfied, Reed picked up his guitar again and played a few more tunes, some upbeat rags. When he noticed David's eyes drooping, he placed the guitar in its case and stood. "Well, David, I'm ready for some shut-eye. How about you?"

David stood and took the bucket of water next to the fire pit, pouring half of it over the coals as Reed had done each night before. Reed shoveled dirt in, while David poured the rest of the water over it. It was as if a small door of trust had finally opened after a week of trying.

"Thanks, David. You did a good job there. Let's go on in."

David walked past him and in the front door. When he crossed the threshold, he looked back. No smile, just a restful, childlike face. David disappeared around the corner toward his bedroom and Reed's heart clenched. He turned toward the open door and scanned the forest around him. His eyes narrowed and he said to the night, "Whoever you are, if you come anywhere near my place to hurt this boy, I'll blow your fucking head off."

Chapter Four

Reed woke to an ear-piercing scream. He ran to David's room, afraid of what he'd find.

"No! Stop hurting her." David twisted in the covers, throwing them off his small flailing body. "I'll go back with you. I promise I won't run away again." His fists beat against the pillow. "Stop it! Stop it! You're hurting her." He kicked the sheets off as if trying to escape. "No! You're killing her!" His breathing accelerated like a bullet train picking up speed, faster and faster and faster, until Reed wasn't sure if his small lungs might burst from the effort. Tears streamed down David's cheeks, soaking the sheets beneath him.

Reed bent over and rubbed David's back in light circles. His first instinct was to pull him onto his lap and just hold him, but he didn't want to startle him awake or frighten him in to running away. He continued the slow circles, speaking softly. "It's all right. I'm here."

Though David had been having nightmares each night since he arrived, this was the first time he'd said anything intelligible during his dream; and he'd never cried out before. In fact, Reed hadn't seen him cry once since his arrival.

He continued to brush slow circles across his back, breathing slowly, coaxing David to breathe with him, to ease out of his nightmare. If he was lucky, David wouldn't remember the terror. Reed certainly wished he didn't remember any of his own.

"It's all right, David. I'm here. I'm protecting

you."

"Please don't die, Mommy. Please don't die." His voice shook as if the storm of tears was drowning him.

There were a few minutes of silence as David finally caught his breath. His heart rate slowed and he turned over. His eyes peeked out below lashes, as if opening them would be painful. He groaned, and in one fluid motion, rolled into Reed's lap, curling his legs into him as he leaned his head against his chest. Damp tears silently soaked through Reed's T-shirt and into his heart.

"You yelled about your mother," Reed said softly.

David clutched Reed's shirt in his hands as if his life depended on it.

"Was that her body in the woods?"

David nodded and pressed his face hard into Reed's chest. His clutched hand shook. Then his entire body tensed. Unsure whether David was trying to hold in the emotion or drawing up to spring from his lap, Reed loosely wrapped his arms around David and rocked from side to side. He wasn't sure if this was the right thing to do with a ten-year-old boy, but he'd heard it worked with babies.

David's arms clutched Reed's chest; heaving, choking cries convulsed his small body. Sobbing interspersed with hiccups as David tried to catch his breath among the flow of tears.

The pain of David's loss tore at Reed harder than any of the losses he'd faced with his unit. How could any kid be expected to handle this? Reed hugged David closer and rocked him as he struggled to keep his own tears in check. All he could do was keep repeating, "That's okay. Let it all out."

About an hour later, David quieted. Spent, he finally fell back to sleep and Reed carefully returned him to bed, pulling the cover up to drape loosely around David's small shoulders. Reed stood and looked across the small lump in the bed to the clock on the nightstand. 4:12. Only two hours before dawn.

No sleep. Again.

Reed carefully moved to the ladder-backed chair in the corner of the room and slumped over with his head in his hands.

How can I help this boy? How can I make him whole again when I can't even fix myself?

If the dead woman on the trail was his mother, who killed her? Maybe a jealous ex-husband? A wife-beater? Someone David had lived with, like a father or some other relative, and his mother had found him and taken him away? Reed was all too familiar with that scenario.

He raised his head and watched the shallow rise and fall of David's blanket as he slept. Reed closed his eyes on memories of children in Afghanistan. Children he couldn't help. *Shit. What am I doing? I have no idea how to play father. If I screw this up, even hell won't accept me.*

****

When David woke again it was seven. He acted as if nothing had happened during the night. Reed wasn't sure if David didn't remember the nightmare, or if he just didn't want to talk about it.

When Reed headed out to split more wood, David followed this time. Instead of watching from afar, he helped by stacking the logs as he'd seen Reed do on other days. After a couple hours of work, David plopped down on the ground.

"I'm tired."

Hmmm. Talking today then.

Reed put the axe down and sat on a stump. "Okay. We can stop." He let the morning air cool his hot skin for a few minutes. Then he reached for his shirt and pulled it on.

David reached into his pocket and took out his matchbox car. With the tip of his finger he guided it open and down his outstretched leg.

"Would you be up for a short walk?"

David clutched the car against his leg. He looked up the trail to the right, where his mother's body had been found.

"We could go that way." Reed pointed to the trail following the opposite direction.

David drew his clutched hand toward him and held it against his stomach. "Will you bring your gun?"

Reed started. His gun was hidden in the nightstand next to his bed. "What makes you think I have a one?"

David dropped his head and looked at the ground. "I…kind of found it one time."

"Uh huh." Reed purposely relaxed his shoulders and leaned back. "Where'd you see it?"

"In a drawer." David raised his eyes toward Reed, but not his head. "I…uh, was looking for a knife…one I could hide in my pocket…you know, to stop the bad man." He raised his head, his lips trembled. "I didn't touch it though. I promise I won't go in your bedroom anymore."

Reed paused for a moment. "I'm glad you told me *and* that you didn't touch the gun. If you don't know how to use it, you could accidentally hurt yourself…or me. That wouldn't be too good, would it?"

David looked down again. "No, that wouldn't be too good."

"You have to promise me you won't ever take it out or touch it. Okay?"

"What kind of gun is it?" David asked, sitting up straight.

"It's a Colt 45."

"Oh." David played with a stick in the dirt.

"Do you know guns?"

"Nope. Just wonderin'." He relaxed his hand and thumbed a wheel on the matchbox car. Reed remembered buying the Colt just before he was sent to Afghanistan. The Marines issued a nine millimeter Beretta, which was the only pistol they were officially allowed to carry. It was worn with a shoulder holster outside the flak jacket, but he didn't see how that gun would stop anyone with a suicide vest.

He'd asked around what other guys used to get more power, and a few of the older guys admitted to carrying an extra gun hidden in a holster underneath their body armor. Then, when they went out on reconnaissance, they traded out the Beretta for whatever else they were carrying. Most unit leaders knew of the practice and just turned a blind eye.

"You could show me how to use it," David interrupted his thoughts. "Then it wouldn't be dangerous."

Reed stood. The last thing he wanted to do was provide a scared little boy with a gun. He looked hard at David.

David stood and backed up, shoving the car deep in his front pocket.

Ah, shit. He was scaring the boy. "I'm not going to hurt you. You know that, don't you?"

"I…I think so."

"Look at me," he said softly.

David looked up and held his ground.

"Maybe one day, a little later, I'll show you how to use it. Okay? But we'll have to go to a firing range where it's safe. Right now, I don't think it's a good idea. Guns are very dangerous and it takes a lot of practice—not only to use it, but to make sure a bad guy can't take it from you. You need to trust that I'm the only one who can use it until you've been trained." He paused. "Got that?"

David nodded.

"In the meantime, I'll teach you some fighting moves that might help you get away if you ever have to. Okay?"

"That would be good…that would be very good."

Reed reached out and patted him on the shoulder. "Okay, buddy. So how about that walk?"

David looked down the trail, then back at Reed. His shoulders rose toward his ears, and he tucked his lower lip under his teeth.

"Okay, I'll bring my gun."

David blew out a breath and his shoulders dropped. "Thanks."

Reed shook his head as they both walked back to the cabin. He was already getting attached to this kid. He better find some relatives for him soon, because a few more weeks and he wasn't so sure he'd be able to give the kid back.

"Go get a couple bottles of water out of the fridge and some granola bars from the cupboard next to it. Oh, and maybe some apples," Reed said when they crossed the threshold. "Then we'll be on our way. We can stop and have a picnic before we turn back home."

Reed slipped into the bedroom and checked the drawer. The gun was right where he'd left it, unmoved. The kid had told the truth. He checked the clip. Still full. He strapped on his shoulder holster and put the gun in it. Then he put his flannel shirt back on, leaving it unbuttoned.

Crap. What was this world coming to when a ten-year-old kid needed you to carry a gun to protect him?

The kid had every right to be scared. The truth was if this bad guy thought the kid was alive up here, he probably would come looking for him.

****

It was a beautiful early June day, about sixty-five degrees and only a few fluffy white clouds in the sky. Reed knew the perfect place to take David for his first hike. The trail to Little Zigzag Falls met with the Sandy River trail only about half a mile from his cabin. The path through the forest was pretty level and not very long, and the trail ended by the pool at the base of the falls.

They walked in silent companionship through a lush, narrow canyon that followed icy, clear Little Zigzag Creek. Reed listened closely to the sounds the creek made as it tumbled over rocks and logs and flowed along sandy shallows. He could almost hear it converse with itself in different voices. The rhoddies had stopped blooming in early June, but the small creek flowers were still out. At the base of the falls, he steered David inside a cylinder of wire fencing. The falls tumbled seventy-five feet in a series of short drops at the top, then fell in one long cascade down an angled, mossy, chiseled rock face. Once David had his fill they continued their walk, making one switchback to climb to the top of the falls where they sat and had their snack.

For the first time since he'd found David, Reed felt some peace. After last night, it seemed David might have found his own small bit of peace too. The boy seemed to have a hyper-awareness of every plant and flower, every curve of the creek, as if he'd never been in a forest before.

"I have to pee," David said, after finishing his apple and throwing it toward the trees for the deer to find later. "What should I do?"

"Hmmm. Well, you're going to have to go in the woods."

"Are you kidding me? Right here? People might see."

Reed stood. "Not exactly right here. You don't want to go too close to the creek." He looked behind him. The slope was pretty steep, but it seemed there was a somewhat flatter part just a little ways up the hill. He pointed in that direction. "Think you can climb up there on your own? Then you can step behind one of those big ferns and whip it out. No one will see you. I'll stay here and stand guard."

David looked up the slope, his eyes scanning both sides of the area where Reed had pointed. "Okay. Don't watch though. Just tell me if someone's coming."

Reed nodded. He watched David climb to the level landing, then chuckled when David motioned for him to turn around. He turned his back and listened to the roar of the falls.

Screeeeeeeech.

Reed looked to the sky for an eagle or some other raptor.

Screeeeeeeech.

He turned toward the scream and saw David barreling toward him. He ran up hill to intercept him.

"Help! They're here. They're here. The bad men are here."

Reed pulled his gun from the holster and aimed with one hand toward the clearing. With the other hand, he grabbed David, stepping in front of him. "Stay there and hold on to my waist so you don't fall." He searched the hillside, his gun tracking his scan. He didn't see anything, not even a rustle of leaves. He couldn't hear over the roar of the falls. He searched again.

Without turning around, his gun still at the ready, he said, "Where were they? I don't see anyone. Where did you see them? What direction did you see them run?"

David held tight to Reed's waist, his face buried in his back. "I didn't see them, but I saw a lady. A killed lady," he choked out.

Reed continued to scan every tree, rock, or bush for movement. Nothing. He wasn't sure if David might be hallucinating. Maybe being thrust back into an unknown area of the forest caused panic. Reed knew all about PTSD and the flashbacks. Was it possible for David to be experiencing those symptoms? Or had he actually found something?

"Whoever did it must be gone now."

"Are you sure?" David asked, his breath still far too quick.

Reed scanned again, then lowered his gun. "Yeah, I'm sure. If they were here and wanted to get us, they would have started shooting already." He put the gun back in his holster then turned and hugged David close. "Can you show me where the lady is?"

David buried his face in Reed's stomach. "Do I have to?"

Reed hesitated as he struggled with his desire to save David anymore trauma and the need to determine if what he saw was real or not.

He squatted down to David's height and looked him in the eye. "You don't have to take me up there if you don't want. I know it's hard to look at a body…after what happened to your mother."

David held his gaze, unflinching. For once there were no tears.

"It's important for me to see her," Reed continued. "I need to be able to tell the police where she is. You wouldn't want her left out here, would you?"

"No, but…"

"I don't want to leave you alone while I go look. So, what should we do?"

David dropped his gaze and kicked the ground. "I'll show you, but only for a minute. Okay?"

"You got it, buddy."

Reed held David's hand and they made their

way back up the slope. They rounded the bush Reed had suggested David use for cover.

Shit. It wasn't a hallucination.

She was face down on the ground. A black dress was pulled up around her waist, but her panties were still intact. Not the usual way to leave a rape victim. He bent to move her dark hair away from her face. "My God! She's breathing."

"She's alive?" David asked, squatting down with Reed.

Reed carefully ran his hands down both legs, then her arms. He checked for wounds along her back. Then he checked her skull. Nothing seemed askew outside of her clothes. Slowly, he turned her onto her back and performed the same body scan with his hands on her front side.

"David, you might want to turn away. I'm going to cut open her dress and check for wounds on her chest and her stomach." He took out his knife and cut from the neckline to her navel. He looked for knife stabs, blood, any kind of wound. Again nothing.

Reed covered her again as best he could and breathed a sigh of relief. "I don't know what happened to her, but she seems okay. She's definitely out cold though."

"We have to get her away from here. Maybe the bad men thought she was dead and left. They might come back any minute." David jumped up and turned slowly in a circle. "Do you think they're watching us?"

"No. I think they've gone a long ways away. I don't think it was the same people who hurt your mother. If it was, she'd be dead."

He'd like to tell the kid the lady just slipped and fell, but that would be a lie and he wasn't going to start lying to the kid—no matter how convenient. Women didn't go walking on Mt. Hood trails in a dress and heels.

Reed handed David the canteen he'd been carrying. "Do you think you could carry this for me? Then I'll carry her."

"Yeah. I can do it." David slung the canteen strap over his right shoulder and across his chest. "Can you carry her by yourself?"

Reed squatted and lifted the woman into his arms, then juggled her a bit to balance against his chest. Though she couldn't have weighed much more than one twenty, maybe one thirty, dead weight was always hard to carry. If it had been a man, he'd throw him over his shoulders in a fireman's carry, but he didn't want this lady waking up and kicking him in the stomach or the kidneys if she was over his shoulders. He'd make the mile and half with her in his arms. That would give him a fighting chance if she woke up and decided to struggle.

"Let's go," he said to David, canting his head back down the hill. "Think you can lead the way back?"

"Yeah, we go back that way." David pointed back up the hill on the other side of the falls.

"That's right. You're a brave boy. Thanks for helping me with this."

"You can wake her up, can't you? You can make her well again, right?"

"I don't know, kid. But I sure as hell am gonna try."

Chapter Five

Reed sat in the recliner staring at his bed and the woman sound asleep on it. He was still trying to recover from bathing her more than an hour ago after David went to bed.

She was so beautiful. Her silky, ebony hair barely brushed her shoulders. It contrasted sharply with her pearl-white complexion. The full moon's soft, pure light on her skin emphasized her beauty and the perfection of her slightly blushed cheeks and full lips. He groaned as his erection sprang to life once more.

When he'd found her on the trail, he'd been so intent on checking her for bullet holes or stab wounds, he hadn't paid much attention to her body or her appearance. But when he'd arrived home and laid her in his bed, he'd carefully undressed her to make sure he hadn't missed anything. The fact she was still out cold worried him. He'd called Dr. Rusch, the only doctor on the mountain, but he was already busy at the ski resort taking care of a head trauma. Doc had told him what to look for and talked him through a brief exam. He'd said to call if there was any change and he'd get there as soon as he could. Reed also called the sheriff. They only had one patrol car at night and it was eighty miles away on a joint ATF bust. Because Doc wasn't worried, the sheriff wasn't worried. He'd said someone would come by in the morning to take the lady's statement.

After Doc talked him through the exam, Reed had taken a soft cloth to clean off the leaves and mud caked on her exposed skin, hoping she'd feel refreshed when she awoke. He didn't touch her in any inappropriate way, and he hadn't dared remove her panties. Even with extreme care, he couldn't help but notice the softness of her skin, the roundness of her breasts, the way her waist flared down to hips in just the right proportion. He'd tried to be clinical about it all, but dammit, he was a man and far from perfect.

Obviously, it had been too long since he'd had any kind of sexual release. He was sure that when she woke, the last thing this poor women would be thinking about was sex.

Sinking back against the chair, Reed closed his eyes and started reciting baseball stats in his mind. That usually worked to dampen his libido. He concentrated on the early years.

1950 National league batting averages—Musial 346, Robinson 328, Snider 321, Ennis 311…

****

Sometime during the night, Jenna woke and screamed. A man rushed to her bedside and grabbed her arms, pinning her to the bed. She flailed against him, but to no avail.

"What do you want with me? You already killed Tanya. Go ahead. Do it. Kill me! I don't care. Just do it, you bastard."

He loosened his grip and spoke softly, "I don't want to kill you."

"Then what do you want?" Jenna searched through the darkness. All she could see was the shadow of a tall, muscular man. "I won't stop looking into my sister's death. I don't care how much you threaten me."

He turned on the bedside lamp and stepped back. "I'm not threatening you. You're free to go, but I don't advise it until daylight."

She took a good look at him. If nothing else,

she'd remember what he looked like so she could describe him to a police sketch artist—that is, if she got out of here alive. His tawny hair was short, but not shaved like the military. In fact, it was a bit shaggy around the edges. He was tall, at least a foot taller than her, since his head wasn't that far from the ceiling. In fact, his presence easily took up the whole room. He looked fit and tan. She'd guess he was at least 200 pounds. If he wanted to hurt her, he'd have no problem. And his hands. She glanced to them open at his side, as if he was consciously trying to appear non-aggressive. They were large hands. The knuckles alone were twice the size of hers—definitely a working man's hands. This was someone who was used to being outdoors, used to pitting himself against nature. She pulled the blanket tighter to herself.

Jenna glanced around the room. Tongue and groove wood lined the walls and ceiling. The queen-size bed was topped in a heavy blanket with a Native American print. A slight breeze cooled the air through a cracked window on the other side of the room. She shifted and something felt off.

She lifted up the blanket and gasped. "What the hell?" She was in only her underwear and an oversized T-shirt, not her own. No bra. No dress. No stockings.

"You bastard! What did you do to me? Where are my clothes?"

He slowly pulled a chair up to the bedside and she scrambled to the farthest corner away from him, wrapping the sheet around her. His dark brown eyes invited confidences, but she wasn't in the mood for sharing.

"I'm not going to hurt you—believe me. If I'd wanted to hurt you, you wouldn't be talking to me now." He patted the pillow where her head had been. "Please, relax. Come back and we can talk."

"I'll stay right here, thank you." Jenna edged a leg over the side and eyed the door. If he made one move toward her, she'd drop the sheet and run like hell. She didn't care if she was half-naked; it would be better than being raped.

"Start talking," she said. "What happened after you hit me on the head?"

"I didn't hit you on the head."

"Right, and you didn't kill Tanya, and you didn't take her baby." She stared at him, her teeth clenched. She could bite him too, if she had to.

"Who's Tanya?"

"As if you didn't know, you murdering bastard."

Jenna heard a noise and looked toward the door.

Oh my God! She drew in a breath and held it. A young boy stood there, shirtless, with pajama bottoms that were obviously far too big on him—rolled up at the legs and a rope around the waist holding them up. A small fist moved in a circle above his right eye.

She let out her breath and stared. She must be hallucinating. She could swear it was Tanya when she was about ten-years-old, only with short hair. The eyes were a little closer together, but the deep blue color was all Tanya. The high cheekbones and the thin lips were also definitely hers. But the thing that clinched it was the small port wine discoloration on his left side below the breastbone. That was exactly where Tanya's had been.

The boy yawned. "You're awake. Did Reed make you better?"

She looked from the boy to the man. So, his name was Reed. That was important information she might need when she finally made it to the police. She turned her head back. She didn't see any of Reed in the boy. What the hell was this man doing with her sister's child?

She wanted to scream all sorts of questions, but

she didn't want to frighten the boy. Maybe he was a prisoner too.

"What's your name?" she asked, trying to sound normal, non-threatening.

"David. What's yours?"

"Jennifer, but my friends call me Jenna."

"How come?" David asked.

"Well, my younger sister had a hard time saying Jennifer, so she shortened it to Jenna and it stuck." She stared at the boy. "How old are you?"

"I'm not sure, but a couple days ago Reed decided I was ten."

Jenna swallowed. *Could it be? Was it possible Tanya didn't get an abortion after all? Had Tanya turned her life around? Had she become a good mother?*

Jenna couldn't stop the thoughts running through her mind and adding a final question, wondering if she had blown the chance to be part of her sister's life, part of her nephew's life.

"Is something wrong?" the boy asked. "You keep staring at me like I'm an alien or something."

Jenna glanced down. "I'm sorry, it's just that..." She gathered the sheet tighter, then turned to the man who hadn't spoken since the boy entered the room.

"I'd like my clothes now, please, so I can be more comfortable."

The man shifted in his chair. "Ah, hum."

"You can't wear them," David said. "Reed had to cut your dress open to make sure you didn't have any bullet holes or anything. Then he carried you all the way down the mountain. Even though you were heavy, he didn't stop. I had to practically run to keep up with him. When we got back here, he called the doctor and the police. Then he made me wait outside his room while he put you in his bed and took off your clothes and cleaned you up. He said the doctor told him what to do to fix you up."

Jenna widened her eyes and looked from the boy to the man. So, he'd undressed her and put her in his bed. She sucked in her cheeks and took a mental inventory of how her body felt. If he'd molested her, she would know it, wouldn't she? She moved her legs. Nothing felt sore.

"I didn't…" The man looked straight at her.

"He saved you," the boy said. "He saved you like he saved me." Then he looked down and his lower trip trembled. "But he couldn't save my mother. She was already dead. The bad men killed her."

The man moved to the boy and gathered him in, giving him a big hug. "That's right, David. We couldn't save her, but I'm glad I have you."

Jenna noted David didn't seem scared of the man. In fact, it seemed as if David felt some protection being with him. Maybe this wasn't the same man who'd choked her in her car. Carefully, she edged her free leg back up on the bed. Still holding the sheet with one hand, she reached out and propped the pillow behind her and leaned back.

"David?"

He peered around the edge of Reed's chest, then pushed away.

"Yes?"

"What was your mother's name? Her first name, I mean."

David looked up at Reed, waiting for his nod. Then he looked back at Jenna. "Tanya. Tanya Mosier."

Jenna's eyes fluttered and Reed saw her shudder. He immediately moved to catch her, but she didn't faint outright—she just seemed dazed. With one hand on her back as support, he rubbed slow circles with his thumb. The other hand chafed her cheeks until her eyes focused again.

"You okay?"

She turned her face into his hand and closed her eyes with a deep sigh. "Tanya Mosier is…was…my sister, and David must be the child I thought…she had—"

He felt a wash of tears against his hand. He moved to the edge of the bed and gathered her close. She didn't sob as if David had. Instead, she made quiet swallows, as tears leaked through his T-shirt. David moved to the other side of Jenna and crawled onto the bed, holding onto her waist, his cheek against her side.

Reed drew his free hand through David's hair, trying to offer comfort. He couldn't help but feel that somehow he was inextricably linked with both David and Jenna. Whoever had killed David's mother had also dumped Jenna. It was too much of a coincidence that both women had been left on Mt. Hood, only two miles apart. But why hadn't they killed Jenna? Whatever the reason, he'd make sure no one else was killed.

Jenna sat up abruptly, her eyes wide. "I'm sorry, I don't know what I'm doing, I…" She tried to scoot away, but then noticed David curled in her lap, half asleep. She reached toward his tousled hair then hesitated, her fingers hovering above his head. Her hand shaking slightly she withdrew it.

Reed moved to the other side of the bed and lifted David off her lap. "He'll probably sleep through the night now. He's had one rough week." He brushed his lips on the boy's head. "I'll put him to bed and then come back."

She nodded and Reed carried David out the door.

When he returned, Jenna still sat pressed against the headboard, her entire body drawn as tight as the sling shot about to be snapped at Goliath. "Do you mind if I close the door? I don't want to wake him again."

Jenna swallowed and looked up at him, as if she were trying to decide whether to trust him. Then she shrugged. He softly closed the door and returned to the bedside chair.

"Can you tell me about your sister? What you know about how she died? It's obvious you didn't know about David, so I take it you and your sister weren't very close."

Jenna took in a deep breath, closed her eyes and rolled her head in a circle. "It's so complicated. I don't even know where to start."

"Relationships are always complicated. Take your time. I'm not leaving."

Complicated didn't begin to describe how he felt about Jenna and David.

Whoa. Danger. Physical danger he knew how to handle. The other kind…

There would be no other kind.

****

It seemed as if hours had ticked by as Jenna recounted her fight with her sister ten years ago, their history together, the loss of her parents, the husband who left her. She meant only to talk about Tanya, but all her feelings were so intertwined and Reed was so patient, so encouraging, that once she got going it all came out in fits and spurts.

"So, David is more like nine years old," Reed said.

Jenna dried her eyes for what seemed like the hundredth time. "Yes. I think Tanya was just three months pregnant when she came to me in early spring ten years ago. I think it was mid-April or so."

She watched Reed calculate in his head. "Sounds like maybe David's birthday is in October then." A soft smile briefly lit up his face. "I guess we'll just have to celebrate his tenth birthday again."

"Has he told you anything about where they lived or how she was…killed?" Her voice shook as she forced herself to say that last word.

"No." Reed covered her hand with both of his. "He only started speaking two days ago. It's been nearly a week since we found her."

Jenna straightened as a tingle danced down her spine. Had it been only a week since she received that awful phone call? With all that had happened in the last twenty-four hours, it seemed like a lifetime since the police had called her.

"I'm not sure he remembers," Reed continued. "I haven't pushed him at all."

"I know you probably think I'm an awful sister for not looking for her all this time."

Reed shook his head. "Stuff happens with families. Whether you're an awful sister or a great one doesn't matter. She's dead either way and it's not your fault. Blame the murderer. Not yourself."

He made it sound so easy. But he didn't know the whole story. There was plenty of blame on her shoulders. Not the murder, but everything that came before. That's why she had to make sure David was safe. That's why she would never shirk her family responsibilities again.

"You need to know...David is my nephew and I plan to keep him." Reed blinked and stiffened. He looked straight at her, but she couldn't tell what he was thinking. He seemed to have a bond with David. But was it real? Or was it brought on by circumstance? What kind of a man was he?

Then he leaned forward and took her hand, chafing the back of it. "Of course, you should. I'm glad to know he has someone who cares about him."

"I do." Jenna's eyes watered. Both for the struggle she saw in Reed's face and for herself. She would see her sister in David the rest of her life. "I do care—more than you can ever know."

"Good. With all that he's been through, and the nightmares he still has, I wasn't about to put him into the foster care system. I know too well how hellish it can be sometimes."

His jaw tensed as he clenched his teeth together. Jenna looked into his eyes for an explanation of the pain that obviously sat there, but his straight ahead stare seemed to say the subject was closed.

"I'm not sure what the next step is. I have to do something legally to make sure I have custody of David. The police don't even know he exists." Her jaw dropped open as she put the pieces together, and she scooted back against the leather headboard. "Wait a minute. Do the police know about David? When you reported my sister's body, did you tell them about David?"

Reed leaned forward, but then retreated when she stiffened her spine and gave him her best I-can-hurt-you-if-you-come-any-closer look.

"It's complicated."

"Try me."

"Like I told you before, David wouldn't talk when I first found him. In fact, he ran as fast as he could, and when I caught up to him, he screamed and kicked and clawed until he got away." Reed stood and walked to the foot of the bed, his hands in his jeans pockets. "That first day he reluctantly agreed to come back to my house. I think he only did it because of the care I took with the woman…his mom. When I picked up the cell phone to report the body, he grabbed it from me and ran before I could even get out the address. The sheriff and I looked for him, but couldn't find him."

"Then how did the police know where to find you?"

"I may appear to live like a hermit, but the local sheriff and the fire crew know me just fine."

Jenna's eyes widened and she tucked in closer to the headboard. Did he have a record? Was she sitting half-naked in the bed of someone who could get violent if crossed?

"I told you before; if I wanted to hurt you, I could have done it before bringing you here."

She nodded once, but still didn't let down her guard.

"I was force recon in the Marines. One of my buddies is ATF at the Portland office and he knows lots of cops. Plus, when hikers get lost up here, I usually volunteer to go looking for them."

"Force Recon? What's that?"

"Special Operations. We're the Marine's answer to the SEALs, only better."

Jenna's shoulders dropped as she let out a long-held breath. "How long?"

"I just retired from the corps a year ago. I was in twenty-years—just enough to get my full retirement. Two tours in Iraq. My last tour was in Afghanistan."

Jenna wasn't sure whether to feel protected or scared. She'd heard stories of soldiers who came back with PTSD, and how special-ops guys particularly saw a lot of action and could one day turn into killers back home. She stared hard at Reed.

"Yes, I'm dangerous," he said, as if reading her mind. "But not to you. Not to David. But if I find who did this..."

Jenna swallowed at his unfinished sentence. She believed he could kill and have no remorse for doing so. She'd never known someone like Reed. She'd grown up a peace-loving, almost hippie child. She'd never even held a gun and didn't want to. She was against capital punishment and she couldn't even imagine dating someone with the violence Reed held so close to him.

Yet, she was drawn to him. She shook her head. No need to go there. Her feelings were just confused because of everything that was happening. It was natural to want protection from evil. But there was no need to make it all romantic. There was no way she was going to fall for an ex-special-ops type. Absolutely. No. Way.

"I'm sure you're tired. Why don't you get some rest?" Reed went to the closet and got down a pillow and another blanket—this one with a window-pane quilt pattern.

"I don't need any more blankets," Jenna said.

Reed's lips quirked up on one side. "But I do. The couch gets a little cold once the fire goes out."

Jenna hopped out of bed. "Oh, geez. I'm sorry. I'm in your bed."

She caught him staring at her legs. "Oh, God." She pulled the sheet around her. "I mean…I'll sleep on the couch. I shouldn't put you out of your own bed."

He brought his eyes back to her face.

"It's fine. Believe me, the couch is much more comfortable than where I was sleeping a year ago."

"But I insist." Jenna did not want to be in debt to this man any more than she already was. "It's the least I could do after all you've done for me."

A smile quirked at the edges of Reed's lips. "How about we both sleep in the bed, then?"

Jenna scooted back again, then noticed his smile widen. Well, she could call him at his own game. "Could I count on you to be a gentleman?"

"I'm never a gentleman, but I also never force myself on a woman." He sat on the edge of the bed and removed his shoes and socks, then his shirt came off. "The bed would be more comfortable, though." He stood to remove his pants and turned toward her, quirking an eyebrow as his fingers hovered on his zipper.

She knew it was a test. She wasn't sure she should take it, but she didn't want to put him out on the couch. Okay. So, maybe—just maybe—she wanted her protector next to her. She owed him for finding her, for carrying her down the mountain, for taking care of her. The least she could do was let him sleep in his own bed. No reason to read anything into it. No reason at all.

She lowered herself under the covers, pulling them up to her chin and turned her back to him, making sure a part of the sheet was tucked under her as one more barrier between him and her. "Sleep in your own bed," she said softly.

She heard the zipper on his pants go down and each foot step out of the pants legs. She didn't dare turn around. She didn't want to know if he was wearing briefs or boxers. She didn't want to know if he slept in underwear or nothing at all. She closed her eyes tight.

She felt the bed give as his full weight was taken. She heard the bedside lamp click off. Though her eyes were closed tight, she felt him lean over her shoulder. He chuckled.

"No need to worry, sweet Jenna." His lips grazed her temple so lightly it felt like a breeze from a window. "Though I will certainly have lustful dreams, I will not tempt you tonight. So sleep soundly. This may be the only night I can make that promise."

Jenna tightened her grip on the sheet. She believed him, but now she was worried about herself. She wasn't sure she could fall asleep with him beside her. Just as she was fighting the battle with exhaustion, she heard his heavy breaths and knew he was asleep. For just a moment, she let go and allowed herself to relax…just enough…to drift off.

Chapter Six

Jenna sleepily opened her eyes and found herself staring at the back of Reed's head. She knew immediately where she was and who lay beside her. A confusing rush of emotions swamped her. Impressions, feelings and thoughts—all coming so fast she couldn't sort them out. Events were sweeping her along, not giving her time to analyze or think or make deliberate decisions.

Had he moved at all since going to sleep? He must have been exhausted. That vulnerability filled her with both tenderness and a fierce sense of protectiveness. She wanted to lay her head against his back. Then she remembered his words last night. The last thing she wanted to do was tempt him.

Well, maybe not the last thing. She shook her head. *Stop thinking like that.*

She wanted to run her fingers through his short hair. It wasn't cut anywhere near as short as most Marines. It was a little shaggy but not long. She wanted to lift the sheets and discover what he wore to bed, but then she remembered his statement about lustful dreams. What would she do if she found a bulge in his underwear? Or worse, without his underwear? Heat gathered between her legs and rose up her stomach, across her chest, all the way to her face. The abrupt sharpness of her own sexual need pulsing through her was devastating, adding another layer of fear.

She hadn't wanted to have sex with anyone since her divorce ten years ago. Sexual release, yes, but not *with* anyone—and for a long time, she hadn't even wanted that. She'd dated several men, but none got close enough to push the relationship to a sexual level. There were times when she'd wondered if her friends were right when they teased that not having sex for so long made her a virgin again.

To so suddenly want—need—to be caressed, to balance on the edge between lust and control, to feel the rawness of penetration made her spin.

Why Reed? Why now?

She barely knew him, and he was exactly the opposite of any man she would ever choose to date. Was it the fact that she'd recently suffered a big trauma? Make that two or three traumas. She'd read articles that suggested men and women in stressful circumstances often find themselves wanting sex. That's why so many babies were born nine months after blackouts or following a natural disaster. People turned to each other for that intimacy—for that close comfort.

That must be it. She edged herself back under the covers. It was cold. The fire must certainly be out now.

It wasn't that she really desired him, she comforted herself. Her sudden body heat was just a reaction to stress. On the other hand, for a few sleepy moments, pondering the resurrection of her sexual need and the delicious unknown of a possible new relationship, she wouldn't mind forgetting her situation for a few hours.

Reality check, Jenna chided herself. She knew that giving up control...of anything...only ended in heartache. She'd learned that with her sister. She'd learned that with her love life. The last thing she needed in her life was a violent, controlling Marine with secrets. But whoever killed Tanya was determined to kill her, and maybe David too. She'd do anything to protect David—even if it meant spending more time with Reed. She listened intently to the silence. It was so different from her condo in the city, where the constant stream of traffic lulled her to sleep each night. Soft light streamed in the window, still muted in the remnants of the dark before early dawn. Reed's face looked quiet in repose, his breathing regular and deep. She snuggled back under the covers. She turned her back to him, afraid to watch him while he slept. Afraid she might touch him.

Reed reached toward her under the blanket and put his hand on her hip, silently pulling her closer. Realizing now that he was not naked, but wore some type of cotton boxers, she let her hips snug up against him, spoon fashion. Tears stung her eyes as she nestled close. This was what she'd missed most after the divorce, the quiet companionship in the night, the knowledge that she wasn't alone. They hadn't so much as kissed, yet somehow she and Reed were already linked.

"Go back to sleep," he whispered softly. "You need all the rest you can get."

Oh God, he's awake. She wanted to turn toward him. She wanted to feel his arms around her. She wanted to nestle safely into his chest. For once, she wanted to know for sure she wasn't alone. She trembled on the verge of turning, but then stiffened at the realization of what she was asking. If he held her, if he put his hands on her body, she suspected they'd do more than just holding. He was a man and he wanted her. And she knew, if she turned toward him right now, she'd give him whatever he wanted.

Was it bad to want him to touch her? To feel his fingers sliding along her thighs, caressing her and working into her center. She wanted it so intensely she had to bite back a whimper.

As if reading her thoughts, he wrapped a strong arm across her stomach, inching her T-shirt up as he pulled her into a protective embrace. "I want you, too, but now is not the time. You're safe. Go back to sleep."

A little bloom of contentment unfolded inside her. He wanted her too. She smiled as she drifted off.

****

Reed listened to her slight snore as she fell into a deeper sleep. He doubted he could sleep now though—not with her butt snuggled right against his cock. No sane man could sleep next to that milky white skin, next to the sweet, fruit-laced woody scent he inhaled on every breath. There would be no getting back to sleep for him or he wouldn't be accountable for his actions when his dreams started up again.

He liked the way she fit against him, the feel of his arm across her bare stomach, the feel of her silken legs against his skin. *Oh, shit.* It wasn't a good idea to think of those legs. He closed his eyes to shut out the picture already playing in his mind, but it didn't help. Instead, his imagination clarified the vision of those legs over his shoulders and his body rising above her. He saw the roundness of her breasts and the erect dusky pink nipples standing at attention when the breeze from the window swept across them. His cock swelled with the pictures in his mind.

Fuck! He'd promised her she was safe. Maybe, if he just didn't move, she'd never know. She wiggled her butt against him and he groaned as she settled in closer. His cock now nestled solidly in the indentation of her panties.

He tried to carefully remove his arm. Maybe he could slowly inch away from her. He tried pushing back. She automatically scooted back against him again.

Crap, this was damn unfair. He wasn't a saint. None of his buddies would believe he was lying here with a luscious woman and not taking advantage. He was sure, if he softly stroked her, she'd respond and he could probably get inside her before she woke up enough to stop him.

But that wasn't his style. He'd meant it when he said he didn't force himself on women—even when it seemed pretty obvious she wanted it. But with her asleep, she wouldn't be making a conscious choice. He didn't want her reacting out of stress, getting into the whole protector thing. If that was all she was feeling, she'd regret it after all was said and done.

He let out a deep sigh. This was definitely a first for him. What was the record for a hard on without any action?

Shit! Wouldn't it figure he'd be the one to set that record—though he certainly wouldn't be sending it in to Guinness. He'd be the laughing stock of the Corps.

Finally, she rolled forward, almost three quarters on her stomach, and he carefully slid his arm from her. He eased toward the edge of the bed and glanced at the clock. Only forty-five minutes had passed, but it was the longest damn forty-five minutes in recent memory. He no longer trusted his control. His cock still hard, he slipped into the bathroom for a cold glass of water. After a second glass, his lust began to subside but returning to his bed was still out of the question.

Reed stripped off his boxers and turned on the shower to warm. He wished he could blame his lack of control on not being with a woman for over a year, but he wouldn't lie to himself. It was Jenna. Her loyalty to her sister, in spite of their rocky relationship. Her confidence in taking in David, knowing it would change her life. Her determination in the face of danger. He'd never known a woman like her. Even her daring to sleep next to him in spite of her fears was courageous. Then when she snuggled against him...*damnit!* Definitely no control. He had no control at all.

Toweling off from the shower, Reed pulled on his sweats and a T-shirt and then slipped quietly out of the bedroom to make coffee. Once the drip started, he found his cell, plugged in his Bluetooth earpiece and dialed Jason. Yeah it was early, but Jason was Corps so he'd be in the office by 6:30.

"You must be desperate, rat face," Jason answered the phone on the second ring. "The last time you called me this early you needed me to spring you from jail."

Reed chuckled. He'd been known as the ladies' man in the Corps. But Jason had nicknamed him rat face to make sure he never got a swelled head about it. He didn't mind, the nickname wasn't nearly as bad as Jason's—Cheeks.

"I'm even more desperate this time, Cheeks, but it won't cost you bail money."

"Must be a girl, then."

"How'd ya know?"

"Rat face, you're so boring there are only three things in your life—booze, women, and kicking ass. You can usually handle yourself on the ass-kicking part, so I knew it was one of the first two."

The coffee pot dinged and Reed poured himself a cup. "Yeah, it's a woman and I need your lawyering skills on this one." He inhaled the aroma of strong coffee then took a long drink for fortification.

"Shit. You didn't finally knock someone up, did you? You know with DNA they can prove paternity these days real easy. There is no getting out of it."

"Cheeks, you know I'm always careful about that stuff."

"Yeah." Reed heard papers shuffling. "So, what is it? A pre-nup? With all your millions, you're finally getting hitched?"

Reed laughed at the thought of millions. He was comfortable with his retirement and his occasional gig with the mountain rescue guys, but he wasn't rich by a long shot.

"You know that ain't gonna happen," he said. "I figure getting burned once was enough."

"Old age creeping in, rat face? What is it…three months and you'll hit the big four-o?"

"Hey, you're close behind; besides, forty isn't so bad. I figure I know what I like and I still know how to use all the equipment."

Jason laughed. "Yeah, with that face of yours, all the old crones will probably be begging for your attention even when you're ninety."

"Seriously, Cheeks." Reed lowered his voice in case David woke up and suddenly came into the kitchen. "I do have kind of a problem with a woman…and a kid…and a murder."

"Holy shit. Hang on a minute." Reed heard a door close in the background. "We're private now. So dump. What are you into?"

Reed ran down the situation in his usual sparse military briefing style—sketching out the important details and leaving out anything unnecessary to the mission, particularly the part about the luscious body he just left in the bedroom without so much as a stray touch.

"Okay, so DNA is part of the problem." Jason paused, but Reed didn't say anything.

"I'll start the birth records search," Jason continued. "It sounds like the dead woman probably stayed in the Portland metro area, so it shouldn't be too hard to find the hospital or clinic where she gave birth. Then we have to see if there's a father listed on the record. If so, we have to contact him. Fathers have the right to stop any custody or adoption hearings, if they can prove they can care for, and want, the kid. We'll probably have to do a DNA test, just to prove that…what was her name?"

"Jenna…" Reed gulped as she walked out of the bedroom, her hair wet from a shower and a towel wrapped around her sarong style. It covered her from just below the shoulders to mid-thigh, but still, he knew what was beneath it and there was that one part of her he hadn't seen yet.

"Jenna? Is that her real name or a nickname?" Jason asked in his ear.

"Who you talking to?" Jenna asked. "Do you have anything I can borrow to wear until I can wash my clothes?"

"She's there, isn't she?" Jason asked in his ear. "I can tell by your shallow breathing. Is she naked or are you just imagining things? I'm starting to feel like this is a porn call here."

"Just a minute," Reed hissed and muted the phone to give Jenna his full attention. "I'm talking to an attorney friend about helping you get custody of David."

"Oh." She wandered over to the coffee pot. "Can I have some?"

"Yeah, sure." He clicked the Bluetooth to talk again.

She opened a cupboard and reached to the second shelf for a mug. It was just a little tall for her. The towel rose giving him a better view of tight lean thighs. Just as he thought he might see more, she fingered the mug off the shelf and the towel lowered to mid-thigh again. She poured a cup and walked barefoot to the fridge, pulled out the milk carton and poured some into the cup.

He stepped close and reached over her head to the top of the fridge. "Sugar?" he rasped, his throat suddenly dry as sandpaper. Citrus shampoo wafted from her hair. His shampoo—but it smelled sweeter on her.

"No thanks." Her eyes looked up at him.

"Thanks for last night."

"Uh…no problem." He lied. He bent his face toward her.

"Hey, rat face did you forget about me?"

He jumped back. "Shit!"

She chuckled.

"Sorry," he said to Jenna. "Just a minute."

"Rat face, are we going to finish our conversation or are you going to jump this lady's bones? I really didn't want to let my imagination play with all the silences I kept hearing."

"Yeah, thanks for pulling me back from the brink," Reed said. "Just a sec."

He muted the phone again and turned to Jenna. "You can, uh, borrow some sweats—second drawer in the chest. I know they'll be a little big." He looked her up and down. "Or a lot big. But at least you'd be warm. Okay?"

"Thanks." She ambled back to the bedroom.

Reed sighed as he watched the backs of her knees, the curve of her shoulder, and the swing of her ebony hair. Damn! He'd been a saint this morning.

"I'm back," he said into the phone. "She came out in a damn towel. Fuck. Life is really unfair sometimes."

Jason laughed. "I'm sure you'll find a way around your inconvenient ethics pretty quick; anyway, while you were salivating, I was starting the paperwork. We have a contract with a reputable company that gives fast service for DNA tests. It's in Gresham. Just a sec and I'll get you the info."

Reed heard keys clicking.

"Okay, it's Vienoy, Inc. 122 Division Street. She can go to any doctor to have the swab done, and take the kid, too. Then have them send both of the samples to Vienoy for processing."

Reed wrote down the company name and

address. Then he repeated it back.

“Thanks, Cheeks, I owe you for this.”

“You owe me so much, rat face, you'll never be able to pay me back.”

“Yeah, don't I know it.”

“Keep me posted,” Jason said, his tone more serious. “This sounds like some wicked shit going on. I know you can sometimes be a lone ranger, but I don't think you should be on this one alone.”

“I won't be,” Reed promised. “Not with a woman and kid involved. I'm calling Stain in on this, and then I'll get back to you with a plan.”

“Right, we've always got your back.”

As Reed hung up, he couldn't help thinking that his back wasn't the problem. Right now, he just needed to concentrate on controlling his front.

Chapter Seven

Jenna drove down the mountain, keeping an eye in her rear view mirror. Reed and David followed close behind in Reed's forest green hybrid. She still wasn't sure they'd all fit in her downtown one bedroom, one bath condo. Reed had insisted she not stay there alone and she had to admit she felt much safer knowing he'd be there. But she worried about David's safety. She needed to find another safe place for him until this was over. Unfortunately, so far David was adamant about not leaving Reed's side.

She'd been up to Mt. Hood several times for weekend stays over the past few years, but coming home to Portland this time felt different. In the past, she reveled in the wildness and the freedom of the forest, the canopies of old growth fir and fast running rivers. She'd always felt a sense of being protected by the mountain. But now, with all that had happened, she felt haunted by a looming evil.

When she made the turn at Shorty's Corner and the civilization of Sandy came into view, the landscape changed once again to a patchwork of small farms, vineyards and fertile orchards. It hit her how much the range of geology and nature here entwined with human history, all within a few miles, and now her history was indelibly marked here as well.

Already it seemed that Reed had inserted himself into her life, her investigation, and now her home. She was grateful for the help of his attorney friend, but things were moving way too fast. She was no longer sure if she was actually making any decisions on her own or just being swept along in the wake of Reed's protective energy. She'd have to get that under control. She wasn't the type to be swept away by anyone, especially not by a man. Been there, done that.

She pressed the talk button on her steering wheel and said, "Dial Becca." Within two seconds, she could hear the ringing phone echoing through her car. She loved these new Bluetooth devices.

"Thank God," her best friend answered. "I've been worried about you since the funeral. I tried to call the next day to check up on you, but no answer. I figured maybe you headed out to the coast for a while. How are you doing?"

"Not bad considering someone tried to kill me."

Becca laughed. "No really. How are you?"

"Really. Someone knocked me out last night and then left me on Mt. Hood. Just like my sister."

Becca gasped. "Oh my God. Are you sure? What am I saying, of course you're sure. Have you talked to the police? Oh my God, where are you? What the hell is going on?"

Jenna took a deep breath. Becca was usually a rock, but then no one in her close circle of girlfriends had experienced murder before. "I'm in my car, heading home from Mt. Hood. Reed is following me."

"Reed?"

"It's a long story. I'll catch you up with everything when I get home. Do me a favor?"

"Sure, anything."

"Could you call Leena, and then both of you meet us at my place. I should be there in about an hour."

"Sure. No problem. Can you bring me up to date while you're driving?"

"It'll be easier in person. You still have the spare key I gave you, don't you?"

"Yeah."

"Make yourself at home. Oh, and would you pick up something from Chat Précieux for dinner. Reed's probably calling in his friends too—so we better count on three, five, uh...seven total. Tell Simone I just want easy finger food—nothing fancy—but enough to fill up big hungry men."

"Got it." Becca paused and Jenna heard her careful intake of a breath. "Listen, take it slow, Jenna. You've been to hell and back the past couple of weeks."

Jenna swallowed. "You don't know the half of it."

"I'm just saying..."

"I know," Jenna said. "I love you, too." She swallowed again, holding back threatening tears. "Now get going, we don't have all day here."

Becca chuckled. "Ouch. That whip reaches a long way."

Jenna smiled. "See ya soon. And...thanks." She clicked the phone off on the steering wheel before the goodbyes got too long or silly.

Becca and Leena were her best friends. If anyone could keep her sane, they would. They'd kept her going after the divorce, after Tanya had left, and through building her restaurant—Chat Précieux. When she learned about Tanya's murder, Becca and Leena never left her side until after the funeral, when she'd forced them to finally go home. Even when she was exhausted or bitchy, they'd stood by her. They'd become her only family—her real sisters—for the past ten years.

Becca had just celebrated her forty-second birthday last month. She'd never been married. A career naval officer, Becca just never found the time to settle down with all the traveling and nine-month deployments. When Jenna and Becca met they'd hit it off immediately. Becca was organized, strong, and completely understood the drive that kept Jenna going.

At thirty-six, Leena was the youngest of their triumvirate. Leena's husband had died six years ago. They used to come into Chat Précieux at least once a month, and Jenna loved to just watch them interact. They were one of the few couples Jenna immediately knew were soul mates. He'd been the love of Leena's life, and though she'd dated off and on—mostly off—for the past six years, all other men paled in comparison.

Jenna was counting on them now to help her figure out who murdered her sister and who was trying to kill her. Becca's computer skills would be a great help for research. She knew her way around databases and personal information files better than anyone Jenna knew. Leena was the social connector. An amazing blues singer, she easily traveled along the social continuum of Portland. She was invited into the homes of the rich and powerful for private parties, but was equally revered by the blue-collar community and the poor who found her bluesy sensibility something that spoke to their lives. People automatically talked to Leena without much prodding. She was drop dead gorgeous, so most men told her all kinds of things without realizing the analytical mind behind those auburn curls.

With Becca and Leena on her side, she felt confident the three of them could unravel this mystery. The only question was, could they do it before something else happened. Becca was the only one of the three who knew how to handle a gun or had self-defense training, and Jenna didn't want to endanger her best friends. That was where Reed and his friends came in. He'd said they were all retired Marines—specifically Special Ops. Maybe, working together, they could stop this monster…before someone else was killed.

****

Marius Crane ushered the petite woman out of the exam room with a smile. “We’ll see you next week then, Ms. Cornwall, and we’ll just get rid of this nasty piece of business.” He patted her hand and opened the heavy wooden door to the reception area.

“Thank you, Doctor. I don’t know what I’d do without you. I just can’t afford to lose my figure. My career would be irreparably harmed. You’re the only one who understands.”

“Of course.” He patted her shoulder and applied a little pressure to move her through the door. “Until then.”

Once the door closed completely, he strode to his office. “No calls for the next half hour.” He looked pointedly at the receptionist and shut the door.

The man standing inside was shuffling from one side to the other. His fuchsia shirt stood out against the blue pinstriped suit. Marius preferred a more understated look, but then Shumenko always wore at least one bright color. Must be a cultural thing.

Marius lowered himself into the large leather chair behind his desk. He waved his hand toward the chair on the other side. The man sat on the edge of the seat, his entire body tense and forward.

“Problem?” Marius asked.

Shumenko gestured widely, his accent more pronounced than usual. “The lady’s nowhere. Didn’t check into a hospital. Didn’t go back to her condo. Hasn’t checked in at her restaurant. Nowhere.”

Marius quietly pulled out a drawer to the right of his desk and extracted a folder. Placing it carefully on the glass top, he opened it and perused all the notes the private investigator had given him on Jenna Mosier. Once again, he was surprised she didn’t have a man in her life. *Beautiful and successful, it doesn’t seem possible.* Perhaps if he’d met her under different circumstances he would have made a play. He shook his head. What a waste.

When the PI first reported the lack of any romantic interest, he thought maybe she was a lesbian. But that didn't play either. Normally he'd figure the PI missed something—but not this guy, he was thorough. Marius had used him to track the kid when he escaped. The PI had tracked down Tanya and the kid within two days.

The plan had worked flawlessly. That is, the locating had worked flawlessly. Losing the kid wasn't part of the plan, but that wasn't the fault of the PI. It was the jackass sitting in front of him who did that. He looked up at Shumenko in disgust.

"How could a petite woman get the best of you? I thought you knew what you were doing."

"I didn't expect her to fight. She knows moves. Then she ran and I slipped. I saw her go over the edge and hit her head on the rock. She was bleeding pretty fast. I sat and watched her for at least an hour."

"But you didn't go down and check her."

"I couldn't. I heard voices on the path. You said don't get caught, so I ran." The man stood and paced behind the chair. "I told you we shouldn't go after her so soon. I told you it would look too suspicious."

Marius sighed. Maybe he'd made a mistake this one time. Maybe he should have listened. However, if Jenna Mosier was even half as smart as her sister, he knew she'd figure things out too quickly. Or maybe he'd given her too much credit. She hadn't spoken to her sister in ten years. Hadn't even bothered to look for her. Why would she risk her life for a dead woman? Why not let the police handle it?

"Look, I think we need to lay low." Beads of perspiration increased on Shumenko's bald head as he paced. "The sister was one thing. She could have ruined all the good work you do here. I didn't mind killing her because I know my Marya might live because of your good work." He crossed himself. "God willing." He stopped and leaned on the desk, his face intense. "This Jenna chick, she don't know nothing. I'm sure we scared her enough now. Let's just wait her out."

"If she was scared, she would have reported to the police," Marius said. "No, this is much worse than I'd counted on. She suspects something now—something more—and she's making plans. I can feel it. That's why she hasn't surfaced. I should have been at the funeral. I should have talked to her, told her about my relationship with Tanya—sent her down a different path." He drew out a newspaper clipping and turned it toward the man. "See who's standing next to her at this charity function?"

"Yeah. Some handsome old guy in an expensive suit. Who's he? Her father?"

Marius sighed. "It's the governor." Did the man never watch the news or read a newspaper? How could he not recognize the governor? It was his second term in office, you'd think with his face out there all the time even an uneducated person like Shumenko would recognize him.

Marius took the clipping back and placed it neatly in the folder. "Unlike her sister, Jenna Mosier has money and influence. She's a planner and a stickler for details. If you'd done your job right in the first place and not killed the sister, just taken her out of the country, we wouldn't be in this situation."

"How was I to know she could fight, or that the kid would listen to her and run? I thought she was a typical dumb blonde—all sex and no brains. I was protecting myself. She would have shot me. Then who would my Marya have to protect her? To make sure she gets the treatment she needs? Huh?"

Marius steepled his fingers on the desk. Jenna Mosier would have to show up sooner or later. She had a business to run, friends to meet. He'd just have to be patient. He could do that. Patience was his middle name. He'd been patient when he was at Thompson Medical University. He'd been patient building up Vienoy, Inc. He'd been patient with his work and with all the children he'd grown from those aborted fetuses.

Soon they'd all see what a good man he was. Soon, they'd all thank him for what he'd done. If a few children died, or a meddler had to be murdered, they'd forgive him when he cured their child of cancer, or brought a husband or wife back from dementia with a full mind. They'd forgive him anything then.

He smiled. "You're right, Shumenko. We should just wait and see what happens. Go home. Give your little girl a kiss for me. I'll call you when I need you."

****

When Jenna pulled in to the underground garage of her condo and parked, she didn't move from her car. She took a deep breath and let it out slowly. She was home. At last. But it wouldn't be the quiet respite she'd hoped for. Instead her small place would be overrun with people.

A knock on her window startled her and she turned to see Reed's face looking in, his brow furrowed. "Okay?" he mouthed. She nodded and pulled her key from the ignition, automatically unlocking the doors. He immediately opened hers and offered his hand to help her out.

"I parked in the visitor space you told me about and hot footed it to the elevator. When you never showed, I got worried."

Her heart sped up. She wasn't sure if it was because she hadn't thought to be scared in her own parking garage, or if it was knowing Reed cared—even a little.

"Where's David?" She asked, looking beyond

him, expecting the kid to be hanging on him as if he had been the last 24 hours.

Reed chuckled. “Your friend, uh, the brunette.”

“Becca.”

“Yeah, that’s the one. She charmed him immediately with milk and cookies. Didn’t take much to convince him to stay there a few minutes while I went to find you.”

“She’s the oldest of nine children,” Jenna said. “Though she’s never been married, or had kids herself, she knows a lot about raising them.”

Jenna started toward the elevator, then turned and thumbed the key fob to lock her car doors. Time to face the music. Time to go through the whole story once more with Becca and Leena. Then they had to make a plan—a plan to figure out why this was happening and how they could stop it.

Reed naturally fell in beside her, his hand at her elbow. When they got to the elevator, he pressed the up button.

“I’m not fragile,” she said, moving a step away from him.

“We’re all fragile.”

She looked up at him. The strong jaw, the dark brown eyes. She didn’t see anything fragile about him. He was granite, solid through and through. She saw something shift in his eyes and he leaned toward her, as if to kiss her. The elevator ding interrupted his motion and he moved back as the doors opened, but no one entered. They rode in silence to the fifth floor. When they exited, she turned to her left and headed to her corner unit at the end of the long hall.

She’d bought the condo when the building was renovated four years ago. Her restaurant had been getting rave reviews and she was making more money than ever before. The Embassy building was a historical landmark in Portland. Built in 1925, it had needed a complete remodel to come up to code. When the owners decided to renovate but keep the historical quality and go condo, she knew it was the perfect situation for her. Within walking distance of the restaurant and all the other amenities in the Pearl District, she never worried about staying late at work. Though it was only 900 square feet, her southwest corner unit was spacious by downtown standards.

It was the large entry and the hardwood floors throughout her unit that had first caught her eye. But it was the French doors between the dining room and living room that had sealed the deal even before she'd noticed all the other beautiful architectural elements. Large floor-to-ceiling windows in each room, custom bookcases, and an updated but vintage kitchen gave it a warmth and charm rarely found in a downtown space. The unit even came with a deeded parking and storage space. Most of the time she didn't even need her car, keeping it parked in the garage, since she could get anywhere in downtown Portland via the Streetcar, the light rail, or the bus system. And the Pearl was wonderful for walking and shopping. She stiffened her back as she approached her unit. How long would she have to be gone? How long until she'd be safe again?

She stopped at her door and Reed almost slammed into her.

"Just savoring the moment," she said, her back to him. "Before all hell breaks loose again."

He didn't say anything, but she could feel his breath on her neck.

She turned and looked into his eyes. "Do we have to go in?"

A sad, sort of half smile answered her.

She held his gaze, sure he could hear her heart beat. He bent toward her and brushed her lips. The kiss was so soft and quick she could almost convince herself she imagined it. But the look in his eyes told her otherwise.

"We're both fighters, Jenna. I'm not leaving."

Reed backed her against the door and lowered his mouth.

A loud retort suddenly echoed behind them.

"Down! Get Down!" Pulling her roughly to the ground, he flattened himself on top of her.

The sound wasn't the whine of an incoming artillery shell. Damn, somehow a sniper had gotten a range on them. He peered between the rail slats.

Where am I? They must be on base. *Where's my weapon?*

Reed saw a man in camos running across the street two stories below, blood spurting from his neck. The man took another step and then toppled.

"Get down!" Reed bellowed at the remaining standing soldier.

The woman struggled under him. He held her down, listening for the next crack of the sniper's rifle.

Where am I? On top of an adjacent building?

A thud sounded like far-off bombing.

"What is it?" the woman asked.

A door opened in front of him. A tall redhead looked down, her brows raised.

"Jenna?" She looked at Reed. "What's going on? You okay?"

"Get down!" Reed yelled. "Sniper!"

Feet pounded in the building behind the door. An arm pushed the redhead to the ground in front of them.

"Ouch! Stop that," she said.

"Reed?"

It was a familiar voice and Reed sighed with relief. He wasn't alone in this crazy war. Cheeks was one of the best in his unit.

Body rigid, waiting for the deadly fire of a Russian AK-47, Reed tried to think. *What should our next move be?*

Cheeks let the red-haired woman up and pushed her inside. "Go on, I'll take care of this," he whispered. "Reed? Hey, rat face."

Reed looked up at Jason standing above him. *Why is he dressed in civvies?*

One second, they were under fire from insurgents. The next, he was on a carpeted concrete platform, atop a furious, frightened woman in front of an apartment.

"Fuck!" He rolled off the woman. She struggled to a sitting position but she didn't move to stand.

Fuck. Fuck. Fuck! He'd heard a car backfire. That's all.

But he'd seen blood spurting from a soldier's neck, crimson mixing with dirt on the road. He closed his eyes. *Shit.* Maybe not. More dazed than he usually was when he snapped out of a flashback, he stared at the woman he'd held pinned down.

"Jenna? I'm sorry."

He looked up and Jason reached a hand down to Jenna to help her stand. She shook her head.

"I'll see you inside," Jason said. "Whenever you two are ready." He closed the door again.

Jenna's wide eyes held his without flinching. "Are you all right?"

"No. Yes." He scrubbed a hand over his face. "Fuck."

"It's okay," she whispered. "Just stand up."

Adrenaline still pumping, physically battle-ready, he got up and offered her his hand. She took it and stood easily.

Neither of them moved, and he sure wasn't in a hurry to walk in that room knowing Cheeks would have told everyone about what just happened.

Jenna touched his arm. "You…PTSD…"

He interrupted her, his hand turning the knob. "Let's go in and get this over with."

Jenna swallowed. Obviously, he wasn't going to talk about it right now. She nodded, raised her chin and went in ahead of him, ready to protect him from whatever whispered confidences were being shared among her friends.

"Hey," Leena said. She raised her eyebrow at Jenna. When Jenna didn't respond, Leena shrugged and raised her hand to show the ice bucket she carried. "Just running down to the lobby for some ice. It seems that caffeine is the addiction of choice around here—in soda that is." She looked frankly at Reed. "Hmmm...you're just as hunky as your friend Jason. He arrived while you were running down the elevator for Jenna." Then she smiled and squeezed past them, moving leisurely down the hall.

Jenna turned toward the living room and heard Becca's voice, followed by a low chuckle that obviously wasn't hers. She found Becca staring at her laptop, and the man who'd come to Reed's rescue a moment ago was looking over her shoulder. He was broader than Reed, with a full head of tawny hair.

"I can't work with you scrutinizing my every move, jarhead," Becca said, pushing his face away.

But he put his face right back where it was. "You going to work now, squid?" he asked. "You know Marines do all the real work. Navy just takes joy rides in big boats."

"You're talking through your brass ass, JAG. You may have been hard working once, but now that you're a soft attorney, you don't know what work is anymore. Now back off and let me show you how to make this thing sing." She tapped a few keys. "Now, what was the name of that database you have access to?"

Reed interrupted. "Jason, this is Jenna."

The man stood, and Jenna then realized he was even taller than Reed—who she had guessed was just over six feet. He took her hand and firmly shook it. “Hard to believe that rat face could hang on to such a beautiful woman more than twenty-four hours. Most women learn real quick he’s got nothing special and move on to someone with the real goods.”

She turned to Reed. “Rat face?”

“A name given to me out of envy,” Reed said. Then he looked back at Jason. “I was being nice when I introduced him. His real name is Cheeks, since it was a bullet in his ass that got him sent home early and a chance to go to law school.” Reed pressed a finger into Jason’s chest and jabbed. “Just to set things straight, it hasn’t been twenty-four hours yet so don’t get hasty.”

Jason smirked. “Uh huh.”

“He may look all brawn,” Reed said. “And definitely has the worst pick-up lines, but there is a good brain beneath it all. Cheeks is the one who’s drawing up all the legal papers for you to have custody of David permanently.”

With everything else on her mind, Jenna had almost forgotten about the papers as they drove down the mountain. “Thanks. It means a lot to me that you’re willing to take care of this so quickly. Can you give me a ballpark figure of what it’s going to cost?”

“Depends.” Jason winked.

Jenna smiled. Were all of Reed’s friends flirts? “Depends on what?”

“On if you can hold rat face here for longer than seventy-two hours.”

“I thought twenty-four was the record,” Jenna said.

She saw a grin pass between Reed and Jason. She knew she was probably being set up, but she was also enjoying the game.

"I forgot about that one three-day weekend," Jason said. "So the new record would have to be four days."

"And what's the payoff?" Jenna asked.

"My fees are gratis."

Jenna looked up at Reed. It wasn't that she didn't have the money, but she didn't mind the excuse to get to know this impenetrable man. She wasn't sure playing this game was a good idea given how uneasy she'd felt this morning waking up next to him.

She cocked a head and smiled at Reed. "Hmmm. Do I scare you?"

Reed grabbed her around the waist and pulled her against him hard. She put a hand on his chest to push him away, but he backed her into a low dip and she screeched. One wide, strong hand reached behind her and supported her head, and in one smooth move, he covered her lips with his. A soft heat filled her mouth, and she couldn't help but open to him. His tongue thrust in as if announcing a victory and she responded with equal confidence. Then the kiss turned to fiery desire as he brought her back to her feet, his mouth never leaving hers. Her fingers automatically twined in his hair and she was now the one wanting to crawl inside his skin. She felt the room spin away from her as he wrested control back. Just as she thought he would tear her clothes off, he stopped abruptly.

"You scare me, Jenna Mosier," he whispered in her ear. "But I scare you even more."

Jenna traced her fingers from his head down his neck and onto his shoulder, her eyes never leaving him, searching for the man behind the wall of granite. It was true. She was scared. Scared of his aggressiveness. Scared of his overt sexuality. Scared of what she wanted to do with him, to let him do to her. Most of all, Jenna was scared she could penetrate that granite wall but still never really be allowed to know the real Reed Adler. In spite of all those fears, she was even more scared to miss the opportunity to find out.

****

Reed walked around the condo complex one more time. He needed some time out. He'd left everyone at Jenna's place, researching Tanya's life and trying to discover why anyone would want to kill Jenna's sister, and what David might know if only he could open up, remember. Who was he to prod David to remember, when all Reed practiced was how to forget?

His stomach churned as if he'd swallowed a fist full of nails, each one pricking his conscience as they mixed and spewed acid pain into his throat. When would his mind stop fighting the war? When would he feel confident he could protect anyone again?

He'd thought insurgents were shooting at them and he'd knocked Jenna to the ground. He wanted to lie to himself and call it a life-saving instinct that had to be retrained—the bang of a mortar, the crack of a rifle, you hit the deck. Soldiers returning from every war had the same instinct. Some of them were able to bury it and take up their lives again. Be normal. Others were permanently mentally ill and could never lead a normal life. He was somewhere in between. He'd thought he'd been getting better. He'd thought he'd been pretty successful at putting it behind him over the last six months.

Obviously, he'd thought wrong. For a minute, he'd been transported back to Afghanistan and the small base near the Kotal-e Salang pass. He shook his head. He hadn't been completely at Kotal either, some part of his mind knew where he was—right here in Portland—but that part of his mind didn't have any control over his actions. At first, he'd known it was Jenna his body was protecting, but then he'd seen the soldier on the road with blood spurting from his neck and the woman beneath him became a burka-covered Afghan. The blood he'd seen had been as real as if he cut himself open right now. He could still close his eyes and see it all play out in his head.

Leaning on his rifle, Reed looks up the pass, wondering if today's going to be like every day this past week. Boring. No insurgents had come across the border since his unit arrived two weeks ago. The Marines had secured the pass for the past month. His sergeant is telling a dirty joke and turns to see Reed's reaction. The sergeant sees something in the distance and lifts his weapon, aiming toward a boulder high on the hill on the other side of the road. He shouts a warning to the corporal below. The corporal runs toward them.

Crack! The corporal jerks as the round enters his neck, a fountain of crimson spews on the dirt as he falls.

Flat on the ground, Reed looks at the corporal, his mind unable to take in the shock in the man's eyes—the knowledge that he is dying and that Reed's face is the last one he'd see. Reed leans in when the corporal struggles to say something, but Reed can't hear it above the answering fire. The corporal sprawls in the dirt, blood staining the packed earth and rocks nearby. He was only nineteen. It was his first deployment.

Somebody opens up with the M-60, with a burst that sounds like a chainsaw at full throttle. Reed backs up on his stomach to better cover. He doubles back over the hill, finding two men with guns. Without thinking twice, he exacts his revenge, firing three rounds into each of them. When he stops firing, he finally looks at them. They were only boys, probably no more than twelve or thirteen.

That had been the beginning of the end. When

he left Iraq, he'd been back at Lejeune for only four months and then they sent him to Afghanistan. He didn't know he had PTSD, or why he hesitated when faced with young boys and guns in the street. All he knew was he couldn't do his job. He was a risk to his unit. He didn't want to kill another woman in a burqa who might, or might not, be carrying explosives, or another woman who might turn out to be a man. He didn't want to be faced with the decision of shooting at a car at a checkpoint because it was going too fast, killing the parents and children, only to find they had nothing inside—no intent to harm him, just escaping the same terrorists he was fighting.

When Reed returned to Lejeune after the third deployment, he retired. He knew he needed help and he'd seen the psychologist for six months as ordered. Then he'd moved to Oregon—to get as far away from military life as possible. He'd thought the time to grieve alone had gone well. His home on Mt. Hood was the perfect location—a place where he could escape whenever he needed time away from the real world. After six months, Mike and Jason followed him to Oregon. His letters extolling the virtues of craft beer, high mountains, and the Pacific Ocean drew them. Having his buddies to go out for beers, to keep things normal, had really helped. The flashbacks had lessened. He still had nightmares, but he hadn't had a flashback in at least two months.

The events surrounding David and Jenna must have triggered something. He'd have to be careful, or he'd be a worthless protector. And they'd all end up dead.

Chapter Eight

"Bingo!" Becca pointed at the laptop screen open on the kitchen island. "There was a request for a birth certificate filed one month ago by Tanya Mosier for a David Mosier born on or about October 7th ten years ago. But the vital records office responded with a null finding."

Jenna peered over Becca's shoulder. "Then Tanya knew David's birthday. But no record? What does that mean?" She turned toward the kitchen and saw David standing perfectly still, his face ashen. The room went silent.

Jenna walked slowly toward him, but when she was within an arm's reach he ducked and ran to Reed's side, burying his head in Reed's stomach.

"Do I have to say, Reed? Do I have to?"

Reed wrapped his arms around the small body and hugged David tight, his eyes looking to Jenna. She could see pain reflected there. Was it Reed's own pain or his empathy for David's?

Oh God, was David kidnapped? Stolen?

When David finally released his hold, Reed squatted down to David's height and looked him straight in the eye. "Hey buddy. You don't have to do or say anything…if you don't want."

David sniffled, but remained stiff and unmoving, his eyes never leaving Reed's face.

"But if you never talk about what happened, then we can't ever catch the bad guys." Reed paused. "It's up to you. We'll do whatever you say."

David dropped his head and heaved a big breath

as if releasing a heavy burden. "Okay, I'll try. But it's still all confused." He pointed to his head. "Up here."

"How about we all sit down first and have a bite to eat?" Reed said. "Then you can just take your time, talk as you feel ready."

Reed offered his hand and David nodded. Together, they walked to the sofa and sat next to each other. No one wanted to break the tenuous hold on fear they shared.

Jenna hustled to the kitchen for soft drinks and bread. Becca followed her back out, balancing plates and silverware with butter, peanut butter, and jam.

Soon everyone was making PB&Js and teasing each other about choices—butter or no butter, jam on one side or both sides, cut in half on the diagonal or straight.

Bam. Bam. Bam. A fist pounded the door.

David shrieked, grabbed Reed and buried his face in Reed's side. "Don't let him in. Don't let him in!"

Reed carried David to Jenna and motioned for them both to go back to the kitchen.

Her heart in her throat, Jenna squeezed David's hand. "It's okay. Killers don't knock." She hoped.

Reed put a finger to his lips to signal silence. Then he nodded toward Jason.

Leena grabbed a butcher knife off the cutting board and held it down at her side, standing in front of Jenna and David.

Becca closed the computer and turned toward the door. Her chin held high. Her back straight and feet braced in a position ready to spring forward.

Jason moved to the peephole. His shoulders dropped as he let out a breath. "It's okay. It's Stain." He pushed the lever and opened the door wide. "You're late."

A tall, solid mass of muscle in khaki shorts and

a Marine Corp T-shirt strode through the door. "Traffic was a bitch, then I couldn't find a parking place, and...whoa!" He scanned the room, giving each of the three women a once-over. "Rat face didn't tell me he'd found dates for each of us."

Reed moved forward and punched the newcomer in the shoulder. "At ease, Marine, they're not dates."

Jenna moved out of the kitchen with Leena close behind. "I'm Jenna. You must be...Stain?" She extended her hand.

Reed cleared his throat. "Mike, Jenna." Mike squeezed her hand with a firm shake before letting go.

"Stain was our go-to guy for dismantling IEDs. If he ever screwed up, all that would be left of him was a stain in the road."

Macabre sense of humor. Did all Marines have weird names?

Mike beamed at her. "I never screwed up. So, this is who has rat face's panties in a wad." He peered around Jenna to Leena. "You don't really need the knife, beautiful. I don't bite...except when asked."

"Oops, forgot." Leena eased backward and returned the knife to the block on the counter. "I'm Leena." She extended a hand and Mike bent over it, brushing her knuckles with his lips. She blushed, withdrew her hand quickly and put it behind her back. "And, uh, biting is not my thing."

"Then you haven't been bitten by the right man." Mike winked.

Jenna's eyes widened in surprise. Leena never blushed around men. Being in the entertainment business, she'd heard all the lines and easily let them roll off her back with a bemused giggle. *What's this about?*

Reed moved back to the sofa with David firmly attached to his arm. "Find a place on the floor, Mike.

David was just about to tell us a story."

David's chin was practically on his chest. He obviously didn't want to talk. His chest rose and fell with a big breath and his shoulders sagged.

Reed waited until everyone had found a seat. He didn't want to force David to look at anyone, or to remember anything too painful. At the same time, he wanted to keep David and Jenna safe and didn't think he could do that without having more information. He positioned himself next to David, letting him get his bearings. Letting him gather his courage in his own way.

Reed tipped David's face up to look him in the eye. "It's okay, just take your time. Start whenever you like. If you get too scared, you can stop. Okay?"

David didn't take his eyes from Reed. "I don't really remember being a baby."

Reed smiled. "That's okay; I don't remember being a baby either."

"That's 'cause you never were a baby, rat face," Jason chided and everyone laughed. Except David.

"What I mean is..." David looked around the room, then dropped his chin again and looked at the floor, as if the memory was easier to find there. "I remember other kids being born—kind of. We all lived together in this big place, like a school. There was one big room where we all slept with beds that you could make go up and down...and lights at the head of it...and nurses who took care of us. Every few months, a new baby would be brought in to join us." He looked back down. "A lot of those babies died within a couple weeks. The nurses always said they just weren't strong enough. Then the doctor would come in and tell us we had to help the other babies. Babies we never saw. The nurses would poke our arms and take some blood for the other babies and then leave again."

Reed grimaced and looked to Jason and Mike. *Is*

anyone else as confused as I am?

“Were you sick, David? Was this a hospital?”

“No, I wasn’t ever sick.” David paused for a long moment. His lower lip tucked under his teeth and his eyes blinked rapidly. “If I wasn’t feeling good, I never said anything,” he whispered. “People who got sick never came back…some of my friends…” He stuck a thumb between his teeth and worried it, his eyes half closed as if he were holding back tears.

Reed gritted his teeth. It was sounding stranger with each sentence.

“How many other kids lived with you, David?” Mike asked.

David removed his thumb and looked up and to the right. “I don’t know, about thirty or so. Sometimes more.” He looked at Reed, his lips downturned. “One time about fifteen kids, all the same size as me, got sick at the same time. But I didn’t.”

“What happened when they got sick?” Reed asked.

“They died.”

Jenna gasped. “Always? They always died?”

David looked at her and nodded. His shoulders slumped and he curled into Reed as if asking for protection. “Sometimes I saw them die. Other times, the doctor would come and get them and then we’d never see them again. But I know they died, too.”

Jason leaned forward, his voice a whisper. “And the time fifteen died? What did the doctor do?”

“He got real mad and he took them all away. Three of them were my best friends and they were barely alive when the doctor and nurses took them. I was worried about them. So, about an hour later, I snuck out and went looking for them.” David paused and swallowed.

Reed held his breath, bracing for what horror David must have witnessed.

"They were all…lined up on those rolling beds, I think they're called gurneys, in front of a big fireplace," David choked out the words. "The doctor gave each of them a shot and…they stopped breathing. Then…" David's breath came out in short pants, and tears streamed down his face. "Then…he put them in the fire…and…and burned them." David wailed his distress and sobbed.

Fuck! Reed rocked the boy, barely able to hold back his own tears. He looked over to Jenna. She, Leena, and Becca were holding each other's hands. Silent tears falling.

What kind of a mad man are we dealing with? Reed looked to Jason and Mike. He could see it in their eyes. There was no question about asking for their help. This murder was more than one man killing Jenna's sister. It sounded like an entire fucking institution. An institution that used children for God knows what before disposing of them.

****

Marius poured himself two fingers of Macallan's single malt. He twirled the amber liquid in the glass and closed his eyes, letting the tangy aroma fill his senses before taking pleasure in the rich oaky taste. The scotch swirled its heat around his mouth and swept its comfort south as he swallowed, soothing the serrated edges of his mind.

God, that's good.

He moved to his favorite club chair and lowered himself into it, slowly pushing back until he was surrounded by the leather wings. He set the scotch on the marble top of the table beside him. Sliding his hand over the top ridge of the rounded arm, he rubbed the chocolate brown leather as he stared into the crackling fire and let the heat seep through him.

He'd worked hard today. He'd harvested six new children and was particularly pleased that the two-year-old group looked healthier than ever. If they lasted one more year, he'd begin his first human trials of the stem cells. As promised, the first subject would be Shumenko's daughter. She'd been born with a particularly difficult case of cystic fibrosis. Though current treatments gave most patients an eighty percent chance of living until they were forty or so, her particular diagnosis made it unlikely she'd live past twelve or thirteen.

He owed Shumenko a try. Of course, his treatment might also make her worse, but he would keep that bit of information to himself—that was the price of great research. Some had to die for others to live. Just like those fifteen kids who died last year. But specimen forty-nine survived. Why? That was the key. He had to be found. Without him, Marius' research was dead.

He took another sip of his scotch. He would not worry about that now. Shumenko was plenty motivated to find the kid and Tanya Mosier's meddling sister.

Marius' cock swelled at the sweet anticipation of success. All those who doubted him would soon hail him. He savored another sip of scotch, and another. Each time rolling the warmth about his mouth and then swallowing. The heat awakening his senses as it traveled into his system.

Bzzz. Bzzz.

Damn it! He pressed the button on his phone that rang to the gate. "This better be an emergency," he said to whoever was there.

"I...uh...think it is," a high-pitched, shaky feminine voice responded. "You told me to let you know if anyone heard from Jenna Mosier."

Marius laughed at his good fortune. *Perfect timing.*

"Come, Adrianne, and tell me all about it." He buzzed her through the gate.

His head nurse was completely loyal to him and

his cause. More than that, she was madly in love with him. Unlike Tanya, Adrianne was nowhere near his equal but she had her uses. His cock surged in anticipation of Adrianne's loyalty.

The tightness and stamina of her twenty-five-year old body made her a pretty good fuck. And she did anything he asked, no matter how unusual. Her own pleasure was completely dependent on his satisfaction. Tonight, he would allow her to please him. His cock tightened at thoughts of her tied to his exam table, her legs fixed in the stirrups begging for him to take full advantage of her.

A few minutes later, she rushed into the room, stumbling at the transom, barely catching herself before falling to her knees only a foot inside the door. She stood quickly, her curly blond locks a messy cascade about her shoulders. Her ample breasts tugged at the buttons on her blouse as her lungs fought for breath. Her full lips—lips he planned to put to immediate use—trembled.

"I'm...sorry to disturb you so late, Dr. Crane." She fluttered fingers to her lips.

"It's no disturbance...if it's good news." He gestured for her to approach the chair. "Maybe you can join me in a celebration if you're a really good girl." He parted his robe and stroked his cock, showing her his power.

Adrianne's eyes widened, as she whispered, "You know I'll do anything you ask." She licked her lips suggestively. "Anything."

Her eyes darted around the room as she fidgeted with the top button of her blouse. He chuckled to himself at her needy weakness. If this news was as good as he hoped, he wanted to draw out the tension, to make her beg to speak. It would make his satisfaction so much sweeter when she kneeled in front of him.

She shifted from foot to foot. Her hands fluttered

to splay across her neck. Her pupils dilated in the dim light and she chewed her lower lip. When it appeared she was about to dance out of her pants, he finally signaled Adrianne to speak.

Instead of saying anything, she fidgeted in her handbag and drew out a piece of paper. Her hand shaking, she stepped closer and held it out to him.

He frowned. "Lab reports?" His sexual anticipation deflated like a ruptured wineskin. "That's all you have for me…lab reports?"

He scanned the results. A DNA match indicating blood relatives. "And what does this have to do with Jenna Mosier?"

Adrianne smiled and handed him the second piece of paper. "Her attorney ordered this one to prove Jenna Mosier *is* David Mosier's aunt."

Marius scanned the request for the DNA test. Then he returned to the lab report. How had he missed the DNA sequence for the boy? He should know it by heart.

"Ah yes, specimen forty-nine. So, Tanya named him David?"

When he'd started his affair with Tanya, he didn't know she was one of the many women he'd helped with an abortion. How could he? Tanya was Vienoy Inc's primary patent attorney. He'd thought he'd finally found a woman who met his needs—both in brains and in bed. After a particularly amazing weekend of research success and sexual celebration, he'd made the one and only mistake of his career. He'd shared his brilliant plan with her. His plan to create organs for dying children. His plan to cure all childhood disease. His plan to finally have all of his research vindicated.

Instead of begging to become a permanent partner in Vienoy, she'd called him a monster. She'd accused him of hurting and killing innocents. He'd argued the specimens weren't human. Tanya vehemently disagreed. To prove her wrong, he took her to the research lab to show her the good care nurses took of the specimens—better care than any animal in most facilities. Though he'd considered keeping the specimens in cages, he'd decided they needed exercise to fully develop—to grow the tissue and muscle he needed to extract. He always followed experimental protocol. He always kept meticulous records of his work. And when the end was near, they were euthanized before the pain became unbearable. Euthanized. Humanely.

Tanya had shakily pointed to specimen forty-nine. Marius saw the resemblance the minute they walked in the room and knew he'd made a mistake. He hadn't known. He'd never actually looked at the specimens. He saw them for what they were—an assemblage of parts to be tested and analyzed and cataloged. Tanya had knocked him out cold and tried to escape with all the subjects. Fortunately, Adrianne saw him go down and called security. They'd saved all the specimens, except one. Number forty-nine.

That was why Tanya had to be stopped. Stopped before she ruined decades of good work. Work that would be hailed around the world, no questions asked about the years of study or the methods used. Tanya had signed her own death warrant with that stupid show of sentimentality for a child she'd never even known existed.

Adrianne danced forward, interrupting his thoughts, shaking even more papers at him. Her voice breathy with excitement. "We have the address, the background check on the sister, the temporary custody order for David to stay with Jenna Mosier, everything." She walked forward and fingered his robe open. Kneeling in front of him, she placed her hand boldly on his cock. "I did good, right? You can get number forty-nine back and finish your work now."

Marius groaned as she stroked. This was perfect news. He had to call Shumenko, get him to pick up the specimen.

She dropped her head and opened her mouth, bringing back his erection. He'd call Shumenko later. He deserved to celebrate first.

He'd learned his lesson with Tanya. Women didn't need brains if they were beautiful and could do this. When she finally swallowed all of his magnificent seed, he patted her head like a good child. He gestured for her to stand and strip. Then he led her to his private exam room. This was her lucky night. He would celebrate with her body for several more hours.

****

Jenna stirred her chamomile tea and looked out the window of Chat Précieux onto the vacant street. It was nearly midnight on a Sunday and none of the shops were open. Her staff had left the restaurant three hours ago and wouldn't be back until tomorrow morning.

She turned back to the dimly lit room and sighed. This was her place, something she'd worked hard to build over the last ten years. Jenna had set out to establish a café that could be both a small romantic getaway and a place for families or a group of coworkers. She'd been smart from the beginning, employing one of Portland's best-known eclectic chefs, Simone Douay, who was now her business partner.

Simone had received great reviews for her menu of subtle elegance—one that paired fresh produce and local meats with deeply satisfying flavors. Each dish was prepared simply but in an unanticipated way, like the vegetable lasagna, a melt-in-your-mouth combo of sparse strands of fresh pasta perfectly integrated with roasted fresh vegetables and cream sauce. Simone prepared the printed menus, which changed monthly. The food critic for *The Oregonian* described the cafe as one using locally grown ingredients with multi-ethnic influences and a French flair. He'd given them four stars.

Just last year, they'd finished an expansion and renovation to include a new exhibition kitchen with counter seating, a full bar with seating, and a private dining room with a small kitchen where cooking classes were held. The expansion had already paid for itself with the increase in clientele.

Along with the expansion, Jenna had redecorated. She'd changed from the muted greens and blues to a red vertical wash on the walls, which contrasted nicely with handsome, dark woodwork and tables to give the space a warm, homey feel. She sucked in a breath as she realized what she might be giving up, what she might never see again. Her chest tightened as if a slipknot were being drawn closed, inch by inch suffocating her dreams.

Reed moved to stand behind her and massage her shoulders. "What's wrong? You're as tight as a new guitar string."

Sighing, she tried to concentrate on his hands, tried to loosen her shoulders. She wouldn't mind having those hands all over right now—helping her forget her worries for a couple of hours.

He turned her to face him, his fingers trailed along her brow and down to her cheek. He brushed a feathery kiss along her lips. "Anything I can do to help?"

She wrapped her arms tight around him. "Just hold me."

He squeezed tighter, activating a release valve for some of the fear binding her chest.

"I'm scared," she admitted. "Scared to leave the restaurant. Scared to find out they can run it fine without me. Scared that I'm giving up everything I fought so hard to build."

Reed tilted her face to look at him. His eyes searched hers. "Scared that you'll never solve Tanya's murder?"

Her breath hitched and she swallowed.

"Scared that something will happen to David if you don't?"

She nodded and buried her head in his chest. Of course he understood her. He'd probably spent most of his life scared. Moving from one mission to the next, and then re-living the worst ones over and over again. He understood her perfectly.

"Scared is good," he said. "That means you'll be careful."

She shuddered against him, letting the rest of the fear go—for now.

He led her to the closest booth and gently pushed her into a seat, then slid in next to her. His large hands still held hers, a thumb circling the back of her knuckles, giving her time to calm down. To find her voice again.

"Is David okay?" Jenna asked. "Did he agree to stay with Becca for a few days while we follow our leads?"

"Yeah," Reed answered. "When I told him Jason would be with them too, that seemed to do the trick."

Jenna nodded. "Yeah, Jason does come across as pretty good at protecting people." She smiled up at him. "Reminds me of you."

He chuckled. "Don't tell Cheeks that. He wouldn't appreciate the comparison." He squeezed her hand. "Jason has all of your papers filed now."

"Thank you," she whispered.

She'd insisted on drawing up a codicil to her will. She left instructions that her entire share of the restaurant would go to David if anything should happen to her. She also appointed Leena his guardian. She didn't want to believe the will would be needed, but given recent events it was the only sane thing to do.

Reed was staring at her again. "What?" she asked. "Did I forget to comb my hair? Brush my teeth?"

He stroked the back of her hand as it held the coffee mug. "No. You're perfect."

"Sure. And you're Harrison Ford."

Reed chuckled. "I can live with that." He paused and his eyes darkened. "I'm worried about you. The papers. Your restaurant. You know that whatever's happening is bigger than your sister's murder. You're scared, and you should be. I just think we should leave it to the police and get you and David hidden until everything is over."

She swallowed. One part of her was really happy with that idea. "And what about you? Are you going to leave it to the police, too, and come protect us?"

He looked away. "I've already made arrangements with Jason and Mike to take twelve hour shifts with you."

She gritted her teeth and pushed at his chest. "You've already made arrangements?" He turned back, his eyes a blank. "Without asking me?" She pushed at him again. "Let me out."

He reached for her hand again, but she snatched it away. "Let. Me. Out." His chest moved in a sigh, but he slid out of the booth and let her escape.

She stood and faced him. "Who do you think you are?"

"I'm the person who carried you down the mountain," he said, his voice low, measured. "You don't know what these types of criminals can be like. You don't know how to deal with them."

"And you do? How does being in force recon in Iraq or Afghanistan prepare you to do police work?"

"I'll be working with the police. I know tracking.

I know combat." He paused. "I'll make sure justice prevails—one way or the other."

"You mean you'll kill them."

"Only if I have to." He looked her in the eye—that dark, vehement stare. "I will make sure they never hurt you or David again."

She looked away. Paced. Each step took a little more air out of the room. "I hate all this. I hate that my sister is dead. I hate that someone is hurting children." She stared at him and shuddered like a hooked fish, grabbing for oxygen. "I hate the look in your eye—like you could actually tear someone apart."

"That's who I am, Jenna. I'm a trained killer," he whispered with a steely edge to his voice.

She shook her head hard. "No. I won't believe that. You are not a killer. Not outside of war. I've seen a different man."

She wanted the caring man she knew, the one who softly caressed her when she cried, the one who knew how to take care of a ten-year-old boy. She didn't want the killer part of him. She didn't want that violence so close to her. She didn't want to accept that she could care for anyone with such clear violence inside. It scared her.

He grabbed her shoulders, his fingers digging in. "I am a killer," he repeated. "Don't ever forget that. I could easily kill anyone who would try to harm you or David. I'd do it without a second thought. No regrets."

"I don't believe that."

"Believe it. That's exactly who I am. That's everything I am." He spat the words like an epithet.

He released her abruptly and she stumbled backward.

"He'll be back, Jenna. He'll be back and I pray to God I'm nearby."

She backed away, as if putting distance between

him and her would remove the violence. Negate his words.

"Why not leave it to the police? Let them do their jobs. You don't have to be part of this, Reed. You've done your part. Now leave it for the professionals."

She waited through the silence, watching the struggle on his face—the clenched jaw, the narrowing eyes, the expansion of his chest.

"I can't. I'm responsible."

She threw up her hands. "Responsible?" She stepped toward him. He drew himself up, an unmovable wall of muscle and granite. Her finger stabbed at his chest. "How are you more responsible than me?" Her face moved within inches of his. "Tanya was the one murdered here. *My* sister. Remember? If anyone is responsible, it's me."

He stepped back and raked both hands through his hair. "Damn it, Jenna! I was the one who found David. I was the one who found you. You're both my responsibility now. I know how to deal with vermin like this. You don't. Why can't you just do as I ask and be safe? I can't do my job if I'm worrying about you."

Jenna half turned and looked away. She clenched her fists close to her side instead of pounding them into a table. Or into his chest. She gritted her teeth, willing herself not to speak without thinking first, without calming down.

This is exactly what she'd feared. That he would take control of her life. That she would be kept in the dark. Well, that wasn't going to happen. What kind of a person would she be if she let Reed fight her battles for her? She would be that weak, crying woman who had been left alone ten years ago after her divorce. Well, that woman didn't exist anymore and Reed Adler was not going to send her back to that.

Reed's audible sigh made her turn toward him again. He pulled out a chair and rotated it. He sat, his legs straddling it, the wooden ladder back like a jail cell between them.

He gestured to another chair. "Sit down, Jenna. Please. I'm sorry if I upset you. I'm just trying to be realistic here."

She counted to ten and took a deep breath. She could be rational. She could be calm and state the facts clearly. But she was not going to sit.

"Okay," she said. "My turn. Hear me out before saying anything. Agreed?"

He didn't move. Didn't nod or shake his head.

"I'll take that as a yes." She paced in front of him. "First, David is safe right now. He's with Becca and Jason. So, you don't need to worry about him."

"Yes, but..."

She held up a finger. "No buts. Let me finish. I can't just sit around and let you do this anymore than you can sit around and let the police do it alone. Either we're in this together, or we're in this separately. But I'm not going to be shuffled off to some safe place to hide while you take all the chances."

He stood and stepped around the chair. "Jenna..."

She stiffened her spine and put out her right hand, palm facing him. He stopped. "Don't 'Jenna' me. Together or separate. Your choice."

"That's not a choice."

"It's the only one you have."

His shoulders lowered, but his posture remained stalwart. "Okay. Together." He pointed a finger at his chest. "But I'm in charge. You do what I say."

Jenna looked him in the eye. "I agree you have more experience with this type of stuff, so I'll do as you say...unless I think you're taking too many risks."

"It's my way or no way," he insisted.

"Then it's no way."

He didn't budge. She held his eyes, her jaw clenched with determination. After what seemed like several minutes, she saw that he wouldn't back down.

"I'm not changing my mind."

He still said nothing.

"I'm going to the ladies' room. Maybe when I get back we can settle this."

"There's nothing to settle. I've set my terms." His body was as immoveable as a stalled Abrams tank.

"We'll see." She turned her back on him and headed to the rear of the restaurant.

Damn stubborn man. She knew he wouldn't back down easily, but she had to make him understand her side. She didn't want to go investigating on her own because she didn't know the first thing about it. But she certainly wasn't going to be left behind either.

A man in a pinstriped suit and a neon green shirt stepped from the men's room into the hall. Before she could ask what he wanted, he drew an ugly black weapon from his pocket and whipped her around with his hand over her mouth and her back against his chest.

"Make a sound, and I'll shoot." He jabbed the gun into her side.

She nodded her understanding, her heart skittering like a wild bird caught in a trap.

"Come. Out back," he said, the accent heavy. The man pulled her toward the back door, her feet scraping on the wood floors as he forced her backward.

She'd heard that accent before. *Russian? Ukrainian?*

Sheer disbelief that this was happening right

here in her restaurant made her shake her head.

"You will come." He pressed the gun between her ribs until it hurt. "Or I will hurt you."

She swallowed and nodded. She thought about kicking or punching but immediately disregarded it. She wasn't stupid. That gun could kill her faster than any attempt to escape. She would go with him to protect Reed. Whatever happened to her, she knew Reed would protect David. That's all that mattered now.

She tripped down the cement stairs at the back door as he pulled her into the alley behind the restaurant.

A car pulled into the alley. When the headlights hit them, the man waved the gun at the car and a scream flew from her throat to warn them. Tires squealed as the car backed out of the alley at full speed and careened around the corner and out of sight.

The man jerked her to the ground and rolled her on her back. He straddled her torso and pointed the gun to her forehead, both hands on the trigger.

"I'll kill you for that."

Bile rammed into her throat as the barrel pushed hard into her head. She closed her eyes. She was dead. Surely, she was dead. She mumbled a garbled prayer in her mind, not sure what to pray for except that her death be quick and painless, and that Reed get David the hell out of town.

Chapter Nine

"Jenna?"

The man turned at the voice behind the door, grabbed her hair in his fist and yanked her to her feet. She couldn't help but yelp with pain.

"Who's that?" the man asked, his gun back and jammed hard into her side as he pulled her behind the alley trash bins.

"Jenna, where are you? Are you okay? I heard a scream, did you fall? Did you hurt yourself?"

Oh God, it's Reed. If he came through that door unprepared, he'd be killed. No matter how good his training, there was no way he could win against a bullet.

"It's…it's my boyfriend," she said. "We were having dinner. He's probably worried that I didn't come back to the table.

"Get rid of him," the man snapped. "Remember, my gun is trained on you. If he makes one false move, I'll kill you both." He pushed her into the pool of light cast by the flood lamp above the back entrance.

She stumbled forward, her scalp prickling with fear, her legs shaking so hard she was afraid she might fall. She had to keep it together or that man would kill Reed. She was sure of it. He'd probably kill her anyway later, but at least she could save Reed right now. She needed to think. How could she alert Reed to her situation with that brute listening to everything she said?

She pulled herself up as straight as possible,

locking her knees and lifting her chin. "I'm here, Reed," she said, her voice a slightly higher pitch than usual. She cleared her throat to bring it back down. "I…I just needed some time to myself. Go on back to the table and I'll be there in a minute."

He stepped through the door. His eyes scanned the alley like a sniper, but his body remained still. "Come back inside, Jenna." His voice had just the right amount of pleading to be convincing. "Let's talk. I don't like you out here alone. It's not safe."

"I…I can't." She stepped closer, placing herself between Reed and the gunman in case he decided to shoot. She shifted her eyes toward the trash bins, hoping Reed would get the message.

Reed held out his hand. "Come here, Jenna. I don't want to shout our problems in an alley for others to hear."

She shook her head. "No…I can't." When he stepped forward again, she held up her hand, palm forward. "I'm just so scared of…getting married. My divorce was so awful. I just need time to think about your proposal."

His jaw clenched and his eyes stared straight through her. She mouthed silently, "Trash. Gun."

He strode straight at her and tugged on her arm, trying to pull her behind him. She stiffened. She knew he was trying to put himself in the line of fire.

"No," she said very loudly and yanked her arm away. "Don't try to force me to make up my mind this minute. I won't do it. I need time."

Suddenly, Reed's body language changed completely. He looked down at the ground as if he was sorry. His hands went to his pockets and he stubbed his toe into the ground. "Damn it, Jenna. I thought you wanted to get married," he said loud enough that anyone in the alley could hear.

Her heart soared that he'd understood and

followed her lead for once. "I love you. Really, I do," she said, a little too loud. Her heart ached as she uttered the words. For a moment, she wondered if there might actually be truth in them. *No. Not possible. I'm only acting a part. I barely know him.*

"It's all so sudden," she continued. "Just give me a little more time to think. I won't be long. Please. I'll come back in and give you my answer in a few minutes."

Reed bent toward her and whispered, "Stall."

Then he smiled and said aloud, "Okay, sweetheart. I'll give you ten or fifteen minutes. Will that be enough?"

She nodded.

He took her hand and drew her to him talking loud enough for anyone to hear. "I love you, Jenna. Don't make me wait too long." Then he moved his lips to hers.

Desperation crawled up her throat as he imprinted himself on her—first moving so hard and so quick, she was sure she'd be devoured. When he softened his touch and thrust in his tongue, she twined her fingers in his hair to pull him back—not wanting even a millimeter of space between them. Her tongue searched his, caressing, dancing, needing to explore every part of his mouth, knowing she may never see him again. He melded his body to hers, so close she no longer knew which heartbeat thumped in her ears. Her other hand raked along his arms and his shoulders, memorizing every muscle.

Warmth pooled in her stomach and moved between her legs. She moaned her desire into his mouth and he returned her insistence with more pressure; her confidence grew. Her fear changed to challenge. She would not let this be the last time they embraced. She would fight to live with every breath.

As if he knew she was ready, he softened his

kiss, feathering the last one to barely touch her lips as he released her. He winked, then turned and walked back through the alley door without looking back.

Jenna stood still, trying to marshal her stilted brain into action.

How am I supposed to stall? What does Reed intend to do?

She turned back to the alley and her captor stepped out of the shadows.

“That was pretty good,” he said as he waved the gun at her. “So he proposed to you tonight?”

She nodded, her lips still swollen from his kisses. She didn’t have to fake the tears in her eyes.

“For a moment, I thought I was going to be treated to his tearing your clothes off. That would have been a picture.”

Jenna gritted her teeth and stood tall. “Look, I don’t know what you want, but I just want to get married and live happily ever after. I promise I’ll forget this ever happened.”

The man laughed. “No way. I saw your boyfriend. He’s not the type to forget.” The man shook his head. “Nope. It’s too late for you now.” He put his arm back around her shoulder and pulled her to him, the gun again pressed hard into her side. “You have courage, lady. You must really love him. At least you’ll die knowing you saved your boyfriend’s life.”

He stepped behind her and motioned to her left with the gun. “Start walking. I’ll tell you when to turn.” The barrel now buried in her back urged her forward, pushing her up the hill into the darkness.

She took a deep breath and started forward. Her restaurant was at the bottom of the street. She’d walked this hill several times during the day without a problem. But now, in the dark of night, with a gun threatening her, it seemed the climb was ten times more difficult. She tried to slow the pace. Stall, Reed had said. She had no idea what Reed's plan might be; she just hoped it involved lots of police and that it happened soon.

"Hurry it up." The gunman pushed her from behind, shoving her forward so forcefully that she hit against the fence on one side.

"Stop it!" Jenna flared, whirling to face him, an unreasoning anger burning through the panic. "If you're going to kill me, you might as well get it over with. I can't walk any faster and you pushing me into fences isn't going to change that."

The man stared back at her, no expression on his face. "Keep moving or you'll get your wish." He ground the gun barrel into her temple.

Oh God, Jenna thought in despair, *what on earth am I doing?* Without another word, she turned and began climbing again, but at least the brief surge of anger had steadied her knees.

At the top of the hill, the man pushed her onto a side street off to the right. Another alley, only darker.

"The black SUV," he said, throwing his arm back over her shoulder and holding her close to his side, the gun now buried in the top of her rib cage. She knew if he pulled the trigger now, the bullet would go straight through her side to her heart.

The car beeped twice. Ten more feet and she'd have no choice. Her blood turned to ice water at the thought of being driven away where no one would ever find her again.

She lurched forward and purposefully tripped, falling flat on her chest, her face to one side. He yanked on her hair and she yelped.

"Get up. Get up right now."

Slowly, she got to her knees. Her head canted back trying to relieve the pressure of him pulling on her hair. Once she stood, he let go of her hair and placed the gun barrel in the small of her back. Three more steps and they were at the car.

"Get in."

Gripping the handle of the SUV, she pulled the door open.

"Don't move," Reed said.

She froze. *Where had he come from?*

She'd heard nothing—never saw him anywhere along their route. From his command, she knew Reed was behind them, but she didn't dare turn around.

Reed moved in front of her, his pistol aimed directly at the man's forehead. "Let her go," Reed said calmly, his eyes cold and hard, the gun in his hand steady.

The man smiled. "You shoot me, I kill the woman."

"Maybe," Reed responded. "But you're aimed at her back. There's a good chance she could live from your shot. You, on the other hand, are dead."

Reed paused, and the killer's gun pushed into her back a little harder, exacerbating what was probably a bruised rib. But she kept the pain to herself. She stood her ground, waiting for Reed's next move.

"So, what do you choose?" Reed asked the man. "We can either have one dead person, and one with a chance to live, or everyone can live and you can drive out of here."

The man inhaled deeply. Jenna tried to follow what must be going through his mind. The bottom line was the man would have to trust Reed not to pull the trigger once he was disarmed.

She heard a click from the gun on her back and her knees shook. *Did he just cock the gun?* Reed's piercing gaze hadn't looked at her, hadn't left the man's eyes.

"Now drop the gun and kick it away," Reed said.

Jenna flinched as the weapon hit the pavement with a heavy thud. It didn't go off. She wasn't sure why, but she was thankful.

"Hands up," Reed said.

The man backed away from Jenna and Reed pushed her to the side while still keeping his gun aimed at the man.

"Jenna, pick up the gun." Reed said.

She stared at him, her eyes wide. Their gazes met for a brief moment. His was still calm and expressionless, as if he did this every day, but the gun remained steady.

She scrambled for the weapon, gingerly picking it up by the handle. "Will it go off?" She asked. She'd never touched a gun before and thought she'd heard it cock.

"The safety is on," Reed said. "Bring the gun to me."

Holding the pistol in her left hand, the barrel pointed toward the pavement, she handed it back to him. He put it in his waistband.

"Good, now I want you to frisk him."

Jenna had no idea how to do that. She'd seen it in movies, but she never really knew what was happening.

"Pat his entire body, feel for lumps that might be a gun," Reed said.

She patted his chest front and back then moved to his torso. When she got to the intersection between his torso and legs she stopped.

The man chuckled. "Afraid I'm bigger than your boyfriend?"

Her cheeks puffed out and she patted his front thoroughly, probably a little harder than she had to, but nothing was there.

"I can't feel a thing," she said to the man, looking him in the eye. "Perhaps you don't have anything between your legs."

Reed chuckled. The man sucked in his cheeks, and she heard a puff of air storm out his nose.

She moved down the killer's right leg as she'd seen them do on TV. She gasped when she found something near his foot.

"That's an ankle gun," Reed said. "That's common. It's probably velcroed around his leg. Lift up his pant leg and unstrap it."

She did as he instructed, then brought the gun to him. He dropped it in a pocket.

"Now check him again, all over."

She went through the same procedure, but found nothing more.

"You're doing great, Jenna. We'll make you into a cop yet," Reed said. "Now, go to the driver's side of the car and search for any other guns. Search the floorboards, the glove compartment, between the seats…anywhere you can think someone might hide a gun."

She opened the driver's side door and searched with shaking hands. She found a large, fat gun in the glove compartment. It reminded her of the trailers she'd seen for Dirty Harry movies. She gingerly placed it on the driver's seat. A second smaller pistol was wedged in the seat pocket behind the passenger's seat. *Criminy.* What might have happened if she'd gotten in the car with all these guns? He probably would have killed her before they even stopped anywhere. She put the second gun on the driver's seat as well and moved to the back door.

"Nothing more," she said. "I don't see any more."

It hit her then that this man could have killed her at any time from a long distance. He didn't have to physically get her and walk her to his car. He must need something from her—information perhaps—or she would be dead already.

"Who are you?" she asked, proud her voice didn't shake. "What do you want with me?"

The man didn't move. His face was blank, without emotion.

"Talk to the lady," Reed said.

"Kill me," the man answered.

Reed's cheeks sucked in and he pushed the gun into the man's right temple. "Gladly."

Jenna's eyes widened. "No!" she said, her voice barely above a whisper. "Don't do it. You gave your word he could leave."

"He doesn't care about my word, Jenna. Do you think if he'd promised not to kill me he would keep his end of the bargain?"

She doubted he would. But the gunman was evil and Reed was good. To kill someone in cold blood was evil. She couldn't let Reed do that.

"We can call the police," she said. "Let them take him in."

"It's his word against ours. How do you think this looks to the police? I have a gun on him."

"Please, Reed. You can't sink to their level. You're better than that."

"He'll come back, Jenna. If I don't kill him, he'll come back."

"Maybe he won't. Maybe he's scared now."

The man chuckled again, and Jenna questioned her request. Reed was probably right, but she couldn't watch him kill someone in cold blood—no matter how bad the man might be. Certainly, for Reed to do that, he lost a part of his soul, too.

"Finish searching his car," Reed said. "Bring me the pistols and put the rifle in the bushes behind me."

She ran back to the driver's side where she'd placed the other two guns. She continued her search, making sure to check under seats, under mats, and even in the cargo area of the SUV. She found no other guns.

She put a pistol in each hand, carefully putting

one foot in front of the other making sure not to stumble. He used his free hand to take the larger one and put it in his waistband. He pushed a button on the side of the smaller gun and then handed it back to her.

"I've taken the safety off and the gun will shoot. Put both your hands on the gun, with your finger on the trigger. Aim toward the man. Keep your hands steady with your aim and walk across the street. Whatever happens, don't take your gun off him. If he moves to hurt you or me, shoot him."

She placed both hands on the gun and aimed it as instructed. Her eyes blurred as tears filled them. She'd always been against all violence. She'd known men with guns before. They'd always assured her that if her life were in danger she'd have no problem shooting someone.

Now her life really was on the line—the first time she had to really decide. She lowered the gun from his chest to his knees. Maybe she could shoot his knees and not feel too bad.

"Hold the gun up higher," Reed instructed.

Her hand shook as she still pointed the gun. "I…I don't think I can shoot him." Her voice cracked with the tears choking her throat.

"Aim at the car tires then," he said. "Do you think you could shoot at the tires and stop him from getting away, if he tries anything?"

"Yes." She took dead aim at the right front tire. "Yes, I can definitely do that."

"Good, now keep your aim and move across the street. If at any time I yell 'Drop,' you hit the pavement and shoot those tires. Got it?"

"Got it," she said, her voice clear and confident. She kept a death grip on the weapon as she walked sideways and across the street.

Reed waited until he was sure she was safely away from the corner. *Shit!* He knew there was no way she'd even hit the tires from that distance, but at least she was out of range. He looked at Jenna across the street, still holding the gun in front of her. Probably still crying. Hell, it would be so easy just to kill the bastard. But she'd never understand.

With one hand on the man and the other still holding a gun to the man's head, he said, "We're going to walk around to the driver's side now. You will get in and roll down the window. Slowly."

Together, the two of them shuffled to the other side of the car. When the man turned to sit, Reed's aim shifted to his temple. The man took out the key and started the engine, the door still open. He reached to the electric panel and rolled down the window. Reed shifted his aim so the man could shut the door and Reed aimed through the open window to the man's head.

"Now, I expect you to very slowly move out of this alley and head home," Reed said. "If you blink, I kill you. If you say anything to Jenna, I kill you. If you do anything unexpected, like step on the gas, or move the car toward me or Jenna, I kill you. Do you understand?"

The man nodded, his eyes forward.

The engine turned over and Reed walked alongside the car, his gun still pointed at the man's head until they got to the corner. Jenna kept up on her side of the street, though he noticed the gun was pointing more toward the pavement than the tires now.

"I said I'd let you go in exchange for Jenna's life, and I am. But remember this—if you *ever* come near her again, I'll shoot you dead without a thought. There are no second chances."

The man nodded his understanding and Reed stepped away from the car. The car turned the corner, sped up, and disappeared. Reed finally lowered his weapon. He looked across the street in time to see Jenna sag to the pavement, the gun in her hand skittered to one side. He ran over.

"I'm okay," she said, her voice thick with shock, almost soundless. She cleared her throat and said, "I'm fine."

"You did great." He secured the safety and the gun, adding it to the collection he already carried.

With a choked sob, Jenna wrapped her arms around herself. Silent tears streaked her cheeks.

His heart clutched. He wanted to cocoon her in his arms and kiss the pain away. But he understood the need to take a moment for yourself when you realize you could have been killed. She'd been amazingly courageous. Anyone without his experience had a right to fall apart.

After a few minutes, Reed kneeled in front of her. He placed his open hand on her crossed arms. "Come on. Let's go home." He put his other hand softly under her elbow and helped her to stand.

Once on her feet, he waited for her to decide what she needed. When she leaned into him without speaking, he put his arms around her and held her as close as he could with her own arms still wrapped between them. He rubbed his hand in circles on her back, swallowing back his own fear.

Reed rested his head on hers and inhaled, reveling in the sweet citrus smell of her hair, thankful he was here at this moment with her. Thankful she was alive. Safe. If that monster had shot her…

No, I won't go there. Not now. Not when she needs me. He'd deal with those fears later. In the dark. Alone.

Eventually, she loosened her hold on herself and her arms encircled his waist, clinging to him for support. He hugged her closer, raining kisses near her temples, at the tops of her ears, all while keeping an eye on their surroundings in case the man doubled back. He would wait with her as long as it took—all night right here on the street, if that's what she needed.

Suddenly, Jenna's energy seemed to have leaked out of her. Her arms loosened from his waist, and she fell like a rag doll against him.

He lifted her into his arms, and her head rolled from side to side against his chest as he walked down the hill. "Jenna, I'm taking you home now," he said, hoping she was conscious enough to understand. "Then we're getting you out of your house to somewhere safe. You and David, together. Safe."

She nodded against his chest. He knew she was in shock right now. That's the only reason she was agreeing to anything. He'd take advantage of that, get her and David secured in a safe house. Then he'd call Jason and Mike, and even the police. They'd handle it without her. She'd give him shit eventually, but he didn't care anymore. No more excuses.

And if she didn't cooperate? That was not an option. He was going to make damn sure whoever was behind this didn't find her. Nothing like this would ever happen again. He wouldn't allow it.

****

White light streamed in the window. Jenna rolled over and buried her head in her pillow. She didn't want to wake up. She didn't want to remember last night's nightmare—almost being killed, so much violence…Reed.

She sat straight up. Reed! Where was he? She remembered him tucking her into bed but then what? She rolled out of bed and strode into the kitchen. As if there were a camera watching her, he walked toward her extending a mug of coffee.

"Cream, no sugar, right?"

She nodded as he loomed over her, blocking the

sunlight at the window.

"Sleep well?"

She took a deep draught of the coffee. "Hmm…thanks."

"We need to talk."

Jenna shook her head. "I need some time to myself. I need time to think."

Reed's eyebrows scrunched together. "Think about what? I already have a plan. Get packed and I'll tell you about it on the way."

She needed to center herself first. Things had been happening way too fast these past couple of weeks. She needed time to herself—time to think and plan before Reed tried to take over. Tried to shuffle her off to safety.

"I'm taking a long bath."

He quirked a brow at her.

"Alone," she emphasized.

He laughed. "Did I say anything?"

"You didn't have to." She waved her arms around the small space. "Relax, watch TV. Whatever. Just give me some time. Okay?"

Jenna left him sitting at the breakfast bar. She could feel his eyes watching her as she strode to the bedroom, closing the bedroom door behind her firmly. She should probably lock it, but there was still a small niggling fear that anything could happen. If the murderer came back—somehow found her apartment—being locked in the back wouldn't be smart. She'd just have to trust Reed not to disturb her privacy unless it really was an emergency.

Jenna turned on the tap in the master bath soaking tub and reached for the bath oil—a combination of lavender and honeysuckle. Measuring out two capfuls, she trickled it into the hot water as the tub filled. She'd allowed herself no more than a quick shower at Reed's cabin. But now that she was home, she deserved a long, leisurely soak, a chance to gather herself before figuring out what to do next. For all she knew, she might not be back here for a very long time.

Steam rose from the water to obscure the edges of the bathroom and she gave herself a moment to pretend this was a normal day. To pretend her sister was still alive. To pretend people weren't trying to kill her. To pretend that somehow she had known David all of his ten years. She sighed. Would anything ever be normal again?

She closed her eyes and inhaled the balsamy undertones in the bath oil. It immediately reminded her of Reed—that mix of balsam wood with leather and pine. God, what was she going to do about him? Every moment she spent with him clearly spelled danger for her heart. She was grateful for everything he'd done for David. For her. But she had to keep her distance or she'd fall so hard she might not recover when he finally walked away. When she'd been sleeping next to him at his cabin, even with all that happened to her, her hormones were begging to have him inside her.

Thank God he was an honorable man, because them together—sex—that was an absolutely stupid idea. Reed was in her life for one reason only—he felt responsible. When this sordid mess was finished, he'd be gone in a flash. If it weren't for everything that had happened in the last week they would have never met. They were totally wrong for each other. His world was filled with violence. Her world sought only peace. And the last thing she needed in her life was confusing lust with love and getting hurt in the end.

She sighed as she stripped and stepped into the tub. She lowered herself slowly, letting the heated water build around her as it continued to fill. Jenna wished she could just grab David and disappear somewhere. Canada might be good—she'd always loved Vancouver, B.C. She sighed, knowing that wouldn't work. If she ran, she'd never have complete custody of David. They'd be on the run. She'd always be afraid someone would find out and take him away. The best thing she could do, for the memory of her sister, was to keep David safe and loved.

Jenna toed off the water with one foot, sighing with the pleasure of lavender and honeysuckle surrounding her. She closed her eyes and imagined herself in a warm meadow, the sun beating down on her face. She let herself relax for the first time in more than two weeks. Inhaling deeply, the lavender offered brief moments of forgetting. Of healing.

****

Reed braced himself when the bedroom door opened. Jenna stood in the entry challenging him, her eyes narrowed, one hip pushed against the frame, her T-shirt emblazoned with the words "Don't mess with me." Somehow her dare made him want her all the more. That she could even rise to the occasion was an amazing accomplishment considering all that had happened to her this past week. In his experience, most women would be cowering in a corner or would have run far away by now.

Her still damp hair had wet her T-shirt just enough to make her nipples stand erect. He wanted to mess with her all right. From the moment he'd brought her home and bathed her in his bed, all he could think of was spending all day with her, naked. He wanted to see her clothes thrown messily across the room as he undressed her. He wanted to see her hair splayed across his pillow as he rose above her. He wanted to see her out of control coming again and again beneath him, on top of him, in every way possible.

Jenna marched to the table and brought herself up to her full height, though she was still a head shorter than him. "I'm not going to be shipped off to some safe place in Timbuktu while you play the macho Marine and run off to get yourself killed. This is my battle, not yours."

"I'm not going to get killed," he said, keeping his voice quiet and even. She opened her mouth, but he continued before she could say anything. "And it's not like I'm shipping you half way around the world. If you can't think about yourself, then at least consider David. If anything were to happen to you, where would he be? He'd be without a mother *and* without his aunt. He'd have no family at all."

She swallowed and her head lowered just slightly. "I've taken care of the arrangements," she whispered. "Leena will take him."

He reached for her but she stepped back. "I'm sure Leena would be a fine mother, but she's not you. She can't tell David about his real mom. She can't share childhood stories with him and make him feel a part of a larger family."

Jenna's lip trembled. "You're not playing fair."

"Life isn't fair, Jenna. Do you think the man who is trying to kill you is thinking about being fair? Do you think the people who held David and are doing God knows what to other children are thinking about playing fair?"

"No…but…" Tears welled in her eyes. "I admit I'm scared, but you can't shut me out. I need to know what's going on. I need to be part of helping catch this guy and anyone who's behind him. I need to be sure he's not going to follow me and David the rest of my life."

"And you can't trust me to do that for you?"

She swallowed as she looked up at him. "No. I'm sorry, but I can't. I can't trust anyone but myself. I learned that ten years ago and it's a lesson I'm not likely to forget."

Reed sucked in his cheeks. Men really were

assholes most of the time. Including himself. He admired her guts, her passion. He wouldn't let someone else do the investigating if he were in her situation. He let out a breath.

"Okay, but we are doing this on my terms."

"Meaning?"

"Meaning you and David will be living at my place, along with Jason and Mike. Whenever we're out together, at least one of them will be with David. If I say I have to go somewhere without you, you won't put up a fight. You'll understand what I have to do is too dangerous for both of us to go."

"If it's so dangerous, why should you be the one? Why not me?"

He stared at her hard, making sure she saw the violence in his eyes.

She gulped. "Because you can kill someone and I can't."

"Exactly. I also have a hell of a lot of experience moving quickly, silently. You don't. You always being with me makes it even more dangerous…for me."

She stiffened and he could see the anger building. Then she turned her back to him and stomped away, her fisted hands pumping at both sides. "I hate that! I hate that I have to even think about it. That it's come into my life."

She walked, stiff-backed, to a window. Her shoulders stiffening and loosening, moving toward her ears then drooping, journaled her struggle with his demands, the strictures—struggling against the violence in him she couldn't deny. But he couldn't care about that right now. What he cared about was her not ending up dead.

"Where will I sleep?" she asked, her voice soft, defeated, speaking to the window instead of him. "Your place only has two bedrooms. David's in one and you're in one.

Reed moved to her and turned her toward him. He needed her to see his eyes. He needed her to see this wasn't easy for him. "You can sleep with me. We managed it before. We can manage it again." He wasn't sure if he could keep his hands off her, but he sure as hell wasn't letting her out of his sight. Sex could take the edge off—calm her...calm him. Or maybe it would make everything worse.

Her brow furrowed and she tucked her bottom lip between her teeth. "Do I have a choice?"

"No."

She quirked a brow and stared him down.

"Yes. You have a choice. You can sleep on the floor in the living room with Jason and Mike. I trust them to keep you safe. Take your pick."

She frowned, her hands clasped in her front of her. "I agree to your terms."

"Good." He reached for her and she backed away again.

"I agree...for now. But if I find out you're not keeping me in the loop, our agreement is void."

Reed nodded. He'd won. He would keep her safe. Somehow. "How quickly can you pack?"

Chapter Ten

Reed helped her lug three heavy suitcases to his car. She'd been very efficient and packed quickly while he made phone calls to Jason and Mike to fill them in on the plan. Mike would bring David up with him. Jason had said Becca's research yielded even more information to share. So both of them would be at the cabin, when Jenna arrived.

Jenna wasn't happy about sharing a bed with Reed again. In spite of knowing he was exactly the wrong man for her, she found herself caring about him more each day. And that was dangerous. The only explanation was something like Stockholm Syndrome—the thing that happened when prisoners began to identify with their captors. She was a prisoner of sorts. Imprisoned by the crazy man who wanted her dead. Imprisoned by Reed who was taking over her life. Imprisoned by feelings she already had for him—a prison she had every reason to fear.

She sighed. She could live through a few more nights of sharing a bed without anything happening. They were both mature adults. Just because they slept together didn't mean they had to have sex.

Reed shoved the last suitcase in the back of his SUV and closed the door. "You're following me straight up the mountain."

"Yes sir," she said, saluting.

He grimaced and shoveled a hand through his hair. "No need to be sarcastic. You're not reporting to me."

"Aren't I? You made it clear you were in command and that I didn't have a lot of choices."

He backed her against the car, an arm on each side of her, his face within inches of hers. "Dammit, Jenna. I just want you safe. Why can't you understand that?"

Her pulse accelerated. He was turning her head in circles. Again. She would not let him get to her.

She placed a hand firmly against his chest to stop him before she couldn't think anymore. "I do understand. But you have to promise me something."

"What?" he whispered, still looming close.

"Promise me you won't push me away. Promise me if there is something I can do, you'll involve me."

"Jenna..."

"Promise me, Reed. The more you keep from me, the harder I'll fight to be part of it. You know that."

He blew out a loud breath. "I promise to keep you in the loop. Now, can we get going?"

She smiled. It was a small victory, but a victory nonetheless. "Thank you." Before she could censor herself, she reached up to brush his lips with a brief parting kiss. Instead, he pressed her fully against the car door. He cupped her head between his large hands. His thumbs swept across her cheekbones, over damp lips. He lowered his head. His eyes turned from a dark brown to almost black so quickly she thought surely he'd take her right there—and she knew she wouldn't raise a hand to stop him. But his kiss was surprisingly soft. His mouth barely glanced hers. Repeatedly. Each time their lips came together, they barely connected, yet the touch of his mouth against hers made Jenna melt.

Then her anticipation was rewarded as he moved into her, deeper, using his tongue to plumb her mouth. The pressure in her lower body grew unbearably sweet. She felt herself swelling, throbbing. She thrust her hips forward and rubbed against him. Her breasts, achy and tight, yearned to feel his hands, his mouth, on them. She wanted to be close to him.

"Jenna," he moaned. "We have to leave."

She pulled him closer. Bed. She needed a bed where they could get rid of this tension. Now. "Let's go back inside. We have time."

He leaned away, brushing her lips like a feather. She felt the cool breeze separate them and she wasn't sure whether to be thankful he stopped or to cry out for what she was missing.

"We'll finish this later." Reed brushed her hair to one side. "I promise."

She nodded, unsure why she'd lost control, or what she really wanted to happen.

Jenna turned in his arms and opened the driver's side door of her car, her breathing still fast and shallow. She slid into the seat and faced straight ahead. "I'll follow you."

He leaned in and feathered a kiss along her temple. "Stay close, Jenna. I can't…won't lose you."

She sucked in her cheeks to stop the smile that threatened to bloom as he closed the door. She watched Reed in her rear view mirror as he strode to his car. She turned the key and waited for him. Every promise she'd made to herself just went out the window.

Reed passed in front of her and she nudged the gas. She had a little over an hour to get her mind back to reality before they got to his cabin. She was determined to have all wayward thoughts back in their proper sealed box before she got out of this car again. Before she ended up in his bed tonight.

It took forty-five minutes, but Jenna finally felt in control as they left Troutdale behind and the road climbed Mt. Hood. Her car had no problem keeping up with Reed. She took each curve with a sense of freedom mixed with control in just the right balance. After passing through Welches and Rhododendron, the road steepened. She put both hands on the steering wheel for the final five miles, relishing the thought of seeing David again.

She passed a sign warning the lanes were narrowing from four to two ahead. A large, dark-color vehicle pulled up to her back bumper and stayed there just as the lanes thinned and the curves became more frequent. She swore. *"What's with people who have to crowd? It's not like I'm going to go any faster."* She sped up a little to put distance between her and the large grille stalking her. The next curve was steeper than she anticipated, and on the downside of it, she had to wrestle hard with the wheel to keep her car away from the railing and on her side of the road. Her pulse ratcheted and she slowed to fifty-five. It wasn't worth dying to keep out of that asshole's way.

The black vehicle bore down on her again, this time bumping into her hard enough to jerk her head back.

Dammit! What's wrong with this guy? She checked ahead, looking for a pull-out. She'd be happy to let him pass and get on his way.

Jenna checked the rear view mirror. There was something familiar about the black vehicle.

"Was that the SUV from the alley at Chat Précieux?" Her voice sounded ominous as the whisper filled the empty car.

The vehicle backed off a ways and she tried to calm herself. Okay, she was a little paranoid. No one would be stupid enough to try to kill her in broad daylight.

Boom! The SUV hit her car again and all her doubts disappeared. Her heart kicked into overdrive and she hit the accelerator, pushing the Prius as fast as she could handle. She pressed the phone connect on her steering wheel and shouted “Reed” for it to autodial his cell.

He answered. “Problem?”

“The SUV is back! The bastard’s back!”

Smash. He hit her again and her car did a 360 just before the next curve.

She was dizzy, out of breath, with no idea which way she was facing.

Scrunch! Metal tore from the fender. She saw it fall on the road and the SUV had to swerve not to run over it. She stepped on the gas. Downhill. She was going downhill.

“He’s going to kill me!”

The dark monster roared up behind her and smashed her into oncoming traffic.

Jenna screamed.

An oncoming car hit the Prius’ passenger door and then careened around her. The SUV came at her again.

Crash!

Her car struck the hillside and rebounded. Her air bags exploded, making her partially blind, as the car headed toward the railing. She pulled hard to the left as the car slipped on the next curve, her wheels whispering within inches of the metal barrier protecting her from the thousand-foot fall to the canyon below. She over-corrected and braked as she entered the next curve, but the SUV came up on her side and plowed into her.

Jenna screamed. The door crumpled, slamming into her ribcage. She couldn’t breathe. She couldn’t see. Her arms automatically covered her face as her car crashed through the metal barrier and arched over the canyon.

Her scream of terror echoed through the canyon as the car turned over again and again and again. Bone shattered.

Dizziness. Darkness. Dirt. Blood

****

Reed slammed on his brakes and jumped from the car when he saw the crumpled metal railing and the gaping hole. He scrambled to the edge and traced the path of Jenna's car. It was a sheer drop over the side—no slope whatsoever. The car was upside down on an outcropping of rock, leaning precariously against a tree that was now horizontal to the canyon floor. He wasn't sure how long the tree would hold.

"Jenna!" he yelled. "Hang on. I'm coming."

Shit. Fuck. Piss. I've got to get her out of there now.

He dialed Jason's cell.

"Get David in the car and you and Mike get down here now. I'm two miles south of my house on twenty-six. Bring rescue equipment. Jenna's gone over the cliff."

He dialed 911.

"I need an ambulance. A woman's gone over the side of U.S. twenty-six, about three miles north of Government Camp."

"Stay where you are, sir. Help is on the way."

"Like hell I will. I'm trained in mountain rescue. Reed Adler—check it. I'm going down to check on her."

"Sir, stay where you are until someone else gets there."

"Someone's coming. Track my phone." He set the phone on the gravel shoulder. It wouldn't help if it fell out of his pocket.

Heart pounding, Reed evaluated the situation. His first inclination was to grab a rope and tie it off on one of the guardrail supports to lower himself to Jenna's car. He'd probably slip a lot, though, and once he was over the edge, he wasn't sure he would be able to see anything. He took a deep breath, trying not to let his emotions take over. He had to treat this like any other recovery mission. He'd need a rope, a first aid kit, and maybe some type of sling, in case he had to move her before the ambulance arrived. He ran back to his car to secure the needed equipment. He'd done some rescues in Afghanistan and he'd done one this past winter on Mt. Hood. But each time in the past, he'd been rescuing skilled climbers with gear and some knowledge of how to work with him. He'd never tried to extract anyone from a car before. God, he hoped she was conscious. He could at least talk her through what was happening.

He slung the pack over his head and onto his back. It contained more rope, a rescue carabiner, and a first aid kit. He stepped into his rappelling harness and cinched it up, ready to drop over the edge as soon as Jason and Mike arrived. He paced as the minutes ticked by.

Fuck! She could be dying right now, bleeding out as he waited for someone else.

He gritted his teeth. Patience. The first rule of all rescues was to not go alone. Safety meant more likelihood of success. If he did something stupid, he'd jeopardize them both.

Mike's truck skidded as it made the U-turn and nosed to the side where Reed stood. "David, stay here," Mike said as he and Jason jumped from the truck.

Mike looked over the edge. "What happened?"

"That fucking bastard ran her off the road," Reed said. "When I get my hands on him, I'm going to kill him."

Jason got gear together and set himself up as the belay man. He secured the rope around his waist, then tested the equipment with Reed just as they'd practiced many times. Mike pulled out a stretcher and more climbing gear from the back of his truck and helped Jason secure the rope to the truck axle.

When he was satisfied, Jason said. "Ready?"

Reed grabbed tight and stepped to the edge. "Belay on?"

"On belay," Jason answered.

"Send me down."

Jason slowly lowered him over the edge, while Reed tried to manage the descent and hold the stretcher at the same time. He dropped backward in a blind descent on the rope and plowed through the brush with his butt and back. A branch caught his helmet and twisted his neck. He ducked his head to release the branch, which snapped back and popped him again in the face. "Shit!"

He couldn't see much except the bottom of the canyon. He hoped he was lined up with the rock shelf. The side was thickly tangled with vine maple, ferns, and poison oak. His boots squelched into thick muck, leaving deep footprints. When he hit soft forest duff, his feet slipped and his knees slammed into the side of the wall. Pain shot into his legs. He slid a few feet on his knees but the rope held fast.

Wiry branches reached out and grabbed the stretcher, pulling it back up the hill. He tugged and the vine maple fought back, tearing his shirt. He yanked the stretcher with all his might and it popped free, slid another ten feet, and nearly bowled him over. The rope went taut again. Jason had him. He wouldn't let him free fall.

Reed dangled in midair for a moment. The harness cut into his groin and the weight of the heavy rescue backpack pulled him backward. He clung to the rope to avoid flipping upside down. Finally, he could see the motionless car and the rock outcrop. *Just fifty to sixty feet. I'm coming, Jenna. Hold on, baby. I'm coming.*

Finally, his feet stretched to the flat ground. He tried to steer the stretcher down the cliff, but instead it banged into him. "Fuck!"

Suddenly, the heavy *thwock, thwock, thwock* of a helicopter swamped all other sounds, and the rotor wash pummeled Reed with a blustery whirlwind of leaves and dirt. The helicopter swooped up the canyon, bringing back memories of Afghanistan. He fought against the blurred vision, the roaring in his ears, the blood pumping in his heart and threatening to stop his breathing.

"No! Not now," he shouted. "I will not go back there. Jenna needs me."

He closed his eyes against the dirt spray, bracing himself with a wide stance on the cliff. With a thundering clang, the stretcher crashed on the volcanic rock beside him and slid over the cliff. Damn! It was going to be up to the chopper rescue team to get her out of here now.

His footing was anything but secure. The mud and moss coated the bottom of his boots and he barely stood upright. He wrapped an arm around a tree branch and cautiously unhooked from the rope, then yanked it a couple of times to signal Jason he was off belay. He then tied a rope to himself and to the base of the tree. If the tree went, he and Jenna were dead.

The helicopter buzzed even closer to the canyon wall and blasted him again with its powerful rotor wash. Overhead, a medic twirled precariously on the cable, an umbilical cord stretching from the aircraft. He spun seemingly out of control, dangerously close to the branches of tall conifers below. A gloved hand reached out from the chopper bay and steadied the cable.

Stay low, Reed reminded himself. *Don't look up*.

A few minutes later the cable swung in front of him and he grabbed a hand to stop the man dangling from it. One hand on the tree and one hand on the man, he pulled the medic toward him and helped him hook to the tree. The two of them released the stretcher and secured it as well. Then the medic waved the chopper off and heaved the medical bag across his shoulders.

"Roberts," the man said extending his hand. "Thanks for your help."

"Adler," Reed replied and shook. "Watch it. Slippery."

The guy didn't look much older than twenty, but given the descent he'd just made, Reed figured he knew his stuff. They both shuffled toward the car, keeping a wide stance, a low center of gravity.

"Has it moved at all?" Roberts asked.

"No, it seems wedged against the tree. As long as the tree holds, we're okay."

Roberts looked at the tree, the position of the car, and shook his head. "I don't trust it. I'm going to tie us into the hillside with petons. If that tree goes, we all go."

"I'll keep a hold on Jenna while you re-secure us," Reed said.

Roberts drove in two anchors and then tied off the entire bunch of webbing with an overhand knot before securing his own rope. Then he drove in two more anchors and did the same thing. He cut Reed's rope to the tree and tied him into the new anchors.

"Secure?" Roberts asked.

Reed pulled on his rope. It didn't budge. "Good."

"Okay, let me in to check her."

Reed moved to one side of the door. "I'm going to get a good grip on her. You check Jenna, and if anything starts to slip, I'll pull her out."

"You could permanently damage her spine."

"I know. But I'd rather have her alive in a wheelchair than dead at the bottom of the canyon."

Roberts nodded and gingerly placed his hand on the door handle. "I'm opening the door now."

Reed held his breath. His legs coiled, ready to

spring forward and pull Jenna out of the car. The door opened and nothing moved. "Jenna?" he paused. "Jenna, I'm here. Hang on. We're going to get you out."

She was on her back, unresponsive. Bright red oozed from her scalp and face, coagulating on the ceiling of the car. A loud gurgling, snoring, grunting sound scared him. He'd seen that before as the life leaked out of one of his men with internal bleeding. It meant her airway was clogging with saliva, mucus, vomit, and blood. Every ten seconds, she took a deep gulp of air—an ominous sign. Something in her brain was interrupting the stimulus to breathe.

Reed calculated how long it took him to get down here. Was it twenty minutes? Thirty? Then how long until the chopper arrived. God, maybe forty-five, fifty minutes?

He reached into the car and caressed her cheek. "You hang on, Jenna, you hear me?" His voice choked. "That's an order, dammit. Don't you give up on me now."

Roberts pulled on medical gloves and Reed watched helplessly as he went through the ABCDEs and spoke into the radio.

"Airway intact. Probable brain injury, apnea to breathing signal. Pulse faint and thready. Skin pale and cold. No pools or spurts of blood, but I surmise she's probably lost a significant amount, since the ceiling of the car is splattered. Large laceration and bruise on her forehead. Definite head injury, must prevent spinal cord and brain injuries."

Reed swallowed. "We're getting you out of here now, Jenna. Hang on sweetheart."

"We need a C-collar, blanket, and helmet," Roberts said as he began the head-to-toe secondary survey. "She has no visible deformity of her spine. Her left elbow appears skewed." He cut away a part of her fleece jacket with heavy trauma shears.

Reed sucked in a breath. A bone stuck out of a matted clump of blood, twigs, and dirt. The medic stuffed the fleece back against the wound.

"Shouldn't you clean that?" Reed asked.

"It's a toss-up," Roberts replied. "The open fracture makes it prone to infection that can set deep in the bone. However, if I open the wound and clean it to prevent infection, it would certainly start bleeding again. I don't think she can afford any more blood loss."

Roberts palpated her abdomen and chest. "Without her response, I can't be sure if they're tender," he said. "But the spleen and liver feel uninjured. We'll still ask emergency to check for blunt abdominal injury when she gets to the hospital." He moved down her legs. "Faint pulse in each foot. That's good. If she does have a fracture, at least it's not cutting off the blood to her feet."

Roberts turned toward Reed. "We're ready for the C-collar."

Reed handed it to him and gently lifted her head as Roberts fixed the collar around her neck. Then they worked together to get the helmet on her head.

"We can't get the stretcher in the car," Roberts said. "We'll have to slide her out onto the board. Slowly."

Reed nodded. This was the most dangerous part. They needed to move her as little as possible to prevent spine injury, but there was a chance the little they needed to do would still paralyze her, if she wasn't already paralyzed.

"Let me do it," Reed said. "I'm responsible for her."

Roberts looked at him. "You know what you're doing?"

Reed nodded.

"Military?"

"Marine Corps."

"Okay. I'll hold the board steady."

Reed carefully angled into the car and placed his arms under hers. "Okay, Jenna, you're moving now. We're going real slow here." He inched her out a little at a time, trying to make no sudden moves, trying to keep her as immobile as possible.

Roberts pulled her straight back onto the board. When half of her body was out of the car, Reed reached in further to move her legs out.

The car rocked. The tree creaked and bent further toward the canyon. Reed stopped. Stone cold. His pulse instantly doubled its speed. "Steady. Steady."

"Are you secure?" Roberts asked.

Reed nodded.

"We'll do it together in one big motion. As soon as she's out, lie flat with your arm around her locked onto the stretcher in case the car goes."

Reed nodded again. "On three. One. Two. Three." He lifted her legs and Roberts pulled her onto the stretcher. Reed hit the deck and wrapped his arm around her waist. He heard the creak of metal and he held tight to Jenna and the stretcher. Roberts' face was also flat on the cliff next to Reed, his arm wrapped around Jenna at the knees.

An awful scraping followed as the car shifted, then a thunderous splinter as the tree gave way and the entire cliff shuddered. Each bounce of the car echoed down the canyon and Reed shuddered as he held his breath.

Finally, the ground stopped shaking.

"That's it," Roberts said. "We're getting out of here."

They worked together to secure Jenna to the stretcher. Roberts taped a big wad of gauze over the exposed bone of her left elbow. Then he wrapped the elbow tightly with a gauze roll and stabilized her entire arm with a malleable aluminum splint covered in soft foam. Safety pins attached her sweater sleeve to the front of her fleece jacket and wraps of two-inch cloth medical tape secured her arm to her chest. Roberts crossed her right arm over her left to stabilize both. All the while Reed made sure that neither one of them moved her neck or back. They covered her with a blanket and secured the safety straps across her. Then Roberts radioed for the chopper to come back in.

They worked in tandem to hook the stretcher to the basket and cable. Reed bit into his cheek, holding back fear, as Jenna twirled in the wind and the stretcher was hoisted into the bay of the chopper. Once she was safely in, the cable lowered again for the medic.

"Thanks," Reed said, his voice dry and raspy.

"Her airway is stable, her spine is immobilized. It's the best I can do for now."

"Can I ride with her?"

Roberts looked at him for a moment. Reed knew it wasn't regulation, but dammit he wanted to be with her every minute in case she woke. He wanted her to know he wasn't leaving her. She wasn't alone.

"Okay," Roberts said. "I'll go up first then we'll send the cable back down for you. With your background, I'm sure you know what to do."

Reed nodded and swallowed hard. He had no more words. He just wanted Jenna to live.

Chapter Eleven

Reed turned the corner toward Jenna's hospital room. Last night, Becca had forced him to go home, to get some sleep and a shower before returning. He'd spent three days and nights at Jenna's bedside—talking to her, praying, waiting for her to wake, waiting to know that she'd live the full, sweet life she deserved. But there'd been no change. The doctors said it would take time—sometimes as long as two weeks. The head trauma was severe enough to keep her in a coma. They were waiting for her to wake on her own—waiting for her body to decide it was done with the initial healing. They wouldn't know the extent of brain damage until then.

Reed entered the room. His eyes immediately locked on Jenna's unconscious form.

"Find out anything new?" Mike asked from his seat in the corner.

"Not a damn thing." He strode across the room and sank to the edge of Jenna's bed. "How is she?" The monitor behind her beeped her pulse. Still weak, but regular.

He stroked along her arms, checked that she was covered and warm. "Jenna? Come back to me, sweetheart." Then he clasped her fingers in his, his thumb tracing small circles on the back of her hand. With his touch, her heart rate immediately sped up.

"Better with you around, apparently," Mike said.

Reed ran the back of his fingers along one cheek and the soft skin temporarily pinked up, drawing attention to the nearly translucent pallor of her skin over the last three days.

"She definitely knows you're here." Mike rose. "I'm meeting Jason and Becca to see how their research is going. Call me know when you need me back here."

"Yeah. Thanks."

Mike left the room and Reed released the breath he'd been holding. His chest tightened so painfully that for a moment he thought he was experiencing a minor heart attack, but he knew better.

Pure fear. He hadn't felt it so strongly since his return from the Middle East. Not fear for himself. Fear for Jenna.

It worried the hell out of him that he hadn't considered they'd target her again within twenty-four hours of the first attempt. He should have known. Even the most inexperienced cop would have considered that the first failed attempt would result in something else quickly. He'd been so caught up in protecting her, in convincing her to come with him, in spending one more frustrated night in her bed without touching, that he'd been distracted. He hadn't thought straight. Hadn't considered all the angles.

He fisted a corner of her blanket. *Damn it!* It was his fault she was here in the first place.

Seeing the blue and purple bruises along her throat flooded hot anger through his veins. This combination of anger and fear was something new to him, and he didn't like it one fucking bit. He should have killed the kidnapper when he had the chance. By letting him go, he'd given him a second shot at Jenna—a shot that would have killed her if Reed hadn't been there to get help. He focused on the thought of finding the hit man again and taking him apart, piece-by-piece. Preferably with Jenna whole, well, and a thousand miles away.

"How's she doing?" Leena's voice came from

behind him. He hadn't heard her come in the room.

He released his clutch on the blanket. "About the same. She seems to respond to my touch."

Leena's soft hand rested on his shoulder. "You're in love with her."

The tight clench in Reed's chest intensified. *Shit.* He didn't need love to complicate things.

"No. I'm not," he said, his voice gruff. He looked at Jenna's closed eyes. For the first time in years, he actually wished he was capable of love, but he knew that was never to be. Not after all he'd lost in Afghanistan, in Iraq. Even if he could find a way to fake it enough—a way to make Jenna believe it—she'd never love him back. Who would want to live with someone who had nightmares and flashbacks without warning, someone who could hurt her—maybe even kill her—in the middle of the night because he couldn't distinguish her from the enemy? That's why he never spent the night after sex. That's why he would never let himself get too close. Love? No way. Too dangerous.

Leena chuckled. "Deny it all you want, but I can see it in the way you talk to her, the way you caress her, the way you worry over her."

"I'm worried because she's my responsibility."

"Uh huh, and when one of your men ended up in the hospital, you stayed up night and day to ensure he was healthy."

"That's different. I had a mission to run, then."

"Whatever," Leena said, waving a hand in dismissal.

"Okay, I admit I care about her, but it's not love. I've only known her a little more than a week. We've been thrust together. She's beautiful, sexy, courageous..."

"Sometimes that's all it takes," Leena said.

He turned back to Jenna. *Could it be?* He stroked along her arms again, looking for some sign.

Instead, all he felt was the chest constriction that hadn't left since he'd flown with her to the hospital.

It wasn't love, however much he wished it to be. Lust, definitely. Yes, he cared about her—perhaps even more than he dreamed possible—but it wasn't love.

Jenna let out a raspy, painful cough and all of Reed's attention centered on her. Her lashes fluttered then slowly opened, revealing scared, teary, blue eyes. Her fingers curled around his and squeezed.

"Don't try to talk. Or move," he said. "Just get your bearings. You're in a hospital. Your arm is broken."

She struggled to get herself onto her elbows, but fell back when she realized one arm wasn't working. He admired her steely spirit.

"Someone's trying to kill me," she croaked, bringing her hand to her throat. "W-why?"

She could talk! Thank God. Maybe that meant she escaped any brain damage.

Reed's cell phone rang and, reluctant to let go of any part of Jenna, he quickly fished it from his shirt pocket and looked at the screen. It was Jason. He flipped it open. "Hang on."

He pointed to the water on the side table and gestured to Leena. She stepped around him and poured a small amount into a cup, then added a straw and lifted it toward Jenna's mouth.

Jenna sipped tentatively.

"Go," Reed said into the phone.

"I think we have something," Jason said. "Becca's found a name at Thompson University—someone who's heavy into stem cell research, and particularly its impact on children."

"I can't believe a university would have anything to do with where David was held," Reed said.

"I agree, but scientists know other scientists, and it may lead to something more. Becca and I are going to pay them a visit and see what we can dig up."

"Okay, keep me posted."

"How is she?"

"Awake." Reed looked at Jenna. "And scared." He squeezed her hand and smiled as he looked her in the eye. "But she's going to be fine."

"That's good," Jason said, relief obvious in his voice. "I'll tell Becca. We're leaving in a few minutes."

"Thanks, Cheeks." Reed closed the phone and relayed the conversation to Jenna and Leena.

Jenna moved back from the cup and sagged against her pillow. Leena returned the cup to the table.

"Will this lead us to who was holding David?" Jenna asked, her voice hoarse.

"Hard to tell right now. Jason will let me know what they learn." He lifted the glass back to her. "Can you drink a little more?"

She nodded and a little stronger hand reached toward the glass.

"Start with just a little. If that feels okay, drink more."

With each sip, it seemed that she gained a little more color, a little more spirit. Then she took a long suck on the straw and drained it.

"More, please." She smiled up at him.

She really was going to be okay. He refilled the glass, completely full this time and handed it to her. When she took it, he trailed the back of his hand from her temple to her jaw. "I'm so glad you're awake." His voice barely choked out the words. "I thought..." Swamped with the possibilities of how close he came to losing her, he couldn't finish the sentence.

She drank half of the second glass. “Much better,” she said, her voice a little stronger. “How long? How long have I been here?” Her eyes locked on his, the color deepening. Her jaw set in determination.

“Four days,” Leena answered. “Bruised ribs. Bruised hip. Concussion. Twisted ankle. Of course, the broken arm-elbow thing.” She tapped each finger as she counted the injuries. “Oh, and one love sick puppy. Reed wouldn’t leave your side until Becca threatened to beat him up if he didn’t get some sleep.”

“Really?” Jenna said, her lips quirking up.

“I was worried,” Reed said, a little too gruff. “Don’t make anything of it.”

“I bet Becca could have taken you,” Jenna said. “She’s a third-degree black belt in Jujitsu, you know.”

Reed lifted his brow. “Maybe I’ll have to challenge her to a duel then.”

“I…uh…think I’ll go see if Mike needs any help with David,” Leena said, bending to kiss Jenna’s forehead. “Glad you’re awake, girlfriend. Don’t rush into anything, okay?”

“Thanks,” Jenna said, clasping Leena’s hand. “Thanks…for everything.” She watched Leena until the door closed again.

She turned her eyes back to Reed and, with a grunt, scooted her hips and pushed against the pillows to sit up further.

“Here, let me help.” Reed pushed the button on the bed to raise her head then placed a hand on her back to bring her forward while he rearranged the pillows behind her for support. He ran his hand along the arm that was in a sling, the elbow that had been broken. Even though the bone had been exposed, the surgeon said the break was clean and she’d heal well.

"Thanks," she whispered when she settled again against the pillows. She took another swallow of water. "So, when do I get out of here?"

"There's no big hurry," Reed bent forward and kissed her lips, very lightly, a friendly I-care-about-you-kiss. Not an I-love-you kiss.

She canted her head to one side. "Hmmm. That was nice." Her lashes closed for a minute then opened, her eyes wide. "You're trying to distract me, aren't you?"

He smiled. One hand reached out to smooth the waves of hair away from her face. "On the contrary, you are the one who distracts me. I could sit her all day and just look at you."

Her lips lifted slightly. "Well, that's nice, Reed, but we don't have time for that right now." She lifted her chin and clenched her teeth. "I want to find the bastard who's trying to kill me," she whispered. "And I can't do that sitting here in a hospital bed."

He could smell the mixture of hospital antiseptic and the salty, sweet smell that was all Jenna. The combination left him feeling feral. He traced his fingers along her brow and down her check. Her eyes seemed bigger, even darker in her pearlescent face. His fingers slowed at the side of her throat, at the bruises on her pale, slender neck—the neck that could have broken in the car wreck and left her paralyzed. Or dead.

His hand dropped away and rage hit him full force. And fear. Bone deep fear for Jenna's life. The best thing for her would be to stay in the hospital until they caught the bastard who did this.

"For the foreseeable future," Reed said, his jaw locked tight, "I want you as far away from danger as possible." He wasn't going to brook any arguments with her this time. If necessary he'd arrange to move her to a hospital where he had some control over the staff. "Understand?"

"Of course I understand," Jenna said in the same locked-jaw tone he was using. "But that doesn't mean I agree."

"I don't care if you agree or not. You have no choice."

Turmoil mixed with fear and determination in her eyes. Then the bravado leaked out of her voice. "I'm sorry I scared you," she said softly, reaching up to cup his jaw.

Reed lifted his hand to cover hers, pressing her cool fingers against his face. "I wasn't scared, I was furious…I could kill the bastard who did this to you." He closed his eyes, struggling to put intense, very personal emotions in a safe box where he could take them out later to analyze and deal with in a sane, rational way. She didn't need his violence. She needed his nurturing—his…his caring.

He wrapped his arms around her, gently pulling her as close as he dared without hurting her. Her free arm slid around his waist. He nuzzled against her temple, inhaling the clean smell of her skin. "Don't worry about me; you're the one who almost died."

He should have protected her. Damn it to hell, he'd believed he could. Knowing how close he'd been to losing her made his stomach roil.

After a few moments, he moved her away from him, feeling the loss of her body's warmth like a rip in his soul. His eyes raked her throat and her arm, his anger rising again.

Jenna tilted her head. "It's written all over you. All you can think about is killing him."

"Yes." He could barely voice the word without growling. He knew how she felt about violence. But that was a part of him he'd cultivated over a long period of time—a part that had helped keep him and Stain and Cheeks alive. He wouldn't deny it.

"I'm not sure I want such a murderous-looking

man guarding me."

Murder. Yes, he was more than capable of killing anyone who would hurt Jenna. But would the violence so embedded in him spill over to hurt her too? He would just have to find a way to maintain better control. At least around her. He had to. He didn't want to imagine being without her.

"I'd never hurt you, Jenna. You know that."

He touched her hair lightly. His hand shook. He rose to his feet, his gut mirroring the disappointment he saw in her eyes. He wanted to crush her to him. He wanted to kiss away the pain in every part of her body. He wanted to protect her from all violence and evil. But who would protect her from him. Who would protect her when he wanted to make slow, sweet love to her, inch by inch—leaving nothing untouched.

Fuck. Maybe I do love her. He couldn't find any other word for the way he felt right now.

"I need to lie back again."

Reed lowered the head of the bed, his arm on her back helping her to recline.

Jenna scooted to one side of the bed with a grunt. She reached toward him with her good arm. "Come here."

He stepped toward the bed, unsure what to do, what to say.

"I won't break," she said. "Come lie next to me."

He hesitated. He wasn't sure if he could do just that. He wasn't sure if he could stop without hurting her.

"Just hold me," she said. "Please. Can you do that?"

He answered, with a single nod, and swallowed hard as his eyes misted. He stretched out next to her in the small hospital bed, his arm gentle over her cast and sling. She stretched her sore, bruised neck up to him and her lips softly touched his, quashing his anger. He gently pulled her head closer.

His lips responded gently at first, but as she pressed herself forward, he couldn't help but pour his feelings into his kiss—his fear, his loss, his dread of ever losing her. He wasn't sure who was the real comforter, him or her. She dared him to deepen the kiss. His tongue dipped into her mouth and she answered by capturing it. He groaned, lost in her. Breathtakingly lost.

Chapter Twelve

It was a little after five when Becca and Jason pulled into the Thompson Medical Center parking garage. Crossing the footbridge spanning the street, a rush of wind whipped her loose jacket open and she shivered against the cold. Bending against the force of the wind, she clutched her jacket closed.

"Here." Jason removed his jacket and offered it to her.

"No thanks," she said. "I'm fine."

"Afraid a Marine would show you up, huh squid?"

"Not you, jarhead."

"Ouch. Tromp my ego into the ground."

She laughed. "I didn't think Marines were so thin-skinned."

"We're not. I just like to make you feel sorry for me, so I can have my way with you."

"Uh huh," she said. "It doesn't work." They rounded the edge of the building and the wind increased.

An empty beer can tumbled down the road. The familiar red tail lights and wisps of exhaust fumes stretched down the street as far as she could see, traveling just fast enough not to give them a break to cross to the other side. It seemed everyone was leaving the Thompson complex at once.

Jason held up a hand, like waving down a taxi, and a white van came to a stop. He signaled a thank you and pulled her into a jog toward the portico at the main entrance to the medical center. She sighed a thanks for the sudden respite from the wind. Jason reached past her and hauled open the heavy glass door, his hand on her back pushing her into the warmth of the lobby. He turned toward the reception desk and Becca grabbed his arm, instead towing him to the wooden plaques marking directions to various offices and labs.

"No need to call attention to ourselves," she said and pointed at the fourth marker down. "Looks like the genetic research lab is in the basement, evidently on the same floor as the morgue and pathology.

Jason placed a hand on her elbow and steered them to the elevator. "Do you have a plan you'd like to share?"

"Sure. We pretend we know where we're going, and when we get downstairs, we ask for Dr. Kramer." She punched the button for the basement and the elevator doors closed. She wasn't sure what would happen after that. They hadn't called ahead. *Better to watch for unrehearsed reactions,* she thought.

"And if we get thrown out, or locked up, what then?" Jason asked.

She smiled up at him. "You're the lawyer, you tell me."

He chuckled. "Yeah, well let's not rely so fully on my paperwork skills. Have you thought about the possibility Dr. Kramer could be the one ordering these attempts on Jenna's life."

"We're here," she whispered. The doors opened into a corridor which disappeared into the dark in both directions. Bare fluorescent tubes glowed from the ceiling at intervals of twenty feet or so. The light from each tube met the light from the next with a gray sort of cloudiness in the middle, causing a strange interplay of shadows from the tangle of pipes along the ceiling. Directly opposite them was a hand-lettered piece of paper that listed morgue, pathology, research in order but no directional arrows.

Jason peered into the small window in the door next to the handmade sign. "This must be the morgue," he said. "I see six large metal drawers to the right and in the middle of the room is someone washing a body."

Yuck. Going into a morgue was not her idea of fun. Her only memory of visiting a morgue was when her brother died from a motorcycle accident and she'd had to identify the body. She shivered.

"Still cold?"

"Yeah," she lied. "Well, try the door."

He pulled on the large metal handle but there was no give.

"Damn." She pounded on the door to get the person's attention and peered through the window. When the man looked up, she put on her best smile. An eyebrow rose and the man walked to the door.

"Dr. Kramer," she said as loudly as possible and smiled again.

The door opened and she saw that the man was much younger than she'd anticipated, she guessed somewhere between twenty-five and thirty. "Did you say, 'Dr. Kramer'?" he asked.

"Yes, sorry to bother you." She batted her eyelashes. "He's in stem-cell research."

The young man looked her over than slid his eyes to Jason and took a step back. She frowned when she saw Jason's stiff, overprotective bearing.

"My brother," she said. "A bit protective." She elbowed Jason in the side. "Back off, J."

"His name is Jay?" the young man asked.

"Yes, like a blue jay," she replied. "Really, he's harmless but likes to puff up and chatter a lot."

The young man smiled. "Oh. Okay then. Uh…I don't know Dr. Kramer personally, but research is through the back there." He pointed to the far right corner of the room where another dirty, white, closed door beckoned. "You have to go through pathology first, and then all the way back."

"Thanks," she said, smiling one last time. She grabbed Jason's arm. "Come on, J. We don't want to miss our appointment."

When they'd gotten through the door, Jason stopped her. "That was not funny."

"It worked. Back down your I-can-kill-you-if-I-want look until we get to Kramer, okay. It is not conducive to asking questions. I'm sure you can be affable if you try—even jarheads have a brain."

"Hmph. Once we get out of here, I'll show you who has the better brain, Navy." He strode down the hall. "Just try to keep up."

The hall led to another door, this time with a proper sign that said Pathology. Cracking the door, she got a glimpse of the interior before entering. A long black stone table dominated the room, running most of its length. Cluttered about on the table were microscopes, slides, slide boxes, chemicals, books, and an array of other equipment. Becca pushed open the door and stepped into the lab. The acrid smell of formaldehyde hung over the room. The entire wall on the left had shelving from floor to ceiling. With hardly a square inch remaining, the shelves were full of varying sized bottles and jars.

"Sweet," Jason said, moving to a large jar with a colorless mass standing on the table. "A whole brain cut in half."

She swallowed. There was a reason she'd chosen not to become a medic in the Navy. She really hated her college biology classes. She'd barely passed the labs with all that dissection work on animals. She'd never even wanted to contemplate dissecting humans.

Jason moved to another jar, this one smaller

with an oval shaped tissue. He read, "Breast ductal carcinoma #489-A7 1989. Shit, that's sad."

Becca located another ugly off-white door at the far end of the room. The sign said simply SC Research. "I think this is it. Let's go." She'd had enough of the smells and weird bottles of death spread all around them.

A small, wiry man in a white lab coat turned immediately when she and Jason entered the room. He was slender, skinny actually, and couldn't have been much taller than five and a half feet. She was sure at her five feet, seven inches that she was slightly taller than him. He wore small, square golden glasses—certainly an atypical look for a medical scientist. His medium brown hair was almost to his shoulders and looked as if it hadn't been combed in a couple of days.

"Are you lost?" he asked, his voice sounding impatient.

"Dr. Kramer?" Jason said from behind her, and offered his hand. "Jason Walters."

The man ignored Jason's hand. "Do I know you?"

"No," Becca stepped slightly in front of Jason. "I'm Becca Collins. You don't know us, but I believe you can help us."

The man turned his back and picked up a journal of some type and leafed through it. "Did you have an appointment? I don't see that there was an appointment scheduled for me."

"I'm sorry," Becca said. "We didn't make an appointment."

Dr. Kramer turned around and took a deep breath. "I'm very busy. Go away." He flicked his wrist, shooing them like children.

"We're looking into the use of children in medical experiments and we thought you could help."

Kramer visibly blanched. "Oh, dear God. Not

again. Who? No one working for me. Please God, tell me it's no one working for me."

"What do you mean, not again?" Jason asked.

Kramer sagged into a chair, his head down. "It's been a long time. Fourteen, maybe fifteen years. I can't believe it. Who is it? Who's using children?" His fingers gripped the edge of the table in front of him.

"Who did it fifteen years ago," Jason asked.

"You mean you don't know who's doing it now?" Dr. Kramer let out a breath. "It's not on my team?"

"We're still investigating."

"Are you with the NIH? FBI?"

"No," Becca said softly. "We found a boy who claims to have been in a lab, he can't remember where. He had regular experiments done on him. The boy is about ten years old. Now please, tell us who it was that did this fifteen years ago. He may be doing it again."

Dr. Kramer's shoulders lowered and he motioned for Jason and Becca to sit down across from him. "Dr. Marius Crane. The most brilliant researcher I've ever worked with. Also completely insane."

Becca looked at Jason, her eyes wide.

"You work with Dr. Crane?" Jason asked.

"I did. Fourteen, maybe fifteen years ago. He started this lab. He was doing stem-cell research before most people had even heard of it."

"Where is he now?" Becca asked.

"Vienoy. He started his own company." Dr. Kramer took off his glasses and rubbed the lenses on the end of his shirt. "I saw him about two years ago. He said he'd be presenting a paper within five years that would prove his theories once and for all. I didn't believe him. I told him it was impossible for anyone to present a paper within five years. The limited therapies that have been allowed on humans have been highly controlled, and only with subjects who would die shortly anyway."

Becca turned to Jason. "Vienoy is where..."

Jason nodded, raising a finger to his lips. "What did he say to your disbelief?"

Kramer frowned, then pursed his lips like he'd just sucked on a lemon. "He laughed. He said I always played by the rules. As if that's wrong. He said he had his own volunteers, and his own line of stem cells." Kramer's index finger rubbed against his thumb as if worrying a blister.

"Of course, I didn't believe that either. First, the stem cell lines are very restricted. The government knows exactly where they are—all over the world. There is no chance that Vienoy would have their own. Second, even if he managed to get his hands on his own line, no parent would offer up a fairly healthy child as a human subject—particularly in an experiment that has no university or government backing associated with it."

"Unless they didn't know," Becca said.

"Nooooo." Kramer drew out the word as his eyes widened. He shook his head and stood. "No. He wouldn't go that far. He may be insane, but he would know that if he didn't get informed consent his research would never be accepted by anyone in the field. That's what he wants more than anything else. To be accepted back into the fold."

"What exactly do you think Dr. Crane was going to prove?" Jason asked.

Kramer shrugged and looked away. "We never talked about his current research. When I downplayed his theories, he got angry. He said I was just envious, that I could never expect to be great if I didn't push the boundaries." Kramer chuckled and turned back to Jason and Becca. "Then he offered me a job at Vienoy. If he was so close and so sure about his research, why would he offer me a job? I think he was desperate, trying to lure me away from

Thompson."

"You refused the job," Jason said.

"Of course. He knew I would never take it. The fact he asked shows how out of touch with reality he is these days."

"Maybe he wanted to offer it to you, and when you refused he could hold it over your head when he publishes." Becca said.

Kramer rolled his eyes.

"Evidently, you two have a history," Becca said. "Fifteen years away from each other is a long time. Why would he even seek you out if he knew you'd refuse?"

Kramer laughed, but there was no joy in it. "Only a crazy person could answer that question. Yeah, we had a history. I'm the one who got him fired."

Becca gasped. "But you said he was the most brilliant scientist you've ever worked with."

"I found out he was injecting altered cells into children without their knowledge. At first it was just one or two, and it appeared the children had some improvement. That was what kept me from saying anything the first time. But then they had a relapse and it was even worse than anticipated. Still, that didn't stop him. He said he'd changed the cell combinations. He said it would work the next time. He just needed more subjects. But I knew if I let him get away with it, he would push the ethics boundary further. He didn't care about curing the children. He only cared about proving his theory. He said they'd die anyway."

"Would they have?" Jason asked.

"I don't know. Maybe…probably. But the point is it's completely unethical. We never do anything without informed consent. Never."

"What makes you think he isn't doing the same thing now, at Vienoy?"

Kramer stood. "Look, it was all over the news when he was fired. It wasn't like it was kept quiet. He was escorted off the premises the day it hit. No brushing it under the rug with the usual early retirement party and an African violet for his desk at home. Thompson Medical used the firing to prove to everyone how diligent they were in policing their researchers. It garnered Thompson Medical national publicity and more funding. And it made Dr. Crane a research pariah. No university or legitimate research facility would take him after that. He was finished.

"When he started Vienoy, he was scrutinized by every government agency and medical board that existed. Both state and federal authorities still visit his facilities on a regular basis, often unannounced, to ensure everything is on the up and up. The only way he could be experimenting on any children is if they didn't exist in the system and were housed somewhere with no record. I mean no birth records, no death records, no existence whatsoever. And that's impossible. Even street kids or abandoned children have records somewhere."

He paused, picked up a piece of paper and moved to a computer. "I think he's just lost it. He's not in touch with reality anymore."

Becca looked at Jason. She knew he didn't want her to divulge any of their own knowledge, but she had to take the chance. It seemed that Dr. Kramer was proving to be a major lead for them.

"I know Vienoy has a reputation as a very successful fertility clinic," she said.

"And an abortion clinic," Jason added.

"If he's so bad, how can he run those clinics? I'd think his medical license would have been revoked," Becca said.

"The charges never went before the review board," Kramer said. "Though the hospital used his firing for publicity, they didn't want anyone looking into it too deeply. If they admitted any fault in the deaths of those three kids, they'd be sued into eternity."

"So, legally, he can still practice medicine," Jason said, the disgust obvious in his voice.

"Legally," Kramer confirmed. "But he can't really make a living at it. He's banned from all the insurers for reimbursement."

"Then how does he run Vienoy?"

Dr. Kramer looked up at her. "He doesn't practice medicine anymore, but that doesn't stop him from being the CEO of a large company that does. He can hire doctors and nurses just like anyone else. They can bill insurance. As long as Crane doesn't practice medicine, he's fine to run the fertility and abortion clinics with other doctors and nurses."

"Maybe he's using Vienoy then to continue his research," Becca said.

"Not possible. I just don't see how he'd get away with it." Kramer said. "He just wanted to lord it over me one more time. I never took him seriously. Look, I'm here, at a top research hospital and where's Crane? Washed up. Desperate. No. He's nothing. He's doing nothing." He turned back to his journal, obviously signaling the interview was done.

"We need to get in touch with Crane," Jason said. "Would you help us? He obviously has something to prove to you."

"No." Kramer waved his arm in their general direction. "Go away. I'm busy. I can't think about this. I won't allow it back in my lab. I won't allow it back in my life. Go away."

Chapter Thirteen

"Thanks for coming in, Mr. Adler." Detective Novak pulled a chair up to his desk and offered it to Reed.

"Anything to help," Reed said.

"I just have a few questions."

Impatient, Reed took a breath and leaned back in the chair. He didn't have anything against Novak, except he was too young and eager. He would have preferred the sheriff's office to handle this case. He trusted them. He'd worked with them several times in the past year. They knew him and would never waste his time bringing him in for questioning. Instead, the investigation had been passed to the local cops in Sandy. The only murders they'd ever investigated were biker gangs fighting at the local bar. Not that they were bad cops, this was just way out of their league and involved multiple precincts. Vienoy was in Gresham, Thompson Medical was in Portland. He was sure they were all playing turf games and not getting anything done. But Novak was the contact they'd been given and somehow Reed had to live with that.

In the past two weeks, Becca and her computer searches had found more leads than Novak had. When Jason had passed them on to Novak, he never followed up with Thompson Medical. Detective Novak said he already had a different theory for the case.

"So, is Ms. Mosier doing better?" Novak asked.

"She'd be better if I were home looking after her

instead of down here on a fishing expedition." Reed had just picked up David from Leena's place and driven Jenna and David to his cabin. When he received the call from Novak to come to the precinct, he'd had to scramble to get Mike and Leena back out to his place so he could leave. Though he doubted the killer knew anything about his cabin, he couldn't be sure. There was no way he'd leave Jenna or David unprotected.

"Of course, I understand you'd rather be home." Novak said. "Actually, my questions have to do with your relationship with Jenna Mosier."

"And how does that help you with this case?" Reed's finger pointed to the case folder.

Novak moved the folder to the other side of the desk, as if he was afraid Reed would take it. "It's just background information. It helps me to see the whole picture."

Reed sat forward. "There is no 'relationship'." His fingers made quotes in the air on the last word. "She's a woman in trouble. I'm trying to keep her safe. That's it."

"So, you're acting as a kind of bodyguard."

"That's right."

"And she hired you in this capacity?"

"You know damn well she didn't." Reed grabbed the edge of the desk and leaned forward until he was within five or six inches of Novak's face. "What are you trying to get at, detective? Let me take care of all your questions at once and save us time. Are we sleeping together? No. Are we having an affair? No. Am I the one stalking her? Absolutely not. Do I have any reason to want her dead? No way, no how. Now does that answer all your questions? I'm ready to get out of here and go back to my job of keeping Jenna safe, a job the police don't seem very interested in doing."

Novak looked up at Reed, impassive. "Please sit

back, Mr. Adler. There's no need to get excited. I'm just doing *my* job. I'd hate to have to hold you for questioning because you were uncooperative."

"Damn right I'm uncooperative when you ask stupid questions. You want to arrest me, go ahead. I'll be out of here within hours. You already know my attorney, Jason Walters...the one keeping you up to date on every lead we find." Reed scanned the precinct. Three other officers sprawled at desks scattered in the big room. If he made a scene, it could get uncomfortable real quick.

He sighed and rolled his head in a full circle, working out the kinks. Then he sat back again, trying for calm. As much as he didn't think Novak knew what he was doing, he also wouldn't count him out. The more eyes on this case the better. "Look, I'm grateful to have you looking into this. I just want answers. I want this to end."

Novak nodded. "Look at it from my perspective, Mr. Adler." He opened his case dossier. "My records indicate you were the one who found Ms. Mosier. She stayed at your house for a week, and you've rarely left her side since. You visited her in the hospital, and now she's conveniently back at your house again. Yet you claim you have no relationship. You have your attorney, Mr. Walters, and some ex-Navy woman looking into Thompson Medical with some idea that kids have been harmed. Yet, no one has produced a kid or filed a complaint about a kid being hurt, experimented on, or anything else. So, what am I supposed to think?"

Reed sucked in his cheeks and wrinkled his brow. Novak had a point. He hadn't said anything about David because he didn't want social services involved. If they knew he'd been harmed in any way, they'd have doctors all over the kid in seconds. The local sheriff had made arrangements for Reed to keep David by using his personal reputation, calling in a favor with Clackamas County social services and giving Jason a chance to work the temporary custody order through the courts. Shit, he couldn't blame Novak, but that didn't mean he had to like the guy.

"I need to make a call," Reed said, reaching for his cell phone. "I think we can help each other here."

Novak waved at the phone on his desk. "You can use mine."

Reed laughed. "Yeah, I bet, but this is faster." He pressed the number three and it automatically dialed Jason's office.

Jason answered on the first ring. "Yeah, rat face. How's Jenna?"

"She's fine. Look, I'm sitting here with Detective Novak and I'm wondering where we are with the papers you were filing. Like, can we say anything?"

"Papers?" Jason paused. "I need a little help here, buddy. I've been filing a lot of papers lately. I know you can't spell it out, but can you give me a better hint?"

"Yeah, that's right," Reed said. "The ones about that younger guy I found. The one Jenna really loves."

"You mean David. Judge signed the order this morning. I just hadn't had the time to tell you yet. Jenna has temporary custody."

"That's great." Reed relaxed a little. At least no one could easily take David away now.

"I think it's time we have David meet Detective Novak. It's time we let him have *all* the information."

"You're probably right," Jason said. "I'll call Stain and ask him to bring everyone down."

"Thanks, Cheeks. Good work." Reed hung up.

"David?" Novak asked.

"The proof," Reed said. "I'll bet you can't find any records of a David Mosier in any database nationwide. But his story is terrifying. You want to know about kids and experiments, you wait for this."

"David Mosier? Ms. Mosier told me she couldn't have children and her husband refused to adopt. In fact, she said that was the reason for her divorce."

Reed fisted a hand by his side. Jenna hadn't talked at all about her ex-husband, but he knew someone had deeply hurt her. What kind of shithead left a woman because she couldn't have kids?

"Mr. Adler?" Novak interrupted his thoughts.

"Tanya Mosier," Reed said. "David is Tanya's son—a son Jenna never knew existed until recently. A boy who watched his mother die in front of him and ran to get away from the killer."

Novak quickly reached for his pen, the nib hardly keeping up with the scratches on the yellow legal pad. "Why didn't I know about this boy before?"

"I wasn't at liberty to tell you."

Novak got in Reed's face. "What the hell does that mean? I'm a police officer, investigating the homicide of Tanya Mosier and what now appears to be a double attempted homicide. You are required to tell me anything I need to know."

Reed narrowed his eyes and bit down on his tongue before he said something he'd regret. He stared down Novak, not speaking.

Novak didn't move back even a millimeter. He stared right back. It was an all-balls-out type of stare—the type that each knew whoever broke first was the loser. Reed narrowed his focus on the spot between Novak's eyebrows. He didn't move, didn't dare even twitch a muscle in his face. He'd spent hours sighting down a rifle. He knew he could outlast this guy, and right now, he needed to take control of the situation.

Minutes, or was it just seconds, ticked by and finally Novak broke away. Reed sat back. *One battle down.*

Novak stood. "I'm going to check this out." He jerked open the door and turned, shaking his index finger at Reed. "Don't you dare leave this room until I have the full story."

"Not planning on it," Reed said.

Novak gritted his teeth and walked out.

Reed's thoughts immediately returned to Jenna. He'd seen how she was with David and knew she would be a great mother. Had she pressed for adoption and her ex refused? Reed had heard about men who had a need to reproduce their specific gene pool. He didn't understand it, not when so many children needed homes.

When Reed was being shuttled from one foster home to another, he'd dreamed of finding a permanent family. But it never happened. His mom refused to sign the papers to let him be adopted. She kept telling him she'd stop using, and when she did, she'd come back for him. But then she'd get high again, and she forgot all her promises.

The courts finally took the decision away from her when he was eight-years-old. The problem was everyone wanted babies or toddlers. A precocious eight-year-old was already too damaged in most adoptive parent's minds. Devastated that he'd never have a real family, Reed converted his pain to anger and took it out whenever anyone tried to get close—his schoolteachers, other kids, foster families—by pushing people away.

At age fourteen, no longer willing to be hit by a foster father who thought the way to straighten him out was to regularly whip him with a belt, Reed ran away, determined he would never return to foster care again. Social Services didn't seem to spend a lot of time trying to find him either.

The Corps was the only real family he'd ever had. They'd eventually straightened him out. That's why he'd stayed in so long. He loved the Corps and had always believed he'd be killed in battle—the only way to go. On his last tour he put himself in harm's way a lot. Afraid to stay. Afraid to come home. Until he retired a year ago, he never dared to imagine what life would be like on the outside.

Novak strode back in the room. "There's nothing on a kid born to Tanya Mosier—any kid, except Amber who we already know about."

"Told ya," Reed said. "Curious now?"

Novak slammed a yellow legal pad on the desk and sat down hard in the chair across from Reed. "Start talking. From the beginning. And don't leave out a single detail."

Relieved to share the nightmare of the last two weeks, Reed tried to lay out what had happened with some sort of logic, concentrating on every detail he'd noted at the crime scenes. It was like a puzzle with three missing pieces in the center. He knew the pieces were related, but he had no idea what the central picture even held.

The detective wrote it down. Reed looked it over and made some factual corrections. By the end of the process, Reed admitted the two had worked out an uneasy respect for each other. When Jenna and David arrived, Becca, Leena, Mike, and Jason were also in tow. The group was ushered into a conference room at the back of the precinct. Novak called in two other cops, one an ex-social worker and the other a detective from Portland with a graduate degree in biology. He'd wanted all the experts to hear the whole story.

As each of them revealed their role in the investigation, Reed noticed all three cops taking this case seriously, often in awe at its potential ramifications. Though murder was not a small consideration in Oregon, everyone now understood this was much bigger than one man—and it involved children. Expendable children with no traceable identities. Most cops had kids themselves, which brought the horror even closer to home.

Reed kept his hands on David's shoulders as he sat in front of him telling the same story he'd told before. David hadn't broken down once this time, and he hadn't asked if he was required to participate. In fact, his small body became even more animated as Novak probed further. Reed watched a fighter develop as David's enthusiastic answers showed an eagerness to involve the police.

Novak let out a deep breath and shook his head when David finally finished his story. "David, you said that when you were in this place, where people always gave you shots and took your blood, you didn't have a name. Is that right?"

"I kind of had a name, but it was a number. The doctor called me specimen forty-nine. All of us kids were called specimen something. I think that specimen meant we were all orphans or something."

Reed tightened his grip on David. He hadn't heard that part before. When David had told him his name, he assumed that had been his name all along. He'd never considered...

"Then how did you get your name?" Novak asked.

"My mother gave it to me. She said it was my real name."

"But you never knew your mother before she helped you escape," Novak said.

"I'd seen her a few times," David said. "She showed up usually at night after we were all in bed. I was the oldest, so at first I figured she talked to me because I knew the most."

"Why weren't you scared of her?"

"I don't know, I guess because I could tell she was sneaking around—making sure the night nurse couldn't see her. And she was real nice. Not just to me, but to all of us. Sometimes she would sneak in extra food because I told her we were hungry. Once when I didn't feel very good and the nurse wouldn't help me, she brought me some medicine that made me feel better."

David paused and took a deep breath. "She told me she would help save all of us. She said she was a lawyer and would stop the doctor from hurting us anymore. She said she would find us all mothers and fathers."

"Why did you believe her? Weren't you scared to leave when she came for you?"

"She brought me a picture of when she was little, like me, and she showed it to me. Even though she was a girl, I could tell it looked just like me. Like she was my sister or somethin'. So I believed her." David paused and looked at Jenna, then Reed. "All of us kids wanted to have a real mother and father. The nurses tried to tell us we didn't need parents because of all the nurses being our mother, and the doctor was like our father. But I didn't believe them. The nurses and the doctor weren't like the story books they read to us." He looked across the table to Jenna. "Jenna, now that the court said you can be my mother, can Reed be my father, too? Can I have a real family now?"

Reed looked at Jenna, his arms tightening around David. She wiped a hand across her eyes. He looked away. He couldn't imagine giving up David and never seeing him again. Surely, Jenna would at least let him be a part of David's life, even if he wasn't an intimate part of hers.

"Jenna is your aunt," Reed finally said. "But she's going to be like a mother to you. And we'll both make sure you have a wonderful father."

"But I want you," David said, his lower lip trembling. "Why can't you be my father?"

"David," Jason mercifully intervened when Reed couldn't find any words. "Remember what I said about the court deciding Jenna would be your guardian?"

"Yeah."

"Well, they didn't say anything about Reed. Jenna is related to you by blood and that is why you can live with her. Reed isn't related to you, so he can't live with you. That's the court rules."

"But everyone's living at Reed's house now. So, why can't Jenna just keep living there?"

Reed could see this conversation had no happy ending. "Let's talk about it later, David. Right now, we need to answer all of the detective's questions so we can go home. Okay?" He squeezed David's shoulders.

David turned back to the detective. "Detective Novak?"

"Yes, David."

"You know the law, right?"

Novak cleared his throat. "I'm not a judge, if that's what you mean. I know some of the law, especially when something is a crime."

"So, if Reed married Jenna, then could we all live together? And would that mean Reed could be my dad?"

Novak chuckled. "Yes, I suppose that's right."

David nodded his head once and smiled. "That's what I thought."

Novak looked at Reed, not hiding his internal chuckle successfully. Then he turned to the science cop. "See if you can find a picture of Marius Crane, will you?"

The man nodded and left the room.

"David, the doctor who came to see you a lot, do you remember his name?"

"His name was doctor."

"He didn't have another name? Like Doctor Smith or Doctor Jones?"

David frowned and looked to one side of the

room, as if the answer might be floating in a corner. "Nope. Everyone just called him doctor. One of the nurses called him Doctor Big. But then she giggled like that wasn't really his name."

Reed and Novak exchanged glances. "Did the nurse who called him that have a name?" Reed asked.

"Ummm. I think it was Nurse Adrianne. Yeah, the young one. She was always nice to us, except when the doctor was around. Then she acted like she didn't know us at all."

Novak wrote down the name in his book. Reed noticed Becca was making a note in her laptop as well. Then the science cop came back in with a newspaper clipping and handed it to Novak.

Novak placed it on the table in front of David. "Do you recognize this man?"

"Sure. That's the doctor."

Chapter Fourteen

Still wired from the day's events, Jenna sat on the edge of the bed in Reed's room. She'd just managed to take a shower with a plastic bag over her cast. That was definitely not fun. The bed baths in the hospital suddenly looked very practical. She wasn't able to get into a T-shirt for sleeping, so she'd opted for a cotton poncho she hadn't worn in years. At least it covered her, and the arm cutouts were plenty big to get her cast through.

She scratched at the top of her cast and wished she had something longer—something that would let her scratch all the way down her arm and relieve the horrible itching. She searched the surfaces of all the furniture but nothing looked like it would work. Darn. There was no way she could sleep with the constant prickling and burning.

"I think he's asleep," Reed said as he entered the room and closed the door. "How are you?"

"I itch like crazy."

"Ah. I may have something to help." He opened a dresser drawer and drew out a long wooden handled stick with what looked like a fork on the end of it. "Here." He handed it to her.

She slid it down inside her cast and groaned with pleasure. "Oh God, this is perfect."

He laughed. "A present from Mike when I broke my leg. I itched for three weeks. Make sure you watch out for the stitches though."

He unbuttoned and stripped off his shirt, throwing it in the corner. Jenna's eyes opened wide.

His broad, tanned shoulders glowed, his skin smooth as satin overlaying rock-hard muscle. She ran an appreciative glance down his furring of crisp light brown hair. Small dark nipples beckoned her mouth and she closed her eyes lest she put her lips on one.

She heard him unzip his pants and watched beneath her lashes as he stepped out of them. Jenna didn't move. How could she? He was undressing right in front of her. Like they did this every night before bed. Her gaze flew open and traveled to his navel, following the trail of hair into the tight fitting boxers he wore. The silky sheen showed the curve of his hip, the strength of his thighs. She licked her lips, but couldn't help wondering what exactly lay underneath. Heat rose in her cheeks and she turned her back to him. "I wish you wouldn't do that."

Reed chuckled, his voice low. "I didn't see you looking away."

"It's…" She was at a loss for words and certainly wasn't going to tell him what seeing him like that made her want. If he reached for her, kissed her like he had in the hospital…well, she just couldn't be held accountable.

"Jenna?" He said her name on a breath, a breath of promise and desire. She couldn't answer, couldn't turn around. She wanted him too much.

He stepped behind her, his chest pressed against her back. His arm snaked around her left side, pinning her good arm. His lips grazed her ear and he whispered, "What would you have me do, Jenna?"

She moaned.

"Would you rather have me undress in the dark and then find you in my bed?"

She could barely find her voice. "Wouldn't…"

He feathered kisses down her neck and she sighed, trying to get the words out, "have to be…"

His hand moved just underneath her breast.

Her nipples peaked through her thin poncho. She swallowed. "...in the dark...please...Reed."

"Please what, Jenna?" His thumb barely grazed her taut nipple as he rolled it back and forth slowly. She groaned. "What do you want, Jenna? Tell me what you want."

His hand dropped, tracing a line to the hem of her poncho, his deft fingers crawled beneath it and he reached across her stomach to turn her toward him, his hand pressed firmly against her bare back. His other hand lifted her chin to him and he lowered his lips to hers. She closed her eyes. She wanted to feel him all around her. She opened her mouth inviting him in.

He cupped the back of her head. His fingers lingered on her ear, stroking the fleshy pad before tracing the swirls. She twitched her shoulder as she felt the fire skim down her throat.

Oh God. What am I doing? What if he only wants a one night stand? What if... She tried to push him away but he held tight, his eyes flashing with need.

"I...I don't really know you...I don't know if this is something more...more than just one night."

"What does it matter?" he asked, his voice rough. She felt his heart beating against her. "You want me as much as I want you, I can feel your desire. Why can't that be enough for now?"

Yes, she wanted him. She wanted him more than she'd ever wanted a man in her life. But that was the problem. She didn't want him for only one night, or only one week. And, if it was to be longer, she needed to know if there was any chance of a real relationship—something beyond all the craziness that was happening right now.

She pushed harder against him. "We need to talk first."

He groaned and let her go. "About what? What

could be more important than this, right here, right now?"

"I want more. I don't want a one night stand."

He reached for her again, but she held up her hand. He sighed. "This is much more than one night, Jenna. I'm far too selfish to let it be only one night."

Her heart fluttered and she closed her eyes. Did he care as much as she did? She opened her eyes again and looked straight at him. "Is it just sex? Or something more? Because I want something more."

He stepped back. "Jenna, what are you asking?"

"I…I don't know exactly," she admitted. "I'm not asking for a commitment, like marriage or something. I just want…I just want to know that it's more than sex. That you care…about me."

He raked a hand through his hair. "Of course I care. Please, you're over-thinking this. Let nature take its course and I'll show you how much I care. It'll be good, I promise."

She laughed uneasily. "I have no doubt it will be amazing." Her cheeks heated and she looked to the floor. "That's why I'm scared."

She put a hand on his chest and slowly raised her eyes to his again. "I'd rather not have this amazing sex between us, wanting more and more of you, and finding out too late that you never intended to give any more than sex."

Reed put his hand over hers. This was why he hadn't tried to take things further before. He knew she'd be the type of woman to want more—more than he could give. He could easily lie, make the promises she wanted to hear. But he wouldn't do that. He wanted her to be with him but only with full knowledge of the limitations of their relationship.

"Jenna." He let out a deep breath. "I can promise that I care about you. I can promise our being together will be more than just sex, more than I've experienced with any woman."

"Then that's enough."

Reed shook his head and placed her away from him. He drew her to sit on the bed and faced her, making sure there was at least a foot separating them. He had to tell her the truth. "But you can't expect love from me. Ever."

She gasped. "How can you say that? You don't know what will happen, nor do I." She paused. He could see her shoulders rise and fall with disappointment as she worked through what he said. "Is there someone else?" she asked. "Someone who broke your heart? Someone you're waiting for?"

"No, it's not like that."

"Then what? Explain it to me. No one truly wants to be alone."

He swallowed, wanting to tell her, but he couldn't. He hadn't told anyone, not even the counselor when he was first diagnosed with PTSD.

"The war," she whispered, as if she'd read his mind.

Panic flooded him. Now she'd ask questions, questions about what had happened. Questions that he didn't want to answer—things about war that she should never have to know. How could he talk about how easy killing had become? About the callousness that overtook him when year after year he faced an unknown enemy, an enemy that could even appear as a woman, or a child, and he still killed?

How could he tell her about being so scared he urinated on himself and defecated in his pants? About how, when he was over there, he had to forget everything sane and normal back home because what he was taught was good and right had nothing to do with this reality. And when he came home, how people wouldn't look him in the eye—how they looked at him with pity, knowing he'd killed innocents.

He stood and backed away. Her searching gaze might see too much. Her need was worse than any truth serum.

"The flashbacks," she said. "You're afraid I can't handle the flashbacks."

He stopped his retreat and breathed a sigh of relief. She didn't ask what happened. He didn't need to tell the story.

"That's part of it," he finally said. He took the chair opposite the bed. There was no chance of sex now. But he could give her this, at least this little bit of truth about his life right now. Maybe it would be enough…enough for next time.

"I'd never expect anyone to have to live with that," he said, his eyes on the wooden floor beneath his feet. "It's more than flashbacks. It's nightmares, too. Sometimes, during a particularly bad one, I wake up choking my pillow, trying to kill an Afghani or Iraqi. I wouldn't want to hurt you."

She stood, too, her arms crossing in front, hugging herself. "But you wouldn't hurt me…you couldn't."

"I don't know that for sure. Look what happened at your condo. For a few minutes, I didn't know if I was in Afghanistan or with you. I knocked you down. Hard. You could have hit your head on the concrete and died instantly."

"You were trying to protect me, not hurt me. I was just startled."

"I didn't hurt you that time…but who knows about the next time."

"I think that some part of your mind knew it was me, even in the middle of it. I could see it in your eyes—brief recognition, and then it would disappear again."

He nodded. She was right. Somehow, he was able to hold both the present and the past in his mind at the same moment. The problem was he didn't know how to make the present override the past.

She bit her lip, nodded and took a step toward him. Then she stopped, as if to reconsider.

"How often?" she asked. "The nightmares, the flashbacks…how often do they occur?"

"Nightmares, once maybe twice a month. They used to be every night…when I first got back. But they've lessened now."

"You're getting better then. You haven't had any nightmares since we've…I mean since we've, you know, slept in the same bed."

He chuckled at her pause. Even sharing a bed without sex was scary for her—hell for him.

"I usually hit the floor after you go to sleep," he admitted.

She raised her brow in question.

"I don't trust myself and don't exactly have a reputation for spending the night with women."

"Love 'em and leave 'em?" Jenna smirked. "I guess I should feel special then."

Reed shrugged.

"And the flashbacks? How often do those happen?"

"That one…outside your place…was the second since I moved into the cabin. The first one happened when I found David."

Her brows knitted and she worried her bottom lip. "So, you were doing fine until we came into your life. Because of everything that's happened. Because of Tanya, and me, and David." She moved to the chair and kneeled in front of him. "Reed, I'm so sorry. It's all my fault. I'm the reason you had the flashback."

"No!" He lifted her onto his lap and hugged her close. He couldn't let her believe that. "It's not your fault. It could never be your fault."

He inhaled the sweetness of her hair, the

combination of citrus and sweetness on her body. He ached with how beautiful she was. Her long, pale throat and delicate collarbone called to him. She looked up, her eyes uncertain, shying from his.

"There was…a confrontation…in Afghanistan…" It felt like his throat was closing up. He couldn't breathe. He coughed to clear it. He had to try. He had to give her some explanation. "Young boys, with guns…a woman in a burka…blood…" He closed his eyes, unwilling to let the picture return again.

"You don't have to tell me," she whispered.

"Yes. I do. If there's any chance of us…" He wouldn't say falling in love. He meant to say having sex, having him sleep with her after sex. Yes, that's what he meant. Nothing about love.

When he opened his eyes again, she was watching him. Trusting. Inviting. Offering forgiveness for whatever had happened. But she wasn't the one who could absolve him. No one could. Those who could were dead.

"It's just random pictures."

"How many tours?" she asked. "How long?"

"Marines generally deploy seven months in country. Not like the Army, which extends to eighteen months. I don't know how anyone can stay that long without losing it." He paused. How could he tell her it wasn't the tour length. It was going back again not sure if your mission was really making a difference. Not sure what was worse—running an impossible mission or returning home with no mission at all but sitting at a desk.

"I did three tours. Two in Iraq. And my last one in Afghanistan."

"Oh." Her voice was just a whisper. "I'm glad you don't have to go any more."

His throat felt thick. He couldn't say anything. No matter how much he wanted…needed…to tell her, he couldn't. It was buried too deep. Too painful.

She nuzzled into his neck. "Thank you."

She turned her face up to his and caressed his lips with hers. He groaned and deepened the kiss. She pressed into him further, her hips moving in his lap, her one hand holding his head firmly as she darted her tongue into his mouth with confidence.

"Make love to me," she said.

Was that all she needed? Just a little reveal of himself, his personal battle? Or was this now just a pity fuck?

She moved her good hand down his chest to his boxers, formed it to his cock. Oh hell. Who cared what her reasons were? He couldn't spend another night without being inside her at least once. He needed her more than he'd ever needed anyone in his life. He needed her strength, her courage, her acceptance, if only for a few nights.

One hand beneath her, and the other hand firmly around her waist, he stood. Her arm went to his neck and pulled him forward for another kiss. Her legs wrapped around his waist as she found purchase and ground against him. He moved to the bed, his erection already pushing to be free.

He laid her on her back, his fingers tunneled through her hair, sifting the strands across his pillow as he brushed her scalp.

Her fingers skimmed down the front of his shorts and stroked the full length of him. His cock pulsed forward at her touch. She bent low and placed her lips against the cotton shorts and trailed heat along his length.

A blaze of heat surged through Reed's body, shocking him with its intensity. The torrent of passion and hunger blindsided him. Her hand dipped beneath his shorts and she took a firm grasp.

He captured her hand and withdrew her deliciously tormenting fingers. "Not yet, or I'll explode within seconds." He searched her face for hesitation, but saw only passion in her darkening, navy eyes. Rounded hips arched against him. His entire body burned with a need to be inside her.

Holding his arms stiff above her, Reed crushed her mouth again, unleashing the raw hunger impossible to deny. He savored the cool mint of her lips, her hair's sweet scent of sun-warmed apricot. Her answering heat stripped him of consciousness, dispelling anything that might have held him back. Nothing had ever been like this before. No woman in the past had brought him even close to the intense pleasure of Jenna.

Needing to feel her all around him, he dropped to her right side and pulled her closer. Jenna wrapped her free arm about his neck and shivered against him while the hot spear of her tongue thrust into his mouth, trembling with the same greed he felt. He took what she offered with uncontrolled hunger.

He delved into her willing mouth, pushing away the small fear screaming in his head. *Stop or you'll never be able to walk away again.*

He tore his mouth from hers. It felt like he'd ripped the skin from his heart. "We can't do this. I can't make the promises you want."

She wrapped a leg around him and pushed him over, his back to the bed. Her mouth avaricious upon his, unrelenting. "Yes, we can." She crushed his thighs between her legs and rubbed her panties hard against the ridge of his erection. Moaning deep in his throat, he plunged his tongue into her, returning the bruising force of her kiss with every ounce of strength.

With her leaning over him, his hands were free to snake beneath her poncho and he took full advantage. Exploring and watching her eyes as he flicked her nipples and held the full weight of her breasts in his hands. Wanting to see all of her, he lifted the poncho over her head and gasped as he threw it across the room.

He couldn't take his eyes off her. She was perfection. She arched her back, presenting him with her generous, creamy breasts, tipped with pale cherries. When he took one nipple into his mouth and laved it, she arched further into him pressing both orbs to his cheek.

His hands captured both breasts. He buried his face between them, inhaling the musty, salty essence of her skin mixed with the honeysuckle and lavender soap from her shower. He pressed her breasts together so he could suckle both at once, unable to get his fill with just one. She moaned and churned harder against him.

He wrapped an arm around her waist and rolled her beneath him, being careful of her arm still in a cast.

Eyes heavy with passion opened, glittering feverishly between her thick dark lashes. He was in awe of her beauty. He pressed his mouth to her once more and her warmth beckoned him. Trailing kisses down her throat, his mouth moved to her belly, and she arched offering her pelvis to his touch. He traced a finger from her navel down the center of her panties. He lifted her hips and fingered the elastic, removing them and exposing her to his deeper caress. He nuzzled the joining of her thigh and her pelvis, small kisses tracing a line to her womanhood. He blew hot air against her mound.

Her eyes opened wide and he watched her passion ratchet higher. The pulse at the top of her thigh begged him for more. Gently opening her legs, he tasted her intimately and her sweet scent beckoned him further inside. His tongue thrust and explored her and she cried out his name.

His hands held her hips firmly in place as she convulsed. He alternated between offering warm moisture and nibbled dryness until he found her pearl. He teased it with his tongue and his teeth until she begged.

"Please, Reed. Inside me. Please."

He replaced his mouth with his fingers to bring her to climax. He covered her lips with his to muffle her scream. Fully spent, her knees sagged and he felt moisture leaking from her eyes.

He kissed her lashes, her cheek. Held her until she calmed.

"Not fair," she whispered.

"What's not fair?"

"You. Me. Control. I was out of control."

Reed chuckled. "Yes. Beautifully out of control."

Her eyes searched his. "No. I can't be out of control. I can't." Her voice shook with a pain he didn't understand.

He rolled to one side and held her. "You can with me, Jenna."

She shuddered in his arms.

He rocked her there for several minutes, letting her catch her breath. But his lips couldn't stop tasting her. Her shoulders, her closed her eyes, the pulse at the base of her throat. His hands couldn't stop touching her, stroking her, as if she had awakened a range of senses he never knew existed. Then the full realization hit him and his breath caught, his heart fought against the constriction in his chest. She was right, it was more than sex.

Oh God, he could never let her go.

And still live.

Shaking, he laid her carefully on her back. His own underwear followed the same trajectory as her panties had before, and he stroked her inner thigh to work her up once again. He needed to be inside her. He needed to love her, to explore everything that was between them and break down each barrier, one by one until she had no choice but to stay. She moaned as if in agreement.

Her skin dewy with perspiration and cheeks rosy from the exertion, her tongue traced her lips, thirsty from her shallow breaths. He rose and she reached to pull him back.

"I'll be just a minute," he promised. Moving quickly to the bathroom, he filled a glass of water and sheathed himself in a condom.

He returned and trickled the liquid into her mouth. She moaned with thanks. He lifted her head and helped her replenish. Filled, she placed the glass on the bedside table. He dipped his fingers into the glass and sprinkled the coolness across her breasts and blew cool air. Her nipples begged for attention again, and he answered with his warm mouth.

"Oh God, I'm in love," Jenna said, arching to his taste, the fingers of one hand tangled in his hair.

"As am I," he whispered, surprised at how easily he said it. His mouth closed on her breast once more. His fingers continued to warm her inner thigh and he pressed a palm against her heat as she bucked into his hand.

He dipped two fingers into her center and her body bowed toward him. He was so hard he was afraid he'd explode the moment he entered her.

"Please, Reed," she said, raising her pelvis. "Don't keep me waiting. Please. Now."

He lifted her legs over his shoulders and positioned himself at her opening, inching into her, afraid to go faster for fear he'd lose control. Now that he knew he loved her, he wanted to offer her a slow pleasuring, wringing multiple orgasms out of her. But he wanted her so much he didn't think he'd last more than a minute—if he was lucky.

Her hips arched into him, and he delved deep. "Yes," she whispered. She retracted then pushed up again, sliding the length and forcing him deep once more.

Oh, what the hell. Control was definitely overrated. As she slid back once more, he positioned his hands beneath her hips, cupping her firm bottom and plunging to her very core. She put a fist to her mouth to mute her screams of pleasure. His strokes grew stronger, faster, deeper with each one. Her head thrashed from side to side and she urged him faster and faster. His heart lunged in his chest as he responded to her call. Nothing mattered now except the fire consuming him. Wave after wave hit him as his body spasmed and he collapsed to her side, cuddling her close. As predicted, he'd lasted barely a minute, but what a glorious minute it was.

Chapter Fifteen

Jenna stretched toward the beam of sunlight dancing across the bed, her sleepy eyes not wanting to open just yet as she savored her memories of last night. An arm pulled her close and she sighed, snuggling her bottom against Reed.

"Why did I wait so long?" she asked. "I've been missing so much the past two weeks."

Reed chuckled and swept his lips along her bare shoulder.

She turned toward him. "I never knew it could be like that."

"Hmmm..." He traced his finger down her neck and stopped at her collarbone as if he hadn't noticed it before. Then he pressed his lips to the base of her throat. "We've barely begun," he said. "Last night was too fast. Now it's time for slow." His lips moved to one nipple and he flicked it with his tongue. When it stood hard and erect, he took her breast full in his mouth. He looked up to her and smiled as her eyes closed and she moaned.

"Slow and long," he repeated. He moved to the other breast and gave it the same attention. "And loving." He returned to her mouth, feathering kisses again. "I'm thinking of loving you all day today."

She giggled contentedly. She was hopelessly in love and wanted nothing more than to spend the entire day like this—slowly exploring, tasting, joining. She deepened the kiss. She trusted him completely, offering him everything.

A knock sounded at the door.

Startled, she pushed away. How had she forgotten there were others in the house? Had they heard the sounds of their passion last night? Was it David? No, he'd probably just walk in on them. Did someone else stay? She couldn't remember.

Reed quirked an eyebrow. "Afraid everyone will know what we did?" he asked, his smirk matching the sparkle in his eyes.

She shoved at him playfully. "No. They would have assumed it whether we did or didn't."

"But you're so glad we did." He bent and kissed her shoulder, her breasts, her navel.

"Hmmm." She put a finger to her lips as if considering.

"I can see you're not convinced," he said, his finger trailing to the moistness between her legs. "I guess I'll just have to try harder then."

Her eyes widened.

The knock sounded louder this time, followed by throat clearing.

"Everyone's up." Mike's voice. "David's asking about breakfast and Becca's trying to find something to feed him."

Jenna smiled at the murmurs outside the door, then feet padding away.

"I suggest whatever's keeping you," Mike continued. "Be…uh…hurried. 'Cause I can't hold off the hordes."

She sprang out of bed and searched for her poncho. Finding it, she pulled it over her head.

Reed chuckled. "Uh, cute, but inside out."

The heat rose in her face. She took it off and reversed it.

"I'll talk to Mike," he said, striding to the door.

She stepped back toward the bathroom, out of view but still within earshot. Reed cracked the door open slightly.

"Hordes?" he asked.

"Sorry," Mike said. "We waited as long as we could, but David was getting a little worried. I guess you two haven't ever...slept in so late."

"Not a problem," Reed said.

"Anyway, everyone's here. Jason. Becca. Leena."

"Got something?" Reed asked.

"Yeah, but..." She heard feet shuffling. "Ah hell. It'll keep. Take your time in the shower. We can wait a little longer."

"Thanks, you know where the grub is. Make yourself at home."

Reed closed the door and locked it, winking at her as he strode forward, backing her into the bathroom. Jenna stopped when her back was against the cool glass of the shower enclosure. He pulled the poncho back over her head, exposing her again. He reached into the cabinet under the sink and pulled out the plastic bag she'd been using over her cast. He turned on the shower so the water could warm and then wrapped her casted arm securely.

After lifting her into the shower, he carefully washed her breasts, her stomach, between her legs, kisses following every place he'd washed. Pressing himself against her, he ravished her lips until she could barely breathe. Her eyes widened as his erection grew and pressed into her stomach. He lifted her leg and wrapped it around his waist. He cupped her bottom and lifted her to him. She added her other leg around his waist as he backed her against the wall and entered her, moving in and out ever so slowly. Her inner muscles automatically grasped onto him and worked both of them. Her eyes rolled back as she held tight and let him do all the work.

"The nice thing about making love in the shower," he said, "is that you don't have any cleanup afterward."

Her heart flipped and she gave herself

completely to his ministrations as the water sluiced over them.

****

Becca laid the Vienoy building plans on the table and Reed focused on the basement portion.

Jenna glanced out the window to check on David playing catch with Leena. He seemed content, as if he had no more worries. She wished it were true. She turned from the scene and moved to the table to view the plans with Reed.

"I don't see anything here except the usual underground utilities," Reed said. "Nowhere big enough for a lab or a nursery to hold so many kids."

Jason pointed to a large square on the far right side. "See this? See how the elevation shows it stepped down? This side doesn't have a basement. See how it shows the dirt is built up here and the slab sits on top with the main entry to the facility."

"Yeah," Reed said. "That's not unusual for office buildings. They don't put heating and cooling systems right under the lobby because of the noise."

"But that's not what's really there," Becca said.

Reed looked up. "What do you mean?"

"When we checked it out last week, Jason and I walked the perimeter and it looked just like the plan. But, when we tried to follow the construction of the basement it didn't match up." She pointed to the northeast corner of the plan.

"See this section here?" She traced it to the end point near a berm that appeared to be fenced and covered with foliage. "It's supposed to end at this garden. However, inside the garden are at least six exhaust shafts coming from underground."

"They're hiding something then," Reed said.

"Exactly," Becca said. "And I want to know what it is."

"Hold on," Jenna intervened. "You've already been there once. They know you and Jason. You can't go back without raising suspicions."

Reed looked at her. "Well, you're not going in there either. It's you he wants."

"That's right." She gritted her teeth. "Which is exactly *why* I'm the one who should go."

Reed shook his head. "No. No way."

"You can't stop me." She got close to his face.

"Wanna bet?"

He picked her up with one hand and threw her over his shoulder. She squealed in surprise.

"If I can do this so easily, imagine what someone who means you harm can do."

"That's different, and you know it. I know you won't hurt me so I'm not on alert right now. When I'm at Vienoy, I'll be waiting to strike them before they get me." She pounded her good hand on his back. "I'll strike you, too, if you don't put me down now."

He set her on the floor, his hand giving a quick pat on her rump. "The answer is still no."

She tried to cross her arms but the cast got in the way. Instead, she held the cast in front of her like a shield and pointed at him. "How dare you try to tell me what to do."

"No," he said, facing her down. "How dare you put your life in danger when I've just found you." His voice choked. "I'll die without you, Jenna."

The whole room went silent.

Damn it. Unfair! She wanted to scream and yell and protest. But how could she when he stood there with his heart on his sleeve. A big strong man who looked like he would fall apart if she said boo at this moment.

Mike cleared his throat and moved toward the kitchen. "I uh…think both of you have a point."

"She's not going anywhere near that place," Reed said between his teeth, his eyes still not leaving hers.

"Just hear me out first," Mike said, stepping between Reed and Jenna. "Then you can beat me up if you don't like it."

Reed crossed his arms and his back stiffened. "I'm listening. But it better be good."

"Dr. Crane probably knows more about us than we do about him. By now, he knows that Jenna didn't die and he may even know about you."

"So, what does that have to do with risking her life?" Reed asked.

"He's going to come after her again, anyway." Mike looked Reed straight in the eye. "Or you."

"I can handle him."

"I'm sure you can, but can she?" Mike nodded at Jenna.

She wanted to scream *Yes, let me at him*. But she knew no one would believe her. She knew nothing about fighting or, God forbid, killing. She was in a cast, not even completely recovered from the accident. So she kept silent.

"I say the two of you lay low for a couple weeks until Jenna's cast comes off. Then you go to Vienoy, together."

"What the hell?" Reed shook his head.

"Ask to see Dr. Crane. Tell him you know Tanya worked for him. Ask him if he can help to solve her murder."

"But he was probably the one who murdered her." Jenna wasn't sure she could face him and pretend she didn't already believe that.

"You shouldn't ask her to do this," Jason intervened. "She's not capable of lying."

Jenna looked over at him. "How do you know that? You hardly know me."

Jason smiled softly. "It's written all over you. Every emotion, every thought is practically telegraphed with a neon sign."

"It is not," she said. "I can lie if I want to."

Becca chuckled. “No, you can’t. You’re not good at keeping secrets either.”

She stomped her foot. “What do you mean? I kept the secret about your surprise 40th birthday party two years ago. You were completely shocked.”

“Uh, sorry, Jenna.” She touched her arm, her eyes squinting. “I wasn’t really surprised. I just pretended so I wouldn’t hurt your feelings.”

“You’re just making that up. How could you have known?”

“Remember, you were so excited about decorating the restaurant and the whole black theme? You went on and on about the party you were planning and asked lots of questions about how I would feel if it were me, which of course it wasn’t.”

“Oh.” Jenna pouted. “I thought I’d been so good about covering that up.”

“It’s okay.” Becca hugged Jenna to her side. “Your enthusiasm alone made me love you that much more for being such a great friend.”

“Okay, then. Maybe I’m not so good at keeping a secret,” Jenna said. “But I can do this. I can pretend I don’t know he’s a murdering bastard.”

Reed chuckled this time.

“What’s so funny?”

“I love that you can’t lie. It makes everything fall into place.”

She canted her head to one side. “What things?”

His smile glowed like the high beams on her car in the dark night. “Later.”

Jason looked from one to the other and smiled broadly. “Well, well, well. Rat face is in love. I never thought I’d see the day.”

Mike’s eyes widened and he laughed long and hard.

Jenna couldn’t help but smile. Her lungs seemed to open wider to make room for her expanding heart.

Reed pressed his lips together. “Okay, so you’ve

had your fun at my expense. Just wait 'til it hits you. You'll be ten times worse."

"Won't happen," both Jason and Mike said, each standing a little taller, a little more stiff.

"Let's get back to the plan before I decide to take both of you out for agreeing to let Jenna go."

Jason and Mike sobered and looked back at the building plans.

"So, you two go in the front door with an appointment to see Dr. Crane." Mike pointed to a room behind the clinic offices. "We figure this is his office, right in the center of things."

Reed nodded, his hand holding tight to Jenna's.

"While you keep him busy, I'll try to get in over here." Mike pointed to an emergency exit door on the other end of the building, then his finger traced down a hallway to a square north of it. "This is supposed to be a library, and here is cold storage for the sperm and eggs from his patients."

"And this." Mike continued his trace past Crane's office to the other side, where the plan indicated an exterior wall at the berm. "This is supposed to be the surgery. I suspect this room joins another room—the one we think may house the nursery. That's what I want to find out."

"How long do you think you need?" Reed asked. "How long do we have to keep Dr. Crane busy?"

"At least an hour," Mike said. "Two would be better. Maybe he could take you on a tour. Then we could compare notes."

Reed stood and stretched upright after bending over the table. His gaze swept over Jenna, a question in his eyes. She looked straight back and nodded. She mouthed, *please*. She had to do this. She had to do something to put things in motion again, to stop this man or whoever was trying to kill her.

He pulled his cheek into his teeth and worried. He took a deep breath then looked away. "All right.

We'll do it."

Mike nodded.

"But I'm packing going in," Reed said, bristling. "And if he so much as twitches wrong, I won't hesitate to take him out."

Shivers skittered down Jenna's spine, reminding her of their differences. She now understood why the violence would always be there. It was part of who he was. But she loved him in spite of it.

What scared her more was the violence building within her.

She'd never hated anyone before. Even when she'd found Aaron sleeping with his secretary, she couldn't bring herself to hate him. She'd certainly never wished him dead.

But after what happened to Tanya, after David told his terrifying story, after someone tried to kill her, she wasn't sure she could hold off the hate. That feeling scared her more than the thought she might die. If she allowed that hate to bloom, she was afraid Reed's need for vengeance would somehow overtake her...that she could actually wish to see someone dead.

She shivered at the thought. If that day came—a day where she hated so much she actually took someone else's life—she wasn't sure she wanted to live.

Chapter Sixteen

"She's getting sicker," Shumenko said, his feet wearing out the carpet as he paced in front of Marius. "You've got to help her. The doctors say she will die within six months unless there's a miracle."

Marius tapped his pencil on the desk. He'd known all along the child was a goner, but she'd served her purpose. She'd brought him Shumenko's services. He opened the laptop in front of him and typed the URL to get to the Thompson Library. There'd been an article. He vaguely remembered it, about four months ago. Something about high doses of Interferon coupled with another drug. *What was it?* He needed something active, quick. Something that would at least make it appear she was getting better, just until Shumenko did one last job for him.

Shumenko dropped into the chair in front of the desk and put his head in his hands, sobs choking his words. "This is God's way of punishing me for my wickedness. I should have let her go. I should have accepted her death. Not try to hang on. Not keep her living in pain."

Marius swore. Then he tried the Mayo Clinic's library. He didn't have time for this drivel. Not when he was so close to a breakthrough. While he was waiting for the database to kick in, Shumenko dropped to his knees. He crossed himself and looked to the ceiling.

"Heavenly Father, please forgive your servant. I'm sorry I broke your commandment. I shouldn't have killed that lawyer. I shouldn't have tried to kill her sister. Punish me. Not my daughter. Take my life instead of hers."

"Get up," Marius ordered, disgusted with this sudden display of piety. He knew Shumenko was religious, but he'd never had him praying in his office. This had to stop.

"God is not punishing you for killing anyone," he said. "That commandment is only for stupid people. I do not hire stupid people."

Shumenko did not rise from the floor, but he did stop praying and looked up at Marius. "It's one of the Ten Commandments—Thou shalt not kill."

Marius made a show of sighing. "Yes, I know. But it's been translated so many times the whole text isn't there. What it really means is 'Thou shalt not kill unless commanded otherwise.' You've heard of the crusades, haven't you? Christians killed the infidels who had taken their land and captured their people. Now why would Christians do that if God had not commanded them to kill?"

Shumenko puckered his brow as if unsure of the puzzle.

Marius walked around the desk and offered his hand. He only had to put up with the Ukrainian a little longer. He schooled his features and pitched his voice to be sympathetic. "You killed to save God's children. You are at my right hand, and you carry out my wishes to secure the future of all mankind." Shumenko finally rose and Marius guided him to the chair.

Marius stood in front of him, looking down so that he towered over the man. He changed his voice to be powerful, demanding. "God is not punishing you for killing. He is punishing you for failing. Failing to get specimen forty-nine back. Failing to kill Jenna Mosier. God does not tolerate failure. How many times did he smite the Jews for their failure?"

Shumenko hung his head once more.

"That is why your daughter is dying," Marius continued, his voice changed back to sympathy. "God needs specimen forty-nine to complete the cure, through me. I need specimen forty-nine to save your daughter."

"I'm sorry," Shumenko said, tears staining his cheeks. "I'm sorry I failed. I will not fail again, Dr. Crane. I promise."

Marius patted his head. Maybe he wouldn't have to find the fake drug after all. "God has heard your prayers, and he has given you another chance. Jenna will be coming to visit me next week."

"What time?" Shumenko almost glowed with the chance to right the failure. "I will be here and kill her on the spot."

Marius chuckled. How easy it was to mold those who worked for him.

"It is not yet her time to die. But God has provided her to us for a cover—a cover that will allow us to get specimen forty-nine back. Later, we will take care of Jenna Mosier."

****

Reed parked the SUV in the visitor lot outside Vienoy and Jenna let out a heavy breath. The gray sky suggested it might rain later. He squeezed Jenna's hand next to his. "Ready?"

She shook her head.

This had been one hell of a two-week rollercoaster. After the interview with David, it seemed the police were on their way to arresting Crane. But three days ago, Novak had informed him he couldn't even get a warrant to search Vienoy. Novak and another detective had gone to Vienoy to talk to Crane as a person of interest. Evidently, all it did was piss Crane off. Crane's attorney put all kinds of roadblocks in the way. He filed suits against the Sandy police department, as well as the Gresham cops, and even threw in the sheriff for good measure. Novak agreed Crane still smelled dirty, but he didn't have enough evidence for an indictment. He couldn't get squat. No warrant. No sting. Nothing.

For the fifth time, Reed checked his ankle for the small pistol. He reached his hand to his back, just between the shoulder blades to make sure his Smith & Wesson neck knife was snug in the scabbard, easy to pull out.

Jenna looked at him and sighed. "He won't do anything to us during the day, when everyone knows we're going there."

"A man who has no compunction at killing anyone in his path doesn't care who knows we're here. For all we know, it's a trap. He may already have a plan to get rid of us once we're inside and claim we never showed up."

"But Mike knows were here and would tell everyone."

"If Mike gets out alive."

Jenna shook her head as if she could block out reality and make the world match what she wanted it to be. Reed hoped her optimism would be rewarded. He prayed Crane was smart enough to try to play them instead of kill them. At least this time.

As the time got closer, he'd seen Jenna struggle with the plan. It wasn't the details that were a problem. She was far too smart for that; the issue was her inability to accept all the violence visited on her life, the knowledge that she had little control over it and a deep fear she would become like him. That fear translated to a complete incapacity to protect herself. She wouldn't even take a knife from him for defense. He wished her world had never been sullied with evil and that she'd been able to go through life never questioning the good in anyone, never having to face down men who believed anyone in their path was expendable.

Today, she wore a demure summer dress in a blue that set off her eyes. He loved the small sleeves that kept her shoulders covered and the square-cut bodice that showed off her slender neck. He looked at the arm where the cast had been removed two days ago. Her skin was still sensitive to the touch, and the old skin hadn't completed sloughed off yet. The swelling had subsided, but he knew she still experienced some muscle weakness and would for a while.

Reed took her face in his hands and brushed her lips lightly with his. "I love you."

She looked into his eyes, hers misting over. She swallowed.

He gathered her into his arms. "You don't have to do this, Jenna. You don't have to be any part of this."

She pushed away. "I can do this. I *will* do this. It's the least I can do for my sister." She reached for the handle on the door and pushed the unlock button.

He exited the car himself and ran to her side, all the while scanning the parking lot and entrance to make sure no one was waiting for them, ready to harm them before they even reached the lobby. Seeing nothing unusual, he offered his arm and pasted on a smile for the cameras that were certain to be watching their every move. "Let's go interview the good doctor."

****

"I'm so sorry for your loss," Crane said, his hand patting Jenna's. "I really cared for your sister. She was a great asset to this company. Her…death was a tragedy."

Jenna stiffened in her chair. The man was smooth, but she didn't believe a word coming out of his mouth. Gathering her courage, she wondered how well he really knew Tanya. She would talk to him for two hours if she could, just to give Mike time to find out the truth about this place.

"Thank you for taking time out of your busy day to see us," she said, then lowered her head as she'd practiced with Reed when they'd planned this conversation. "I hadn't seen my sister in some time when I got the news. I'd like to know a little more about her life here." She lifted her head and looked up. "I understand she was an attorney. What exactly did she do for Vienoy?"

"I employ world-class medical researchers," Crane answered. "We do drug trials, specifically for fertility. Your sister helped us to obtain the proper patents before we sold our research to someone for manufacturing."

"I'm…surprised," Jenna said.

"Why, dear? She did it for you, you know. She told me how her sister couldn't have children and no one could explain why. She told me that your divorce was because your husband wanted a child of his own flesh and blood."

Jenna struggled not to jump up and slap him. How dare he talk as if he knew anything about her past, as if he cared about her marriage. *God, Tanya, how could you not know how evil this man was?*

Reed squeezed her hand, hard.

They hadn't practiced this as one of his ploys. Looking away from both of them, she screwed up her courage, determined to play out this game. "How could you have helped me, Dr. Crane? No other fertility specialists could offer anything."

Crane reclined in his chair and smirked. "Of course, I'm the best. I know things no one else knows. My record for finding ways for women to conceive is unparalleled."

He reached toward the bookcase behind him and brought out a large album. "Here, let me show you." He turned to the first page—filled with pictures of smiling babies and their happy parents.

Jenna swallowed. She wasn't sure she could look at these. This was asking too much. Her eyes misted.

As if Crane knew how much it would bother her, he pushed the album further toward her. "Take your time, dear. Look at how many wonderful children I've helped to bring in the world." He turned page after page. Mothers and fathers smiling and holding a newborn. "This could be you. I could do this for you. Would you like to see the letters?"

She shook her head. She focused on a spot on the desk just below the album, unable to look at any more pictures. After she thought she'd given him enough time, she forced herself to put her hand over his.

"I'm happy for them." And she meant it, even though she knew he was trying to be cruel to her. "They are fortunate."

"It's not too late for you, dear." Crane closed the book, then reached and covered her hand with his.

Bile rose in her throat and she swallowed hard to force it back down.

"You are a little old, what? Forty maybe?" Crane paused. "But I've helped women as old as forty-six conceive."

He released her hand and she quickly pulled it back to her lap, wishing she could immediately wash the evil from it. She would not make the mistake of making it available to him again.

Crane looked toward Reed then back to her. "I'm sure your fiancée wants to pass on his genes and I can help with that."

Reed placed his hand softly on her thigh. "I have no need to pass on my genes." Jenna looked at him in time to see his eyes narrowing at Crane with all the hatred and violence he had stored up over the past six weeks. Crane visibly shrank in his chair.

Then Reed turned to Jenna, his face softening.

She could see the love in him as he looked at her. "I want to adopt—lots of kids. I want to give a home to children who really need one—babies, toddlers, kindergartners, ten-year-olds. All of them. However many Jenna and I can care for."

Crane cleared his throat. "Of course...adoption is a noble venture. Not quite as satisfying as having a child who looks just like you, but if that's all you have, it's a good second choice."

Reed's head snapped back to Crane, his jaw firm and teeth clenched. "Not a second choice, a first choice. The only choice I would make, ever."

Crane stood. "Well, it seems there is no need of me then. I'll ask someone to show you out."

Jenna panicked. No, they hadn't been there nearly long enough.

"Please, Dr. Crane. Even though Reed is the most loving person in the world, I'd still like to explore alternatives with you."

Crane slowly lowered himself back to his chair. However, he didn't seem nearly as interested anymore. "Let's cut to the chase, shall we? I know you aren't really here to seek fertility advice. And you probably know that I've already had you investigated. So, let's stop beating around the bush and why don't you just ask me what you really came here to ask me?"

Jenna's eyes widened. She hadn't expected that. How could he be caring one minute, and cruel the next? And now he was arrogant enough to lay it on the table knowing he couldn't be caught. Fine. She'd cut to the chase then. She'd nail the bastard.

"Tell us about your work in gene therapy. I understand you're somewhat of an expert in stem cell research."

Crane sat back quickly. His eye flicked, just briefly, to the side of the room. A lie. Reed had told her how when people lied they always looked away.

Then Crane let out a big belly laugh. “You two are so much smarter than I gave you credit for. I should have known. Tanya was very smart, too. I’m truly sorry she’s no longer with us. I enjoyed her mind, her quick wit, her...well never mind. So, please humor me. Tell me how you know this.”

Reed sat forward, his chest out, his jaw tight. “We visited Thompson Medical University. Your previous employer...where you were fired for ethics violations.”

Crane smiled and chuckled under his breath. “Ah, you must have spoken to Cyrus Kramer. He’s never forgiven me for leaving him and starting my own company.”

Jenna looked at Reed, her eyebrow raised, then turned back to Crane. “You weren’t fired?”

“No dear, I resigned. Check the official records at the university. They couldn’t fire me. In spite of what you may have heard from Cyrus, there were no grounds for the ethics violation. Go ahead, check it.”

“But Dr. Kramer said—”

Crane stood and laughed heartily. “Poor Cyrus. Little man’s syndrome you know. Small dick, small brain, always needing to prove himself. Like all researchers, he wanted to be the one with the breakthrough. The one to win the Nobel Prize. Oh, he was smart enough for a doctoral student, but never smart enough to think outside the box. Definitely nowhere near my level of intelligence. But then few are.”

Arrogant, Jenna thought. *Who does he think he is?*

“When I left Thompson, the poor boy was almost fired. He had no idea of the complexities of my project. Not only did he level untrue accusations against me, but he also led them to believe he understood my research and could complete it on his own. When they asked him to repeat the experiment, he couldn't get the same results. Of course, he blamed it on me—shoddy recordkeeping and all—but they knew the truth. They knew he just doesn't have what it takes. That's why he's never gotten tenure and why he'll always be stuck in that tiny lab in the farthest corner of the medical center. Why they've hung onto the boy I have no idea. He must be screwing the provost's daughter or something equally sordid."

"If you weren't fired, why did you leave?" Reed asked. "It seems you had everything you wanted. A good research career, an international reputation."

"Ah," Crane returned to lean on the back of his chair. "Unfortunately, there was a misunderstanding, but then I'm sure you already know about that."

"Tell us anyway," Reed said.

"You see, Cyrus forgot to get informed consent from some of the children's parents. I thought he'd done the paperwork, which was his job, after all. Not mine. I was the lead researcher in that lab; I didn't need to do the paperwork. They paid me for my brain." He shifted his gaze back to Jenna. "It wasn't until I'd already started treatment with the children that I learned he hadn't done his job. He blamed me, of course. I wanted to fight it, especially when the children began to get better."

"They were getting better?" Jenna asked. "But Dr. Kramer said they all died."

"Did they?" Crane turned and looked out his window. "I didn't know." He sounded genuinely sorry, almost teary. "How awful. You see, when the university refused to back me—even though the children's parents saw me as a miracle worker—I couldn't stay. I couldn't stay at a place that cared more for politics and grant money than actually helping people. Whatever happened after I left was on Cyrus's watch."

He sighed dramatically, then flicked an invisible bit of dirt or lint from his white lab coat. "How sad. I could have saved those children…if only they'd believed in me."

Jenna sat silent, her eyes wide. She'd been lied to before, but never this deftly. How could he sit in front of her and lie straight to her face with so much conviction? She'd never met someone who could lie so easily.

Is this what they mean by psychopath? Did he actually believe what he was saying?

"It all turned out very well for me, actually," Crane continued. "I was far too comfortable at Thompson. I never demanded enough from them—enough money, enough lab space." He gestured widely to his opulent office. "But look at me now. I have Vienoy. I make millions of dollars and I still do what I want to do. Help people."

"So, you do no research on stem cells at Vienoy?" Reed asked, his tone hard.

"I don't. Unfortunately, Cyrus's lies made sure I couldn't continue my career in that line of research. I'm not allowed to do the research that could save millions of children." He looked down at the desk. "I must admit, I was very angry with him for quite some time. But not anymore. Now I'm the hero. I bring beautiful children into the world—children for parents who had given up on conceiving."

"Actually, I feel sorry for him now—stuck in that lab for the rest of his days. I was the fortunate one. I got out." He shook his head. "It's hard to believe he still holds a grudge after all these years."

Jenna groped for Reed's hand, unable to take her eyes off Dr. Crane. Reed took it and squeezed. She searched for a clock in the room. She wasn't sure how much longer she could talk to this man—a man so evil that he showed no remorse.

She had to stall…couldn't give up yet. They

hadn't been here nearly long enough for Mike to do what he needed to do.

"How about children?" she finally asked. "Does any of your research involve children?"

Crane looked her straight in the eye. "Why no, dear. What would ever make you ask that? This is a fertility clinic. We help women conceive children, not experiment on them."

"You also do abortions," Reed said.

Crane leaned back and steepled his fingers beneath his chin. "Yes, for those women unfortunate enough to find themselves unable to care for a child. I consider it a godsend to help a rape victim, or a young girl in high school with her whole life still ahead of her."

"Don't you find that incongruous?" Jenna said. "Helping women conceive while taking babies from others?"

Crane covered her hand once more. She tried to jerk it out of the way, but he held fast.

"It may look like that on the surface," he said. "But I consider it my mission to help women in whatever state of need they may be. Sometimes the same woman I help with an abortion, under unfortunate circumstances, will seek me out years later and thank me. Often showing me pictures of the children she now has. Don't you think it's better a good doctor does the abortion, so the woman can conceive again. Don't you think it's best that a child is loved and wanted instead of added to the thousands of unwanted children we already support in this country and others?"

Jenna wasn't sure. She'd always struggled with abortion. Even though she'd stood by her sister's choice.

"Take your sister for instance."

Jenna's mouth dropped open.

Dr. Crane leaned forward. "Ah, I see she never

told you about us."

"I...I thought she just worked here. She would never..."

"You are the one who didn't know her, Jenna."

Jenna swallowed. It was true. She never did understand her sister. And now she never would have that chance.

He squeezed her fingers. "Her loss was especially tragic for me because I loved her. We were lovers until she died."

"No!" Jenna jerked her hand from his and stood. She wouldn't accept it, couldn't believe her sister would sleep with the man who was surely part of her murder.

Crane looked up at her, the slightest upward curl of his lip. "She told me all about you, Jenna. She told me how you'd helped her when she had her first abortion."

Oh, God, he did know her. She wouldn't tell a stranger that, or even a work colleague.

"She loved you very much, Jenna, in spite of the fact you never tried to find her over the past ten years. But she always knew where you were and all about your restaurant, Chat Précieux. I believe that means precious cat. How unfortunate that you didn't think your sister was precious enough to find. In fact, I believe she was still trying to prove herself to you when she died."

Chapter Seventeen

Reed pulled into the mall parking lot to wait for Mike. He shut off the engine and rolled his shoulders. The entire interview with Crane weighed heavily. One hand rubbed the back of his neck and he glanced at Jenna.

Her eyes stared straight ahead, as if she could see through the dashboard. Her stiff jaw, with cheeks sunken into gritted teeth, mirrored his feelings. There was no doubt Crane was hiding something, and they hadn't even scratched the surface.

"Jenna?" He stroked the top of her shoulder.

She crossed an arm over her chest and laid her hand over his. She inhaled deeply and let it out slowly. "He's so arrogant," she said, still looking straight forward. "He knows that we know everything and doesn't even care. It's as if he's invulnerable." She turned toward Reed and his hand slipped down her arm. "How can that be?"

Reed shook his head. Then the reason burst in like an unwanted rain shower.

"Shit! Insurance."

Jenna puckered her brow and squinted.

Reed clamped his teeth together. "Dammit. He has some kind of insurance. I've seen it before, in Afghanistan."

Jenna's eyes widened and she looked up at him.

"I remember hunting down a particularly atrocious war lord—a man who not only burned and raped to make a point to his enemies, but he enjoyed it. He enjoyed the fear, the humiliation, the power over others."

Jenna shrank toward the door. "Did you find him?"

Reed remembered that day, the day that ended his career—even though the Corps didn't discharge him for another eighteen months, when the PTSD got so bad Reed couldn't hide it any more. He clamped down on the memory. He wouldn't…couldn't go there. He needed all his faculties alert. He couldn't afford a flashback now.

"Reed?" Jenna's touch pulled him back. Her fingers twined in his squeezed hard. "You okay?"

He swallowed and nodded, unable to look directly at her. If he did, he might spill the whole sorry event.

Mike's truck pulled into the parking space next to Reed and Jenna. He got out of his car then jumped in the back of Reed's.

"Get anything good?" Reed asked.

"Yes and no. I verified our map was good as far as it goes. I also verified there is definitely another room where we suspect. However, there was no way to check it out. There's a surgery—an operating room—at the end of the building, just like in the plans. But I could see three doors on the other side. I figured they could be just storage, or they might be something more."

"You know damn well there's more," Reed muttered.

"That's why I figured I'd slip through the surgery and check one out. But just as I opened the door, a nurse came up behind me and asked if I was lost."

"Shit." Reed said.

"My thought exactly. So, I told her yeah, I was looking for my wife. I'd gone to the bathroom to provide a semen specimen and got lost."

Reed laughed at the thought of Mike in a fertility clinic. "That should have taken her mind off where you were."

Mike smiled broadly. "I thought it was brilliant, actually." He paused. "The nurse, I think her name was Lisa, escorted me back toward the lobby and pointed me toward the fertility clinic, instructing me to ask the nurse at the desk. What could I do?"

"You went back in after she left, of course."

Mike shrugged. "Of course."

Reed waited. He knew Mike would fill in the rest in his own time.

"By the time I got back to the surgery, the nurse who'd escorted me to the front was talking to someone else—another nurse, someone who was crying as if her husband had left her or something." Mike leaned forward between the two front seats. "They were preparing surgical instruments—looked like maybe for an abortion—I'm not sure. Anyway, I couldn't make out the other woman's name tag. It was something with Anne on the end. But not a separate name like Debra Anne. Maybe Marianne. I couldn't really see it."

Reed looked at Jenna. "Do you remember any nurse names in the stuff Becca found? Anything with Anne in it?"

Jenna's eyes rose toward a corner of the car, as if the database sat there for her to search. "Oh!" She jerked back to face both of them. "Remember what David said? There was a nice nurse who turned uncaring whenever Crane came in? I think he called her Nurse Adrianne. Yeah, I'm pretty sure of it."

"Interesting." Mike stroked his chin. "If this is the same woman, she may have been talking about Crane then. She was really pissed. Definitely sounded like a lovers quarrel."

"Tell us exactly what you heard," Reed said.

"Something about a guy who didn't appreciate

all she'd put into him and his work, even when she didn't always agree with his decisions. How she'd believed he was her soul mate until she found him with some other bunny hopping on his lap, in his office, during lunch. I figure she was planning to be on his lap during lunch and wasn't any too happy to find competition."

"I'd cut off his balls if I found my soul mate in that condition," Jenna said.

Reed raised an eyebrow and looked at her, trying to hold back a smirk, but not being entirely successful. "Such violence, Jenna. I didn't think you had it in you."

"I didn't say I'd kill him, and the truth is I probably wouldn't cut them off. But I might, at least, kick him where it hurts. It's a nice fantasy." She paused. "It would be a kind of apt justice."

"Ouch," Mike said. "I think you've just been warned, rat face."

"Seems like." Reed smiled and squeezed Jenna's hand. "I'll make sure you never catch me."

She pushed at his shoulder playfully. "I suggest you don't put yourself in the situation at all."

Mike cleared his throat. "Yeah, well this guy evidently was so cocky that, when the nurse found them together, he just laughed and asked her to join them for a threesome. From what I could hear of the conversation, it sounds like that is not the choice she made. In fact, I think there was something about 'over his dead body,' and the nurse stomping away as he laughed at her exit."

"That's good," Jenna said, her eyes wide and lips quirked up. "Real good. Nothing like a woman scorned to help our cause."

Reed pressed two fingers to his forehead to stave off the headache he felt coming on. If what Mike heard was accurate, it probably was Crane the nurse was talking about. He'd certainly be arrogant enough to do something that stupid, and Reed had no doubt that Crane used women and threw them out like everything else he deemed expendable. What little they learned from the conversation, he knew the only one who mattered to Marius Crane was himself. No one else would ever be his equal.

"We can use that on our next visit," Jenna said. "A woman who's been hurt like that wants revenge, and she'll talk to anyone who will help her get it."

"Is that what you did when you found your ex and his secretary?" Reed asked, his voice soft. "Did you get your revenge?"

"In a way," Jenna said. "When I found Aaron and Stacie in our bed, at first I was so angry I did want revenge. But as the divorce wore on, I felt like it was my fault somehow, like I was nothing, worthless—all because I couldn't give him the children he wanted."

Reed rubbed circles on the back of her hand, partly to empathize and partly to stop himself from wanting to wring Aaron's neck if he ever saw him. It was bad enough the guy couldn't keep his pants zipped. To blame it on Jenna was unforgiveable.

"With help from Becca and Leena, I learned I could take control of my life or continue to allow him to have power over me, to make me feel guilty, even though I'd given him a viable option—adopting children. It took a while, but they helped me turn my life around. They helped me realize women were more than baby factories. That's when I took a chance and started my business. I think I did pretty well."

Reed squeezed her hand then. "You know it—'Portland Entrepreneur of the Year.' Man or woman, you were voted the best."

Jenna's smile made his heart flip over. God, he loved her. Then her lips turned down and her eyes darkened.

"So, when's the next visit?" she asked. "I'll do the talking with Adrianne. I understand her. I bet I can get her to come over to our side. I can use her feelings and get her to reveal what's really going on, too—maybe even show us the nursery."

"There's not going to be a next visit," Reed said, staring into Jenna's eyes. "It's too dangerous."

"We've had this discussion," she said, her words clipped. "You can't lock me away and protect me. I go where you go."

"I'm not going. No one's going."

Jenna turned away and looked out the window.

"He's right, Jenna," Mike said. "Crane's too confident right now. There's something else going on, and until we find out what his plans are, we'd be sitting ducks to go in there again."

"But he killed Tanya," Jenna said, her voice obviously choked in frustration. "I know it was him. He also hurt David and who knows how many others. He has to pay."

Reed stroked her cheek. He'd go back and make him pay, but not right now. When he did, it would be only him—maybe Mike and Jason, but he wasn't even sure about that. Definitely not Jenna. Not any more.

She turned, her eyes wet, searching him. For what? A promise?

"Then when?" she asked.

"He'll pay, Jenna. He's already making mistakes, already pissing people off who protect him. When he's pissed off the right person, we'll know…and he'll pay."

The car door clicked open and Mike stepped out. He put his head back in for a moment. "Heading back to your place?"

Reed turned. "Yeah. Comin'?"

"Jason and Becca there?"

"Yeah, they're watching David. I've got pizza we

can bake while we all talk. See if we can piece any more together. Give more info to the cops. Come up with another plan of attack."

"Okay. I'll see you there in fifteen." Mike closed the door and sauntered to his car.

Reed glanced back to Jenna as he turned the key and the engine hummed to life. She was staring out the window again—her shoulders slumped forward. He knew the feeling, one of helplessness. He'd been there many times when he'd had all the clues, all the information, knew who the enemy was, but couldn't go get him. Not without a plan. Not without orders.

He signaled and turned onto route twenty-six and headed east.

He'd always gotten his man in the end. But at what price? How many men had he lost? How many innocents got killed in the crossfire?

He glanced back at Jenna again. Her head now back against the headrest, her eyes closed. He hoped the price wasn't too high this time. It had been once and he swore it would never happen again.

He pressed the accelerator to ten miles over the speed limit. He wanted to get home. He needed to get home before the memories crashed in on him. He needed to be somewhere safe—with Jason and Mike—just in case.

When he'd cleared Shorty's Corner, Reed smelled smoke. Forest fire. He rolled down the window and sniffed again. Close. Unusual.

This side of Mt. Hood rarely got fires, even in the summer; and when it did, it was usually on the other side of the mountain, the dryer side. He thought of the friends he had at the Welches fire station—the full timers and the volunteers who'd probably be fighting it, along with the forestry service.

He glanced at the trees—no wind. At least that

should help. He hoped no one was on the trail wherever it was. Most people would have no idea where to go to get away. It would be easy to be caught in it, to climb in the wrong direction.

As they drew closer, the fire looked like it was in the area where his cabin was located. Reed's heart pounded in his chest. "Damn it to hell. That was his insurance."

Jenna opened her eyes. "Oh my God. You don't think it's…no! David? Becca?"

He pressed harder on the accelerator, and at the same time, dialed the fire department. He had the number programmed on speed dial. They were usually the ones who called him about mountain rescues.

"This is Reed Adler. I think…"

"Reed, where are you?" The dispatcher knew his voice since they'd worked together on every rescue.

"I'm about three miles east of my place. What's going on?"

"Units are already there. Flames all around your house, but haven't breached it. Those big logs have done a good job keeping it out. Last report they've stopped the worst of it. Just hot spots now and they're digging trenches down the hill to make sure it doesn't endanger anyone else." She paused. "Reed, they're pretty sure it's arson. Jerry said gasoline smell is everywhere and they found a can in the woods out back."

"Has anyone been inside?" Reed asked, his breath short, his chest felt like someone was sitting on it. "I had three people there when I left—man, woman, ten-year-old boy." He knew Jason would have gotten everyone out if he could. If he was alive.

"They bashed in your door when they got the flames down. No one was inside. Tires were slashed on a car outside. So if people were there, they didn't get out in that car."

Fuck. That meant either Crane had them, or they were on the run. Or lost somewhere in the wilderness.

"I'm sorry, Reed. I don't have anything else."

"Thanks, Shelly. I'll be there in a minute. I'll talk to the guys on the ground." He pressed his steering wheel to end the call.

Jenna squeezed his thigh. "Becca will keep David safe, I know she will. I've seen her in tournaments. She knows how to fight, knows how to protect herself. And Jason's like you, right? He knows his stuff."

Reed nodded. She needed to believe that, and he wouldn't tell her otherwise. He wouldn't tell her all the things that could happen, even to someone well-trained like Jason. The thousands of ways a professional can kill or disable. Guns, knives, poison darts—even bare hands if they got the jump on you. He just hoped they'd gotten away.

****

Reed started up the trail, and Jenna followed.

He turned and placed both hands firmly on her shoulders. "Stay here. Wait for Mike. Let him know what's going on."

She pushed her arms up between his hands, dislodging them and shook her head. "You're just trying to get rid of me. You're trying to protect me again."

"I can move faster without you. Please, just once do as I ask."

He could see the hesitation in her eyes. His cell phone rang. Caller ID showed it was Mike.

"Yeah."

"Found Becca and Cheeks knocked out cold in a ravine about three hundred yards north of your place, pine boughs for cover. Cheek's come to, but groggy. Becca is still out. Looks like the guy was thinking of coming back. Looks like Becca may have been drugged. Called rescue, you gotta lead them here. Bring blankets."

"David?"

"Nowhere."

"Shit!" He slammed the phone closed and took off running back to the house, Jenna at his heels.

He'd promised David he would be safe. He hoped David had escaped, that he was hiding. But he doubted it. More likely whoever took out Jason and Becca now had David.

"Blankets. Water. First aid," he said as he barreled through the open back door and over to the linen closets. The stench of ash still hung in the air. He handed a blanket to Jenna, got his first aid kit, and filled a canteen with water.

"David? Oh God, not David," she said, trying to keep up with him.

"David's gone. It's Jason and Becca they've found."

He took her hand and waited in the front yard for the ambulance. It was only seconds before they arrived. He recognized the two guys, Alan and Randy—guys he'd worked with before on a rescue. Guys he trusted. All four of them scrambled up the trail.

"You sure do have a lot of accident-prone friends," Alan said, huffing behind with a portable stretcher.

Randy pulled a second stretcher from the ambulance. He looked over at Jenna. "You doing better? I heard your car decided to ditch in the canyon up the road."

She nodded, her arms tightly clasped around the blankets Reed had shoved at her earlier.

"We need a fourth," Alan said, then looked at Jenna. "Unless that arm has healed enough to carry one end of a stretcher."

"Won't happen," Reed said. "But my buddy's

already there. He can handle it. Let's go."

Within a minute or two, the three of them were looking down into the ravine where Mike waved. Reed slid down the thirty-foot drop on his butt with Alan beside him. It wasn't deep, but it was steep. He looked to the top and saw Randy holding Jenna back. Reed didn't hear what he said, but it seemed to work. Randy joined the rest of them moments later.

Alan immediately checked Becca's pulse while Randy squatted next to Jason.

"Solid, but slow," Alan said.

"A little fast, but not much," Randy echoed at almost the same time.

"I'm fine," Jason said, pushing at Randy. "The bastard came up behind me when I saw Becca fall."

Randy ignored him and checked Jason's head and neck.

"Ow. That's gotta hurt," Randy said, his hand poised at the base of Jason's skull. "He must have hit you pretty hard." He turned the head to one side, then the other. "No needle pricks here, though. You should get checked out, just in case. Could be a concussion."

"Take a look at this," Alan said, turning Becca's head slowly to one side. "Pinprick puncture. Like a dart." He looked over at Mike. "You said something about drugs. Why?"

"Just a guess. Jason said when he turned back it was like she fainted."

"Yeah, that was when I got clocked." Jason looked at Reed. "That fire was set to draw us out. They got David, didn't they?"

"Looks like," Reed said between clenched teeth.

Alan ran hands along Becca's arms and legs, neck, side, and torso. "Nothing seems broken and I don't see any bruising. Let's hope we can tox her and figure out what it was." He handed the stretcher to Mike. "How about you help me get her loaded and strapped? Reed can help Randy with the big guy."

"I don't need help," Jason said. "Just concentrate on Becca." He stood and wobbled.

Reed held back Randy when he reached for him. "Just give him a minute. He'll be fine. He's been hurt worse."

Randy moved to help Alan get Becca ready to be carried. He positioned the stretcher and then he and Alan lifted Becca onto it and both of them worked at strapping her in. As a team, the four of them made their way out of the ravine.

"I'll go with Becca," Jason said when they crested the hill. "I should have known someone would be out there. I screwed up. I didn't protect her and David. I'll call you as soon as I know anything."

Reed nodded. The closest hospital was thirty miles into town. It was the same direction he'd be going. Down the mountain, toward Vienoy.

"Jenna, you better go, too," Reed said. "Becca knows you, she'll need you."

"You're going back, aren't you? Back to Vienoy," she said, her voice tired, as if she'd given up, instead of the fight he'd expected.

He didn't say anything. He wanted her safe and out of the way while he went after David.

She shrugged. "I guess there's no asking you to take me along."

When he didn't respond, she simply nodded and walked ahead of him, her eyes focused on Becca's unconscious form.

He let out a sigh of relief. Maybe everything had finally hit her. Maybe now she accepted how dangerous everything was, how far out of her league she'd been. Now it was time for him and Mike to take care of it, once and for all.

He had no doubt David would be held at Vienoy, and he wasn't going to let him down by waiting overnight. First he needed a plan, and with sunset only a few hours away, he needed one fast. They needed to get into Vienoy tonight, find David, and get out. Then they'd have their proof—proof of what Crane and Vienoy were really doing. The police wouldn't do anything until they had proof. Reed just wanted that sick bastard Crane thrown in prison for the rest of his life.

Or dead. Either ending was fine with him.

Chapter Eighteen

Jenna stood against the far wall in the busy emergency waiting room, her spine stiff, her eyes darting to the outside door every time it opened. She didn't know what she expected. Reed coming through the door on a stretcher? Mike? It seemed that ever since her sister's death, everyone she touched was in jeopardy.

She hadn't liked the murderous look in Reed's eyes as he kissed her goodbye and sent her in the ambulance with Becca and Jason. She knew he was going back to Vienoy, but there didn't seem to be anything she could do about it. It was obvious he intended to go without her.

Jenna stomped her foot in frustration. She should be with him. It was as much her problem as his. David was her responsibility now.

"Jason Walters? Jenna Mosier?" A nurse said from the door.

"Yes?" they both answered in unison.

"You may come back now."

Jason held the door for Jenna to precede him and they followed the nurse back to a curtained section.

"Thank you, Doctor," Becca said.

Jenna rushed forward. "You're okay." She hugged her friend. "I was so worried, I—"

"Hey, Navy." Jason stood next to her and smiled at Becca. "So, what got you?"

"Polypeptide," the doctor said. "She was lucky. Even one microgram can cause rapid loss of blood pressure and unconsciousness. More would have killed her."

"Substance P?" Jason said. "Shit, I'd heard of that stuff, but not in the U.S."

"How about Russia?" Jenna asked.

"Yeah, I remember a briefing once that the KGB was looking into it for assassinations. Something instead of ricin, which they've always denied using."

"The man who tried to take me from the restaurant," Jenna said. "He was Russian…no, Ukrainian. Could he? Oh God, I'm so sorry, Becca. This is my fault. I forced Reed not to kill him. I didn't think. I—"

Becca squeezed Jenna's hand. "Hold on. How could this be your fault? You weren't the one who shot a dart into my neck."

"No, but Reed would have killed him. He didn't because of me…because he knew how much it would upset me…and now…"

Jenna had never thought of killing the man who kidnapped her, or the person who sabotaged her car and tried to kill her. She hadn't even considered killing the man who had hurt David—though she definitely believed he belonged in jail for the rest of his life. She knew there were evil people in the world, but she'd always believed that if she were to kill them—whether in defense or in capital punishment—that she would be stooping to their level, their evil would somehow become permanently attached to her. Now she wondered if by not killing, or stopping Reed from killing, she had tacitly became an accomplice to his future deeds.

Now that she could look her best friend in the eyes and realize how close she'd come to death, she wasn't sure any more about her choices. Everything she'd held true was in question.

Becca hugged her close. "Jenna, you are not to blame. You, of all people, are the innocent one here.

I've always respected you, and how you put yourself on the line for others. You are as brave as any Navy SEAL or Marine Force Recon."

"Thanks for the pep talk," Jenna said. "But I'm not brave. I just don't think before I jump. I was afraid for Reed. I was afraid to involve the police. I was afraid that killing was too much for...I don't know any more. I just don't know."

She knew what she had to do now. She would not let Reed and Mike do what she had to do herself. She might not be able to kill anyone, but she wasn't going to put anyone else in danger for mistakes she'd made. She wouldn't be able to live with herself if one of them died.

"Becca, I gotta go. With Jason here, I know you'll be fine."

"Hold on." Jason grasped her arm. "You can't go anywhere without protection. We still don't know who's out there or who might be watching every move you make."

Right. She forgot the code that Reed, Mike, and Jason shared. Well, she wasn't going to let Jason risk his life one more time either.

She smiled and kissed him on the cheek. "I love how you guys always take care of us. I'm just tired. I thought I'd find a place to lie down for a while. When they release Becca or move her to a regular room, you can come find me in the waiting room. Okay?"

Jason canted his head and cocked an eyebrow.

Jenna opened her eyes wide and looked straight at him, repeating silently to herself. *You can believe me. You can believe me.*

It did the trick. He nodded.

Jenna brushed her lips across Becca's cheek. "I'll see you later."

Jenna headed toward the waiting room, passing other rooms where people were hurt, families were in distress.

She heard a woman sobbing, each breath seemed wrenched from her wails. Jenna stopped in her tracks. She couldn't help but turn toward the window. Most of the room was blocked by a curtain, but through a crack, Jenna saw a small woman bent over a thin blonde child, her shoulders trembling as she cradled the body. Dressed in loose fitting clothes that seemed decades old, her head wrapped in a dark scarf, she seemed out of place and alone.

She spoke with a thick accent, her words barely discernible.

"But she was getting better. This can't be. This can't be." She shook the child, as if it might awaken her back to life.

The silhouette of a tall man stood several feet away, unmoving.

The woman turned toward him and shouted, "This is God's vengeance on us for what you have done. It is you who should be dead. Leave us. Take your evil away. Leave us."

Jenna scurried down the hall, feeling guilty for eavesdropping on such a private moment. Back at the waiting room, she immediately called a cab. It had thinned out a bit, but there were still plenty of people waiting to be seen. The taxi company said it would be twenty minutes.

She moved to one of the small sofas in the back, away from the others. She drew her knees to one side and lowered her head to the armrest. She closed her eyes, trying to put the scene she'd witnessed out of her mind. She took deep breaths, even more determined to execute her plan. She worked on regulating her breathing to appear as if she were asleep. If Jason was anything like Reed, he'd come check on her in a few minutes, just to make sure she hadn't skipped.

She heard footsteps stop near the sofa.

"Jenna?" Jason whispered.

She focused on her breath, keeping the same rhythm. *In. Out. In. Out.* It seemed he watched her too long, but she continued to concentrate. Finally, he turned and walked away. She counted to two hundred before slowly rising and scanning the room. She spotted the yellow cab as it drove up to the drop-off circle in front of the doors. She quickly scanned the hall to verify Jason wasn't nearby watching her. Then she sprinted through the door and into the cab.

"Vienoy, Inc.," she said.

"You sure, lady? They'd be closed now."

"Oh, I know. I left my car there earlier. My friend had an emergency and I came here in the ambulance. I just need to get my car and go home."

"Okay." He turned and pulled away from the hospital, the meter counting the miles and the charge.

****

A metallic-green Jeep pulled into the Vienoy parking lot. The reflection from street lamps showed it was most likely one of the smaller foreign toy trucks, not a serious 4 x 4. Reed checked his watch. 11:00 p.m. This might be the break they needed, someone to disarm the back door. He signaled Stain to hold where he was, hidden on the opposite side. A tall man exited the vehicle in dark clothes and approached the door as if he used this entrance frequently. He stopped and looked up to the light Reed had disabled earlier. Reed held his breath. The man shook his head and laughed.

Strange.

Reed let out his breath. Without the light, there was no way the man would know Stain had disabled the camera too. The man stopped and looked to each side, then one hand moved to his waistband.

Gun.

Reed signaled "gun" and for Stain to move in. They would attack the moment he gained entry.

The man entered a code and jerked open the door. Stain barreled into his back and the man caught himself before falling, pulling the gun from his waistband. Reed shot his fist into the man's gun arm before he could turn around, raising it to the ceiling. The shot echoed in the stairwell and footsteps pounded down the hallway above him.

Reed extracted the gun from the man and pointed it at his head. "Turn around," he whispered. "Slowly."

The man turned to face him and it took every ounce of training for Reed not to pull the trigger. This was the same man he'd encountered at Chat Précieux, the same man who'd run Jenna off the road.

"I knew I should have killed you."

"Go ahead," the man said. "I don't care. I'm already in hell."

"Use him," Mike said as he frisked the man for additional weapons. "Use him before we have ten guys on us all at once."

The man nodded, too eager, his eyes opened wide. "Yes, I can help."

A door opened above them and someone shouted down. "Viktor…is that you? Are you okay?"

Reed's pressed his gun hard into Viktor's forehead.

"Sorry," Viktor shouted. "I thought I heard someone at the door, and when I went to investigate, my gun got stuck in the holster. I nearly shot my balls off."

Raucous laughter echoed down the stairwell.

When it subsided, Viktor spoke again. "Don't tell Crane, all right? I'll never hear the end of it."

Another chuckle. "You'll never hear the end of it from us." A mumbled order followed and footsteps retreated overhead.

"Okay, Shumenko. We won't say anything to

Crane. Glad everything's all right."

The door to the upper stairwell closed and Reed let out the breath he was holding. He knew having bullets flying around a stairwell was not a good game plan. Even with just one assailant, someone could be taken out by a ricochet.

He grabbed Shumenko by the collar and yanked him out of the stairwell and through the door. He had questions, and he didn't want them echoing in that closed chamber.

Keeping the gun trained on the man's forehead, he backed him against the wall.

"I can help," Shumenko repeated.

"Yeah, liked you helped Jenna? It was you who tried to kill her in that alley. It was you who ran her off the road."

"Yes." Shumenko swallowed but didn't flinch. "I understand. I would kill me, too."

Reed stared at him in silence. Something had changed. He wasn't sure what. When he'd met Shumenko before, he was cocky, sure he'd get away. But now something was off. His eyes no longer held that confidence. It was almost as if he wanted to die. No, more than that. He was begging to die.

"You want to know where the boy is," Shumenko said, not a question but a statement.

"Yes."

"I can take you to him."

"Why should I trust you?"

"Without me, you will never find him."

Reed paused to think. It could be a trap. Something was definitely wrong.

"Why?" Reed asked.

"My daughter..." Shumenko's voice shook with obvious grief. "She is dead. Crane must pay."

Reed was confused. Nothing made sense right now. He certainly didn't trust Shumenko, but no one could fake that kind of grief. This might be the break they needed. On the other hand, it could be an elaborate scheme Crane had planned in advanced. Shumenko, knowingly or not, could lead them to the slaughter.

Without taking his gun off Shumenko, Reed said, "Stain?"

"Got your back," Mike said.

"Shumenko, you lead. One false move and you're dead."

Shumenko nodded. "Not this door. It's too close to the lobby, too guarded. There's a secret door, at the back, in the sub-basement."

With Mike to Shumenko's left and Reed to his right, with the gun still aimed at his head, the three of them moved as one unit along the perimeter of the building, then down two flights of dark stairs hidden by tall bushes. At the bottom was a door, painted to match the rest of the building. They might have found it eventually on their own, but it wasn't on the building plans they had.

"What's this?" Reed asked.

"The door to the nursery—the children."

"How many?" Mike whispered, his voice rough with anger.

"I don't know," Shumenko said. "Three or four rooms, maybe fifteen or twenty to a room."

"Fuck." Mike shook his head, rolling his eyes heavenward.

Shumenko stooped to the ground near the door. He swept away dirt with his hands, then removed a grate of some kind. Reed peered over his shoulder. A keypad security lock with 30 buttons of letters and numbers was beneath the grate.

"Shit. We would have never gotten in here," he mumbled.

Shumenko punched six keys in rapid succession, then a pause and six more keys. Reed heard the lock click.

Mike pulled the heavy door open and Shumenko entered with Reed on his heels. Mike brought up the rear.

When the door closed, an involuntarily shudder snaked up Reed's spine.

Reed waved the gun down the hall. "Where to?"

"Third door on the right."

"You first."

Shumenko led again. Reed didn't hold the gun as stiffly now. He no longer believed Shumenko was leading them into a trap. Crane had been busy pissing people off—first his lover, now his hired killer. If things kept going this way, someone would probably get to Crane before Reed.

When they reached the door, Shumenko stopped.

"Another security lock?" Reed asked.

"No." Shumenko pointed to the corners. "Cameras…inside."

"What if I go in on the floor?" Mike asked. "Would they see me then?"

"No. They are designed to monitor the nurses and doctors, not the children."

"How far off the floor?" Reed said.

"About one meter."

"Activated when we open the door or always on?"

"One always on the door, a second sweeps the room every three minutes."

"Personnel?" Reed asked.

"Two nurses at the central station. From the station, the nurses can see all four rooms. The children are all on electronic monitors. If a child gets up to go to the bathroom, the nurses know it."

Reed looked at Mike. "I don't want to kill nurses if I don't have to. We don't know if they're accomplices or oblivious to what really goes on here. They may believe they are doing a job like at any private hospital or long-care treatment facility."

"I'll secure the nurses," Mike said. "You find David."

"I will help you," Shumenko said to Mike. "They know me. If I tell them you are with me, they will not be afraid."

"I still don't know how far we can trust him," Reed said.

"I'll take him anyway...and kill him if he tries anything."

Reed squatted on the floor to the right of the door. Shumenko opened it wide and strode in with Mike at his side. Reed rolled through before the door closed and hunched in the darkness against the wall.

Shumenko and Mike went straight to the glass-enclosed room about fifty yards away. The half-walled room was bright with fluorescent lights overhead and glass from the knee-wall to the ceiling. Reed saw two women immediately stand and peer toward the door where they entered. Evidently, their monitors also told them exactly which door opened. Each woman wore light blue scrubs beneath long white jackets and had a stethoscope around her neck.

When Shumenko approached, the two women relaxed. Reed watched introductions and then heard a little laughter. Stain was being his usual charming self.

Turning back to the room, Reed waited for his eyes to adjust to the darkness. Beds were lined up side-by-side, two high, with about three feet between them. In the ones closest to him, he could see small lumps beneath blankets on each bed. He counted eight units along one wall and ten units along the other. If they were all full, that meant thirty-six children in this room alone. The magnitude of the mission hit him square between the eyes. Though he'd come here to save David, he now realized he had to save all the children—the children in this room and all the other rooms.

How can I pull it off? If I leave with just David, how quickly can I come back for the others? If Crane feels threatened, what will he do?

The enemy never hesitated to kill women and children to prove a point, or to place blame elsewhere. He shook his head. He wouldn't put it past this monster either. To Crane, all these children were replaceable.

Reed closed his eyes. If that were true, it meant David was already dead. Crane already killed him. Reed had failed his promise. Reed had failed to protect him. Reed had failed another mission.

The room swirled and blackness closed in around him. He pressed his back against the wall, trying to hold off the kaleidoscope of colors and sensations blurring his vision. *Please, God, no. Not now. Please not now.* Then he slammed back into the past.

Reed and five of his guys held Abdul Fahim at rifle point in front of a cave opening. It had taken three days of searching through ancient ruins, house to house, and then climbing through hills and mountains in northern Afghanistan to find this guy and his gang of men. They'd followed him from farms outside of Balkh.

The glassy eyes of a ten-year-old had driven him, along with the words of a fourteen-year-old girl. Farishta, a Pashtun mother of seven children, had described what happened to her, and to her girls. She had put her children to bed when five heavily armed Junbish soldiers burst into their modest home. Over the next eight hours, one soldier held her crippled husband at gunpoint as the others took her three oldest girls into the room and raped them repeatedly—first Gabina, fourteen; then Bibi Rokhana, twelve; and then Bibi Amena, ten. Then they came for Farishta.

The ten-year-old sat in the corner, her eyes glazed, not speaking at all. Reed wondered how a child that young could begin to understand what was done to her. But it was the fourteen-year-old, Gabina, who had begged Reed to do something. "Please, help us," she said. "The police do nothing. They will come again. And again."

Something broke inside Reed as Gabina's simple request burned in his chest. It reminded him of his childhood in foster homes, of that feeling of powerlessness. He couldn't let it continue. His superiors had said it wasn't their fight. That Abdul and his men had helped rout the Taliban. Women and rape were a casualty of war. But Reed couldn't walk out of yet another village knowing what would happen.

"You are accused of rape," Reed said to Abdul in front of a cave in the mountain.

Abdul laughed. "You cannot accuse me. I have done no more than some of your soldiers. Pashtuns are nothing. Their women are lower than nothing. Your government protects me in this."

"Not today," Reed said.

Abdul uttered only one word. "Almaut—death," and ducked into the cave.

Automatic weapons discharged all around him. Bullets strafed Reed's unit. Men jumped from behind rocks. Reed shot, ducked, shot again. Blood. Blood everywhere he turned.

Gurgling. Kenny dropped, blood filling the hand he held to his chest.

Grenade! Alex blown to the sky.

Adrenaline pumped through Reed. He heard nothing except the roar of blood in his ears. He saw nothing except vengeance. Reed ran like a mad man into the cave, shooting anything that moved. "Abdul!" Each pounding footstep reinforced his mission. Stop the looting. Stop the raping. Stop the killing.

At the back of the cave Abdul faced him and Reed emptied the magazine into his chest. With impunity, he stared straight into Abdul's wide eyes as he melted to the dirt beneath him. He fell on a young woman. Or was it a girl? She wore the clothes of a wife, but she didn't look any more than eleven or twelve-years-old.

His heart slowing, the blood not rushing in his ears as loud, Reed's eyes cleared. He scanned the barely lit cave.

Blood. Two men.

Blood. Four women.

Blood. Children—two girls, five boys, two babies.

Blood.

Every one of them dead.

Dead at Reed's hand.

Chapter Nineteen

Reed's head buzzed as he tasted death and decay, the darkness in the room stifled his breathing. He punched the wall beside him and his hand vibrated from the lack of give in the concrete. The nightmares, the flashbacks. This was the one he'd been denying—the one he never wanted to remember.

The counselor had said there would come a time when he'd give them up. It was his mind trying to deal with the horror of an unconscionable choice. Because he held fast to a moral code that said killing was wrong, protecting human life was his highest duty, he was unable to deal with his actions—his only choice. He'd always been playing the game on a different playing field than Abdul—a man who valued no life but his own.

Tears silently stained his cheeks. He remembered. He remembered the monster he'd become. Sitting in the dark, he shook as if he was in a freezer. Reed battled the nausea threatening to come up his throat. *Everywhere I go, I bring death.*

Jenna wouldn't so easily brush aside his flashbacks if she knew what they consisted of, if she'd seen the carnage. The children's bodies riddled with blood and bullets, the dirt saturated with the blood of innocents. All at his hands. She would spurn him then—she already hated the violence in him.

How could he hope to save David, or anyone else, when he hadn't been able to save himself from this mental prison?

A child stirred in the bunk next to him. A whole, healthy child—a boy, near David's age. Wide eyes stared at him as Reed crunched against the wall.

Reed wiped the back of his hand across his eyes.

The boy nodded. Then he tapped his finger on the bunk above him. A slow, fast, fast rhythm. *Tap…tap, tap.* A pause. Then again. *Tap…tap, tap.*

The child above him rolled over and stared at Reed. Another boy. He smiled, then repeated the rhythm on his bed rail. Soon, Reed could hear the rhythm jump down four beds. Then a different one came back. This time, it was three fast taps and a slow one. *Tap, tap, tap…Tap.*

When it had worked its way back to the bunk in front of Reed, the first boy whispered, "Hi, Reed. David said you'd come to save us."

A string snapped inside him.

Reed willed himself to crawl to the first bunk. He might be playing with a cursed memory, but he was done warring with himself. He could, and would, save David. He would save all these children. Even if it was the last sane thing he did.

More tapping sounded around the room. It was faint but defined. A code the children must have devised as a communication system for themselves. He waited to see if the kid next to him would translate again.

About thirty seconds passed, and the kid opened his eyes again. "David says be ready. Chaos is coming."

Reed pushed himself up and stood against the wall. *What kind of chaos?* He looked back toward the lighted rectangle. Mike was half sitting on a desk, leaning over a computer with the blonde. Shumenko was standing behind her, also over her shoulder. But the other nurse was not visible.

Reed knew he could count on Mike, whatever happened, but Shumenko was still the wild card.

A humming started out soft then grew louder. The children were all climbing out of bed and walking in a zigzag pattern around the room—intersecting, touching, humming.

Mike looked up from the desk and gave Reed a thumbs up. Reed tried to decipher the children's pattern. He concentrated so hard he didn't notice a boy come up next to him and put his arms around him.

"I knew you'd come. I knew you'd find me," David said. "We're all ready." He pulled Reed back down to the floor. "Stay low. My size. We do this walking every night, so the cameras expect it." David guided Reed through the pattern as they edged closer and closer to the nurses' station.

The other children continued in their zigzagging steps, their humming growing louder and louder until the buzz in his ears actually hurt.

"We have to get the other children," Mike said, when Reed reached the door. "The babies and toddlers. You get the kids in this room out. They can all walk on their own. Shumenko and I will get the others." He gestured toward the nurse.

"How many?" Reed asked.

"Ten or eleven babies, I think."

Reed turned to David. "How many are strong like you? How many could carry a baby?"

"Only two or three."

"Bring the babies here," Reed said. He grabbed a blanket off one of the beds and wrapped it around his neck, then tied it at the bottom to make two seats. "Each of us can carry three. That leaves only two for the younger kids."

Mike nodded and he, Shumenko, and the nurse disappeared out the door on the other side of the nurses' station. That was when Reed noticed the other nurse was sitting in the corner. Her eyes were closed, she looked like she was asleep but her legs were out at an awkward angle.

He ran to her and pressed two fingers to her neck. He let out the breath he was holding. A strong pulse. He didn't need any more innocents killed on his watch.

Reed's cell phone vibrated. He looked at the display. It was Jason. *What now?* He wouldn't be calling unless it was an emergency. He knew Mike and Reed's plans.

He flipped it open and put the phone to his ear. "Problem?"

"Jenna skipped. I figure she's coming your way."

"Shit, Cheeks. You were supposed to be watching her."

"Yeah, I know. But she's sneaky."

"Got that right. Dammit, when I get my hands on her…"

"Look, I'm in the car now," Jason said. "I'm pushing the speed limit, trying to catch up and head her off."

Mike appeared with two babies.

"Fuck," Reed said. "Her timing sucks."

There was no doubt she'd come to Vienoy. After what happened to Becca, she'd be out for vengeance. Not the killing kind. She didn't have that in her. But she'd be out for justice. What if she got here and needed his help? What if he was away from the building and didn't know she was here? He hesitated. Another impossible choice. His whole damn life seemed to be a series of bad choices.

"We're moving out with the kids now," Reed said, deciding this was their best chance. "Call the cops, ambulances, fire department. Everyone you can think of. If they all come with lights and sirens, maybe none of us will end up dead."

"Gotcha." Jason cut the connection.

"Jenna?" Mike asked.

"Damn stubborn woman."

"I guess you should have told her what we were doing."

"Then she'd have insisted on coming."

"And your point?"

"Fuck it. Next time I'm tying her up and throwing her in a closet."

Reed placed the babies side-by-side in his makeshift double papoose. One of the nurses was already waiting with two more babies to hand over. Reed read the name on her badge. Adrianne. So, this was the woman Crane had pissed off.

Reed took one in each arm. "What did you do to the other nurse?" he asked, canting his head toward the corner.

"No worries," Mike said. She's just having a nice little rest. We put a little valium in her coffee. She was a little too much by-the-rules, if you know what I mean. We didn't want her getting in the way of our little rescue operation."

Adrianne nodded. "Poor thing. She was Marius' latest conquest...only twenty. She'll thank us eventually. Right now, she doesn't know how much heartache we've saved her."

Shumenko appeared with three babies attached to him. Two in the same blanket contraption Reed had fashioned. And one in his left arm. Right behind him was David with a baby and the boy who'd first seen Reed in the room, who held his own charge carefully in his arms.

Mike hurried back to the other room, tying a blanket around him. When he returned with two more, Reed handed back one of the four he held.

Reed turned to the door through which he came. Adrianne put out an arm to stop him.

"Cameras. You can't crawl around with babies in your arms."

"Right," Reed acknowledged. "Alternative?"

"Morgue. There are no cameras in there."

"Please tell me the kids aren't on display. I don't want all these kids witnessing that."

"No," Adrianne assured him. "They're all in drawers. Tucked away."

She pointed to a door beyond the next room. "When all the kids start moving through here, the guards will pick it up on the camera and start running downstairs to intercept. You'll have to move fast."

"What about you?"

"I'm giving myself the same stuff we gave Sharla, only not as strong. The guards will assume we were both drugged."

"Why don't you come with us?"

Adrianne took a deep breath. "You need me here. When Marius finds out what's happened, he'll be down here immediately and doing everything possible to blame us for it. I've seen his rages before so I've got to protect Sharla. She doesn't know how he can be."

Reed nodded. "Be careful."

"Don't forget," she said. "Straight through the morgue to the back. There's an exit on the back wall. Now hurry."

David hugged Adrianne and then let out a low whistle and all the kids started running, single file toward the nurse's station.

Reed had about half of them into the morgue when a high screeching alarm crashed through his ears. He hurried the rest of the children through. As he looked back, he saw Adrianne slump to the floor and the needle fall next to her.

He swallowed hard, choking back his concern, and slammed the door closed.

****

Jenna's nerves jumped at the continuing alarm. Frantic, she looked for a door. Any door. End of the corridor. She ran toward it. No markings. She tried the lever. Unlocked.

As silently as possible, she opened the door, just a few inches at a time. A supply closet. Toilet paper, paper towels, blankets. She stepped inside and pulled the door closed. It had to be midnight by now. Surely, they wouldn't be looking for supplies at this hour.

She heard footsteps running on the vinyl floor outside and shrank to the back. She bumped into a shelf. Gauze pads and scissors spilled to the floor. She pocketed a pair of scissors. They weren't the best of weapons, but certainly better than nothing. She pulled out the large multi-roll packages of toilet paper and made a place for herself under the shelf. She scooted in and curled into the far corner, pulling the paper back in front of her. Then she messily arranged blankets on top and over her head. She covered her ears to stop the alarm's noise assailing her senses.

Finally, the alarm stopped. Footsteps approached at a run and then passed her door. She waited, counted out minutes, listening for anything else that indicated someone was nearby. Hearing nothing for ten minutes, she climbed out, cracked the closet door open and peered into the hall.

It was eerily quiet, as if nothing had gone wrong just moments before. Then she heard a voice she recognized at the other end of the hall. It was Dr. Crane and another man—not anyone she'd met before. She closed the door again but put her ear to it to listen.

"We don't have much time," Crane said. "That Marine must have called the cops. They've surrounded the building and it's just a matter of time before they have a warrant."

The voices drew closer. She guessed they were halfway down the hall now. The other man spoke with a nasally voice, like he had a cold. "We have to get rid of the evidence. I can't afford to be caught here. My career will be over."

"What career, you imbecile," Crane said. "I'm the one who invested my life, my fortune into this. I'm the one who will lose everything."

"What about the sick ones?" nasal voice said. "The ones they left behind?"

"Euthanize them and we'll move them to the morgue. By the time they're all autopsied we'll be in Asia somewhere."

"I'm not killing any children," the other man said. "I came here to help children, not kill them."

"I'm not killing any children," Crane mimicked like a sarcastic cartoon character. "Don't pull that on me. You're in this just as much as I am. You've administered every therapy. You've documented every side effect. You know why all the ten-year-olds died, except specimen forty-nine. Now we've lost him to that interfering bitch. We'll have to start over. You bring your computer files, and with my genius, we'll be back up to speed in half the time. In Asia, there isn't so much scrutiny around lost children."

Crane paused. "Now man up and get rid of the evidence before your pathetic life is slapped into handcuffs by those police out there."

"No. I'm done here," the nasal voice said, and Jenna heard him step down the hall.

"No one leaves, Bailey," Crane's voice was soft but deadly. A shot rang out, followed by a heavy thud in the hallway.

"Goddammit, I guess I'll have to do it myself," Crane said.

Euthanize? Children? Jenna couldn't allow that to happen. Determined, she put her head down and barreled out of the closet aiming straight for Crane.

He turned and she ran right into him, knocking him over. The gun flew out of his hand as he fell backward and she toppled on top of him. He wrapped arms around her, but she pummeled his chest with her fists and kicked as hard as she could with her legs.

A blue trouser appeared at her side. A beefy hand grabbed her shirt collar, choking off her air and then threw her against the wall like she was a rag doll. Pain shot through her back and up her neck, bringing tears to her eyes. The room spun in front of her and she closed her eyes, working hard to maintain consciousness.

"You okay, Dr. Crane?" the man asked.

"Yes, thank you."

She opened her eyes, but now she was seeing double. She saw two Dr. Cranes stand and brush off his trousers. Then he bent to retrieve his gun.

Crane pointed at Jenna. "That woman shot Dr. Bailey with my gun." He pointed to the gun on the floor. "Pick it up and take it as evidence. Bring her to my office and tie her to a chair while I contact the authorities."

"Yes, sir, Dr. Crane."

Jenna winced when the man roughly lifted her from her sitting position. He yanked her arms behind her and she cried out at the pain in her shoulder, and her half-healed elbow, as he force-marched her to the elevator.

She barely registered the elevator moving toward the top of the building. Was it just yesterday she and Reed had sat in Crane's office? Reed. She hoped he'd found David and they were out of the building and safe. She should have listened to Reed. He was right. She didn't know what she was doing.

The elevator doors snicked open and she screamed in pain as the man yanked her into the hall. *No more!* Jenna stopped abruptly, lifted her foot and slammed it down hard on the guard's instep. He yelled in pain, his grip loosening on her hands. She kicked backward toward his knee and he yelled again as his leg gave way. She sprinted down the corridor.

The guard pelted after her. There was no choice but Crane's office at the end of the hall. She grabbed for the lever and lifted. It popped open. She pushed the heavy oak door into the room just enough to get through. The guard gripped the edge of the door with one hand and wedged his left foot between the door and the casing tugging the door open wider.

Jenna grabbed the scissors from her pocket and gripped them like a dagger. With a quick overhand stroke, she plunged the scissors into the guard's hand again and again.

The big man screamed in agony as he ripped the door open and staggered toward her. He lifted her by the neck with both hands and she flailed as he choked. Her hand plunged the scissors into his neck. He screamed and dropped her. Blood squirted from his neck in short pulsating arcs onto the white carpet.

Jenna watched in horror as the blood splatter formed a pattern of dark red dots in the doorway. He slapped a hand to his neck but it did no good. The blood seeped around his fingers until his hand was completely covered in sticky bright red fluid. He staggered and fell into the room, his breathing choppy as he choked on the blood filling his lungs. His eyes rolled up into his head and his hand dropped to the floor. He gurgled and gagged as his life slipped away.

As if from a far distance, she heard someone clapping behind her. Then she felt the prick of a needle in her arm and her head felt very heavy. She closed her eyes, hoping that David was safe. Hoping that Reed got him out. Hoping they both knew she loved them.

Chapter Twenty

Colliding. Splitting. Recombining. Images took form and motion like an abstract movie without meaning. Out of the confusion, the image of a hand—Jenna's hand—raising and lowering scissors into a thick mass of skin. Then bright red filled her consciousness, dripping from walls. Crane's face broke through the wall of red then receded again. The corridor twisted and turned kaleidoscopically.

Jenna regained her consciousness in fluctuating stages. She realized she was looking at a ceiling, the ceiling of a corridor that was moving. No, she was moving. Jenna tried to move her head but it seemed to weigh a thousand pounds. She tried to move her hands. It took all her concentration just to lift one hand even an inch from the gurney. Sounds darted around her. A telephone. A beeping. A rhythmic squishing. Voices…but they were unintelligible.

She felt someone grip her hands and push them down to her side. But she wanted to get up. She wanted to know where she was. She wanted to know what had happened to her.

Am I asleep? No, she'd been drugged. Suddenly, Jenna knew that. She fought the effects of the drug, trying to lift herself from its grasp. Trying to clear her mind. She could understand the voices. One in particular.

"You're an amazing specimen of courage for a woman," Crane said, removing a strap and placing one arm out to her side on a cold metal table. He then strapped it down again.

"I'm not brave," Jenna said, her voice reflecting her exhaustion. "I'm just a woman who wanted to be a mother, and instead, walked into a horror movie."

He took her other arm and moved it out to the side, strapping it down. She suddenly realized she was naked under the sheet, in an operating room. Or the autopsy room. She wasn't sure which.

"So, where is that brave Marine who came with you the other day?" Crane asked. "You both came in together tonight, didn't you?"

"No," Jenna said, her pulse racing. Something must have happened while she was passed out. *Is Reed okay?* She couldn't remember. She couldn't remember when she last saw him. "I…I came alone."

She felt a cool breeze when Crane removed the drape. She tensed and prickles of fear worked their way from her toes to her head.

"Such a waste," Crane said, his fingers drawing a line from the base of her neck, between her breasts, all the way down her belly, across her pubic bone. He stopped and chuckled as she automatically tensed. Then he continued his touch along her inner thigh to her toes. "You're almost as beautiful as your sister."

Her skin crawled with what felt like small biting ants from his touch.

"It's too bad I don't have more time to spend with you," he whispered into her ear, as his fingers fondled her breasts. "I'd very much like to know if you feel like your sister—inside." His fingers moved between her legs and he fluffed her pubic hair. "I'm sure you're very tight. Unlike Tanya, you've never had children."

She closed her eyes and swallowed back the bile of fear building in her chest. *Please God, just let him kill me and get it over with. Please don't let him rape me, too. If I'm going to die, just make it quick.*

His hand drew slow circles on her stomach and

he sighed. "Jenna. What a stupid name. It's short for Jennifer, isn't it? Now that's a proper name. Did you know Jennifer is a derivative of Guinevere? Arthur's queen? Powerful, beautiful Guinevere. You should never have shortened your name." He blew a breath across her breasts, and her nipples stood up.

She cursed silently.

"You really are amazing," he said again. "You haven't once begged me to stop, nor have you begged me to kill you. You've even stopped asking any questions." He bent to her lips and hovered.

She pulled her lips inside her mouth. If he was going to kiss her, she wasn't going to help him.

He chuckled and stood up again. "I really did love your sister. I actually cried when Shumenko told me he'd found her and specimen forty-nine living together in Welches. I went to see her, you know."

Jenna blanched.

"I gave her one more chance to come back. To be my partner, even though she'd betrayed me. But she refused. We were a team once, and I would have forgiven her lapse in judgment. I never really imagined she would refuse."

He paused. His eyes seemed to look into some space that didn't exist in the room. He let out a big sigh. "She did more than refuse. She threatened to go to the authorities. Why would she do that, when I offered her so much?"

He really was crazy, and Jenna was certain there was no way he would let her live. If he killed Tanya, whom he claimed to love, Jenna had no chance.

"Of course, I had to make her pay for her betrayal. I think it was three days of payment. Or was it four? I can't remember now." He chuckled. "Do you know how powerful it felt to fuck her till she bled? How amazing it is for the smartest woman I've ever known to beg me to fuck her again? By the last day, she was begging me to kill her. Of course, I had to oblige. I wonder how many days it would take until you begged me to fuck you, and then to kill you?"

The bile rose in her throat and spewed out of her mouth, hitting Crane's pristine white jacket from the shoulder down. She choked and turned her head to one side to get it out of her mouth.

She heard water running, then a soft cloth wiped her mouth. He held her head up and offered her a small Dixie cup of water. She swallowed and he lowered her head again.

"The taste of fear," he said, his voice calm as if he was discussing the weather. "I guess you're not so brave after all. You're nothing like your sister—probably wouldn't even last one day."

She turned her head away from him.

He chuckled. "Your Marine boyfriend didn't vomit when I killed him, you know."

Her eyes opened wide. *Reed? Dead? Wasn't it just a while ago Crane was asking about him? Or was that part of her drugged dream? Oh God, did that mean David was still here somewhere?* Tears leaked from her eyes.

"Painful, isn't it?" Crane whispered into her ear. "Knowing everyone you love is dead and that you've done nothing important with your life. You didn't care about your sister. You never looked for her. Now she's dead. Then your boyfriend. So brave, until I started cutting him into pieces. Then he died too quickly. It was sad really. I wanted him to last. He never begged though. I wonder if you will, sweet Guinevere. I wonder."

He walked away and she heard him rummaging in a cupboard. When he returned, he held out a needle and plunged it into a vein. She gritted her teeth. She would not give him the satisfaction of crying out again if she could help it.

He laughed. “No real need for antiseptic if you’re going to die anyway, is there?” He attached a tube and she saw blood being withdrawn. Then another tube, and another. Soon, he had attached a bag to her and her blood was dripping into the bag.

He handed her a small, pliable ball. “Pump, Jenna. Pump for David. He’s the only one you love who is left. He will need your blood to live after the surgery. It’s up to you to save his life.”

Jenna closed her eyes and pumped. She didn’t know if anything he said was true, but she wouldn’t take a chance. Maybe there was something special about David. Some reason Crane needed him alive.

“Do you even know what miracles I have accomplished here?”

Jenna tried to think, but her brain was shutting down. She wasn’t sure if it was the drugs or her mind unable to deal with knowing Reed was dead and soon David, and all the children, would probably be dead.

“You’re nothing more than a murderer.” She wasn’t sure if she’d said it aloud or it was just in her mind. Jenna let her eyes drift close, but she kept pumping out her blood. She’d rather think about her last time with Reed. She’d rather die thinking about how much he’d loved her, and she him.

She felt him take the bag away from her.

“Good job, Jenna. Five pints. You should be proud.”

Crane ran a finger along her cheek. “Do you see now what your sister gave up?” he asked. His voice a whisper.

Jenna refused to open her eyes. Refused to give him the satisfaction that she even heard him.

He pinched her left nipple, and she cried out. Then he pinched the other one. “Nothing like your sister.” He draped her again and Jenna said a silent prayer of thanks.

"Unfortunately, you and your dead boyfriend have ruined things for me. But you can still provide one last benefit to my research. I will take your heart and kidneys with me...for David. You see, in my next test he will develop kidney failure and then heart failure. I would have been able to grow organs for him if you hadn't interfered. But now he'll have to take the next best thing...your organs."

Oh God. She now had a grasp of what David and the other children must have lived through. Perhaps by giving up her organs, she would buy him more time. Time for someone else to find him. To save him.

"Now will you beg me to kill you? Will you beg me to kill you to save David?"

Jenna's mouth formed words but her throat was too dry. She couldn't get them out. She struggled and tried again.

Crane leaned forward to hear. He had to bring his head to within inches of Jenna's lips.

"Say it again, Jenna. I want to hear you beg."

Jenna's mouth struggled to bring her lower lip against her upper teeth to form the first consonant. It spilled out in a whisper. "Kill. Me."

"Thank you." Crane smiled. "I will."

She felt the needle move in her arm and heard the IV bottle thunk against the metal pole as he hung it. She knew the drug that would put her to sleep forever was making its way down the tube. He whistled *Auld Lang Syne* as he walked away from her.

She heard water running in a nearby room. He must be scrubbing for the surgery.

As the drugs filled her head, she struggled to think of Reed. She thought of their last time together, how they'd declared their love to each other. The light above her eyelids dimmed and she fell quietly asleep.

Jenna felt a slap to her cheek. She couldn't open her eyes, but she knew she was still alive.

"Come on, wake up," a woman's voice said. "I can't carry you out of here. Reed can't save you right now. You have to help me."

The woman slipped her off the table and Jenna slithered to the floor. Her limbs didn't seem to be her own. She could barely feel her head.

Soft arms dragged her across the floor. "You can't stay here," the woman said. "When he comes back, he'll kill you."

A siren went off in the room, hurting Jenna's ears.

"The police are coming in now. I'm going to put you in here in case Marius comes back."

She heard a cabinet door open near her on the floor. Then the woman lifted Jenna's legs in, bent them up and shoved her toward a corner. The woman grunted as she lifted Jenna's butt inside. She pressed down on her head and wedged it into a corner. Jenna felt her arm flop on to the floor.

The woman lifted it back in and crossed it across Jenna's stomach. "I'm really sorry. I have to go now. Just stay quiet and you'll be all right. Someone will come to get you."

It was tight quarters. The woman was unable to close the door completely when Jenna heard steps coming into the room.

"Adrianne. What are you doing?" Crane's voice. "Where is she?"

"Who are you looking for?"

"You know damn well who I mean or you wouldn't be here."

Jenna held her breath. She heard the crash of someone falling against the cabinet. The door shut completely with a loud bang. The sound rang in her ears, making her dizzy. Then footsteps left the room and receded down the corridor.

****

Reed ran through the doors just ahead of the police, Cheeks right on his heels. Stain would lead the paramedics and doctors to the sick children's ward. Reed immediately turned left at the hallway and headed for the stairwell, leaving the elevators for the ambulance crews. His mission was to find Jenna. He prayed Crane hadn't found her first.

Jason continued up the stairs to the tenth floor and Crane's office. Reed went down to the basement where he'd earlier helped the children to safety. He remembered there were two operating suites there.

And the morgue.

He swept through each of the three children's suites. The police and doctors were moving the last sick child out when he got there. Once the children were out, the police found the nurse Mike had drugged and moved her to a gurney before a final check of the room.

Reed's heart contracted. Still no Jenna.

He barreled through the door of the first operating room, his gun pointed in front of him. An IV bottle hung from a pole, the tubing snaked to the floor leaking fluid. Straps looked like they'd been ripped off in a hurry.

Fuck! I'm too late.

He heard a groan and turned.

Adrianne sat against a cabinet at an odd angle.

He hurried to her side, checked her pulse and quickly scanned her body. Her pulse was steady, but it looked like her shoulder might be dislocated.

"Adrianne?"

She didn't move, didn't open her eyes.

Reed heard footsteps slapping on the vinyl floors outside the door. Closer and closer they came, then stopped. He turned and pointed his gun at the door.

Jason barreled through his gun also out. He

skidded to a stop. “Shit, rat face! I almost shot your head off.”

“Same goes,” Reed said, his breath shallow. He’d almost killed his best friend. “Crane?”

“Nowhere,” Jason said.

Reed looked back to the nurse who’d helped him earlier. “Adrianne’s only half conscious,” he said quickly. “I can’t find Jenna. I may be too late.”

Jason nodded. “Go! I’ll take care of the nurse.” He paused. “Find Crane and you’ll find Jenna.”

Reed didn’t have to think twice. He bounced up and headed for the next operating room where he heard someone whistling. Slowly, he turned the lever and pulled just enough to see inside. At the far end was a room with a long sink and someone was pulling off rubber gloves and dumping them in a trash container. He was about the right height for Crane. Reed couldn’t clearly see the hair color beneath the blue surgical cap. His stealth approach across the room and through the door was unnoticed.

He cocked the gun. “Crane.”

Marius didn’t turn toward Reed’s voice the way most people would have. He was arrogant enough, or crazy enough, to think he was still in control.

“You’re too late,” Crane said. Then he turned slowly, his arms raised halfway at his side. His lips quirked in a half smile. “She’s already voluntarily sacrificed herself for my research. You might as well kill me now.”

Reed’s breath sputtered and his heart beat accelerated until it seemed to be the only thing he could hear. He focused, forcing down the panic. It might be a lie. *Please, God, make this be a lie.*

“She fought to the end though; you would’ve been proud of her. She fought just like a good little Marine.”

“How?” Reed asked, his cheeks pulled in as his jaw clamped down.

"Simple, really. A little anesthesia. Hmmm. That's not quite accurate. Maybe a lot of anesthesia." He chuckled. "She was beautiful, you know. I had a taste of her before I cut out her heart."

Reed put one hand around Crane's throat and pushed him against the wall, putting just enough pressure on his windpipe that he could still speak, but would know death was near. "Where?"

"The ovens," Crane choked out. "We cremate everyone."

Reed pressed against his windpipe, and Crane struggled as Reed let less and less air in. "Her organs..." he barely got the words out and Reed let off a little. "In the morgue. For David. He needed a heart. You can still get it. Ice it. He can barely live another year without it."

Crane was a damn liar.

Reed knew David didn't have a heart problem. A doctor had checked him thoroughly two weeks ago. Reed knew David was safe.

That meant Crane might have been lying about Jenna too.

Now he just had to find her.

With one press Reed finished him off and Crane slumped to the floor, his neck broken. Crane would never hurt or kill another child again.

Jaw set, shoulders hunched, head down, Reed headed for the morgue.

First, he had to know if Jenna was there. Then the cremation ovens.

At the morgue, he methodically opened each drawer, beginning on the far left of the south wall. All but two were full. Most of them babies, some premature, others three to six months. Seven or eight were toddlers, two or three-years-old.

He checked every single one.

No Jenna.

Closing the last drawer, he leaned his forehead

against the cool metal and took several deep breaths. She wasn't here. But how many children had Crane killed over the last decade?

Cheeks entered the room. "Ah, shit. No. Fuck." He crossed to Reed.

"She's not here," Reed said, his voice barely a whisper. "Crane said she was dead. I wasn't sure if he was screwing with my head. I had to check."

"Stain and I have combed the place and we haven't found anything." Jason put a hand on his shoulder. "Where else can we look? Where would that bastard have stashed her?"

Reed turned and looked past Jason's shoulder, as if willing Jenna to appear. "The ovens," he said. "Crane said she'd been cremated."

"A lie, rat face," Jason said. "I was just there ten minutes ago. They were stone cold. No way was anyone put in there today."

Mike rolled around the door, his breath short as if he'd been running. "Fuck. What are you doing in here? The last place I'd expect to find you was the morgue. What kind of sick mind do you have, rat face?"

"How's the nurse?" Reed asked.

"That's why I've been looking for you. She came to when I got her to the ambulance and said something about Jenna Mosier stuffed in OR and I had to save her."

Reed stood tall, his mind in full gear. "I've checked both operating rooms. Jenna wasn't in either one."

"We better check again," Mike said. "Adrianne definitely said stuffed, like it was a small place."

The three of them ran back to the room where Reed had killed Crane. They worked methodically, opening every cupboard, both in the scrub room and the OR. Nothing.

They turned the corner and entered the second

one. Then he heard a sound. A human sound. Reed raised his hand for silence. It sounded like a light snore. He inched toward the sound.

That's exactly what it was—just like the little snore he remembered when Jenna fell asleep beside him.

He listened for it again.

The sink!

He ran to the cupboard and opened the door.

Jenna's arm flopped onto the floor. His breath caught as he stared at her. Her head wedged in the corner. Her nude body angled around the plumbing trap at the bottom of the sink. Her knees pulled up and leaning against the cold water valve. Her feet stuffed sideways.

Her chest moved and the snore issued forth again. It was beautiful. She was alive. Wonderfully alive.

"Yeah, paramedics," Cheeks was saying into the phone. "I think it's some kind of anesthetic, but it must be wearing off."

Reed worked one hand behind her head and the other beneath her knees. He lifted and pulled an inch at a time until he worked her out of the cabinet. When her entire body was freed, she rolled toward him and he cradled her in his lap, rocking back and forth.

Mike tapped his shoulder and he looked up.

"Uh, you might want to cover her a little." He handed Reed a hospital drape, and Reed molded it around her, never letting go.

When the paramedics came, they had to pry her away from him. As they examined her, Reed continued to hold some part of her. Her hand, her head, her foot. He moved as the paramedics moved. He had to touch. He had to be reassured her body was still warm, breathing, alive.

Reed moved with them to the ambulance. He

held her hand all the way there, talking to her, telling her how much he loved her. He refused to let go even in the emergency room.

He vowed he'd never let go of her again.

Chapter Twenty-One

Jenna half-heartedly fought against Reed as he sat her in his SUV and clasped the seatbelt around her. She'd told him to leave her alone. She didn't want him around. She was afraid. Afraid of what she'd become.

He put the car in gear and drove into the dark night, due west.

It had been two weeks since he'd found her scrunched into that cupboard at Vienoy. Other than recovering from the anesthetic, the blood loss, and a few bruises, Jenna was uninjured—physically that is. But the psychiatrist had kept her in the hospital for the whole two weeks. She'd said Jenna might be suicidal. Her mind couldn't yet process everything that had happened.

Jenna sighed. She might feel like she deserved to die on some days, but she wasn't going to kill herself. She just wanted to be left alone. Left alone to forget everything that happened. Left alone to forget Reed and all the violence he'd let into her life.

Reed drove on in silence. Jenna pressed her head against the cool window, her eyes open but not seeing. "How could you leave David? He needs you," she said, her voice almost a monotone.

"David's fine. He's staying with Leena, and Mike is over there almost every day," Reed answered.

"He's not fine." She turned toward him. "He's in pain. Can't you see it?" Her lips trembled, her shadowed eyes stared at his profile."

He reached for her hand.

Jenna shrank from him. She didn't want him to touch her, to hold her. If he touched her, Jenna was afraid she would break into hundreds of pieces and never recover.

"David is fine. In spite of everything, he's probably more sane than either of us."

This had nothing to do with sanity, she thought. It had to do with the rape of her soul.

"Talk to me, Jenna. Help me understand."

"Can't you see it written all over me?" she said, her voice rising. "You drew me in. They all drew me in to their evil." She felt the rage building inside her, like steam forming in a kettle as water heated. Helpless to stop it, the emotion rose from her stomach to her chest, then up her throat, choking her.

"I'm a murderer," she yelled at him. "A cold-blooded killer just like Crane, just like Shumenko." Her shoulders shook with the suppressed rage she'd held in all week. "Are you happy now? I'm just like you, dammit." She slumped back in the seat. "Just like you," she whispered.

The world would never again be light for her. *How does he stand it? How does he live each day with this kind of pain? How does he live knowing that nothing will ever be in its right place again? Knowing that any semblance of control of your own life was all façade?*

"You are not a murderer," he whispered. "You are one of the bravest people I know."

Her vision blurred with red haze and she heard an animal sound coming from her throat. Then the rage burst free, and despite the seatbelt holding her in, she launched herself at him, screaming and punching him, slapping any part of him she could reach.

He jerked the steering wheel to the right, pulling them off the road onto the gravel shoulder.

He put the car in park, making only a half-hearted attempt to fend her off.

"You bastard. *You* made me. You and your violence. You and your open vengeance. Not justice, vengeance. I hate you!"

His features blurred in her fury and tears, but she could see enough to tell that his expression hadn't changed, that he was still so damned untouched.

He just sat staring straight ahead while she hit and scratched. Not reacting. The sounds coming from her were feral. The raw, wounded sound of unbearable pain—like an animal trapped in the forest trying to tear itself free, each limb bloodied in the process. The sound started from deep inside and tore its way out of her throat. The band around her chest compressed her heart, exerting such an unbearable pressure, she thought—no, she hoped—it would give out and let her escape into death.

Then she collapsed forward on herself, sobbing so hard she couldn't draw a breath. She hadn't known she could cry like this, not even in the early, desperate days when she'd first awakened in the hospital. Her voice broke and she choked, coughing convulsively.

Reed seized her shoulders and hauled her upright, propping her against the door. Distantly, she heard him say, "Drink this," and he put a bottle of water to her lips. Her throat so raw and swollen, she barely managed a swallow.

She slumped in exhaustion, her eyes closing. She heard Reed on the phone, talking quietly, but she was too numb to listen. She sank into a stupor, so emotionally drained that she was unaware of anything except being on the move again.

She slept, starting awake occasionally and looked out the windshield in total blankness, not knowing where they were or where they were going, not caring, or even fully comprehending. Then the headlights of oncoming traffic hypnotized her to sleep again. She roused when he stopped the car. She watched dully as a man reached through Reed's window and handed him something. Then they rolled slowly down a gravel road and stopped.

Reed came around to the passenger side and opened the door. "Come on."

He reached for her, his arms tight around her waist pulling her forward. She followed slowly. She didn't have the energy to fight him anymore.

They were parked at what looked like the deck of a small A-frame cabin. A cool breeze whipped at her legs, snaking beneath the hem of her dress. The ground beneath her bare feet was a mixture of sand and grass, and there was a loud roaring in her ears.

"I have to be home in the morning," she said, surprised at the raspiness of her voice. "I have to fix David breakfast."

"David's spending the night with Leena." Reed took her arm and led her up three steps to a deck that crossed the entire front of a cabin she'd never seen before. He put a key in the door and pushed it open with his hip. His arm around her waist, he held her tight to his side.

He reached inside and she heard his fingers scrabbling against the wall. Suddenly, a bright light flooded the entry, making her squeeze her eyes shut. After her brain had time to adjust to the light, she opened her eyes again and he ushered her inside. She found herself standing near a chest-high, pale yellow tile counter that separated her from a small, old-fashioned kitchen. Permeating everything was a musty smell mixed with the scent of mixed berries.

Reed went back outside and she just stood there, too beaten and apathetic to care. Doors slammed; then he was back at the front door, carrying two large suitcases.

He walked past the kitchen, across the living room, and into another room at the back of the house. More lights came on. Jenna closed her eyes and waited for him to come back. No matter how often she'd sent him away, he always came back.

He took her arm and led her to the room with the light, and then through the bedroom to another small space. "I figured you might need to use the bathroom."

Jenna stepped inside and he closed the door, giving her some privacy. She peed. She flushed.

She stood for a moment unsure why she was here. The bathroom had the same yellow tile on the counters as the kitchen. A yellow, blue, and white pattern dotted the vinyl floor. The shower, however, seemed newer. It was big enough for two people and had no door. Large, off-white, rough tiles adorned three walls and the floor. A huge rainhead fixture jutted from the ceiling in the middle.

As she stood washing her hands, Reed opened the door again.

"I'll put on some soup," he said as he placed a hand beneath her elbow and led her back to the kitchen.

She sat at the table and looked vaguely around while he poked through the cabinets and found what he needed. After a while she said in her croaky voice, "Where are we?"

"A little north of Lincoln City."

A tiny frown knit her brow as she tried to get her tired mind to sort through the available information. Finally, she remembered that Lincoln City was on the central Oregon Coast. Her brain started putting together all the clues. The sandy grass, the roaring ocean sound. They must be on the beach.

Reed set a bowl of steaming vegetable and noodle soup and a glass of water in front of her.

Dipping a bowl for himself, he sat across from her and dug in.

Cautiously, Jenna dipped her spoon into the soup and sipped at the broth. The very act of lifting the spoon was almost too much effort. It burned her raw throat, but at the same time the heat felt good.

She kept her head down, her gaze focused on the bowl. *Spoon in. Lift. Sip. Spoon in. Lift. Sip.*

She couldn't let herself look at him. She couldn't let herself think about why they were here. Right now, the pain hovered just on the edge of her consciousness, ready to consume her again. *Spoon in. Lift. Sip.*

When she was finished, Reed took her bowl with his and washed the dishes in the sink. Then he put them on a towel to dry. He helped her stand and led her back to the bathroom, where he laid out a towel and a washcloth.

"Take off your clothes," he said softly. "Get in the shower. I'll bring you your nightclothes."

If she'd had more energy, she might have argued with him, or even locked the bathroom door. Instead, she did exactly as he'd ordered. She turned on the faucet and stepped back, waiting for the water to warm. Then she stepped under the soft, warm rain and let it drizzle all over her body. She didn't scrub. She could barely move. She prayed the water would wash away her sins.

She wasn't sure how long she stood unmoving. Reed scrubbed her. Reed washed her hair. Reed turned off the shower. Reed toweled her dry. Her T-shirt and boxers—her favorite nightclothes—were neatly folded and waiting on the counter, along with a toothbrush and paste, her blow dryer, and a hairbrush. Reed stepped just outside the door and waited.

She put on her nightclothes, brushed her teeth and sat on the toilet lid, the hair dryer in her hand.

But she couldn't bring herself to plug it in or turn it on.

"That's okay," he said. "You don't need it tonight. It's warm enough." He wrapped the cord around the handle and put it in a small drawer beneath the counter. Picking a comb out of the drawer, he quietly combed the tangles out of her hair.

Then he leaned down, lifted her into his arms and carried her to the bed. The covers were already turned down. He placed her between the sheets, pulled up the covers and turned off the bedside lamp.

"Good night." He kissed her on the forehead and walked out of the room.

She let out a big breath. She hadn't known what he wanted but wouldn't have stopped him if he'd crawled in with her. She wouldn't have stopped him for doing anything, nor would she have participated. She couldn't feel love anymore. She wasn't worthy of love anymore.

She lowered her head to the pillow and her brain switched off.

****

Each day she woke, wandered the house and beach, ate, showered, slept, and woke again. One day merged into the next, memories disjointed. Crying. Screaming. Nothingness. Throwing rocks into a tree with all her might. Throwing dishes at a wall. Anger. Pain. Nothingness. Begging. Pleading.

Fits of rage would take her unawares, exploding when she least expected it. Afterward, she was always ashamed of her lack of control. She took long walks on the beach, trying not to think. He was always behind her, following. Not close, but not far either. Some days, she hated Reed with such an intensity that it prevented her from even looking at him. Those days he stayed farther away. He never pushed, never asked her to talk. He just let her be—be whatever she wanted that day.

Other days she loved him more than she could bear. She cried and held tight to him. He rocked her, stroked her hair. He whispered his love to her. On those days, she begged him to make love to her, to take her mind away from all this, to let her lose herself in him. He refused. In spite of his words of love, he no longer touched her in that way.

Reed made certain she ate, slept, walked, showered. He did the cooking, the dishes, the laundry, because it never crossed her mind to do them. He never left her completely alone for long. Even the groceries were delivered.

One day she woke and asked, "How long have we been here."

"Two months."

Her eyes widened, her jaw dropped. "But…then this is…October?"

He nodded.

"What about David? Have I talked to him? Did I say anything? Oh my God, he must think I don't love him anymore."

"Do you, Jenna? Do you still love him?"

She paused, searching her heart. She didn't think she could ever love again—not truly love, not love for unselfish reasons. But for David?

"Yes," she whispered. "Yes." Her voice was stronger.

He leaned forward and touched her lips with his index finger. She held it, unsure. Then he withdrew his finger and replaced it with his lips. His lips were soft, undemanding. It was just a moment, but it was definitely a kiss.

"Good," he said. "You're going to live, Jenna. You're going to live a long and wonderful life."

****

The days after her admission seemed sunnier.

She'd called and talked to David a couple of times. He seemed happy. Leena assured her she was having the time of her life keeping up with him. She regaled Jenna with David's accomplishments in school. Toward the end of October, Leena told her about David's casting in the role of Tiny Tim in a community theater production of *A Christmas Carol*. For the first time in months, Jenna really wanted to leave. She wanted to go home. She wanted to see David, to celebrate Christmas with him, to be a family.

Instead of pacing the beach and letting the roar of the ocean dull her senses, Jenna now stopped on her treks and regularly lifted her face to the sun, letting the warmth spill over her. In the mornings, she'd start at the edge of the ocean at low tide, where sea stars and purple sea urchins clung to wave-splashed rocks. Then she'd scamper across a swath of hard sand, and climb over outcroppings of rock just to find the tide pools and marvel at the variety of colors and species. Other days she'd go south, running across the soft sand, all the way up to where salal or beach grass or shore pines began their toehold on the beach. Her world was teaming with life.

One night in mid-November, she stepped onto the deck while Reed finished the dishes and she was caught by the beauty of the deep reds and blues and purples. She ran down the stairs and out to the ocean. Throwing off her sandals, she twirled in happy circles as the tide lapped against her feet. It was as if the skies were blessing her. Her imprisonment finally at an end. She turned to share it with Reed, to invite him closer.

But he wasn't there.

Surprised, she scanned both up and down the beach for him.

When did he stop following me? Why didn't I

notice? She couldn't see the deck from here. She couldn't see if he stood there watching. Did he share in the beauty of the evening?

Suddenly, she felt bereft. For the first time in a long time, she wanted to share this moment with him. She wanted to see him smile. Not for her, for himself.

A tear traced down her cheek. She'd waited too long. Or maybe she'd driven him away long ago. Was he just waiting for her to be well enough to leave? Maybe she'd mistaken all his caring, his patient waiting, for love.

She turned her back on the sunset. With all her other sins, she must have killed his love too.

Chapter Twenty-Two

Thanksgiving. Reed had a turkey delivered while she napped. He was planning a small feast for dinner. A celebration of Jenna coming back to life.

He had stopped following Jenna three days ago, no longer concerned for her safety. Reed hoped they could head home by December first. The only question was if their home would be together. Or separate. They hadn't talked about it. Was it fear of her answer? Or fear of acknowledging the inevitable? No matter how much he wished differently, he knew Jenna could no longer choose him. Her precarious peace could not accept his violence, and he knew he would never be completely at peace.

Reed enjoyed sitting on the deck, particularly in the evening as Jenna strode the beach. She often stopped now to pick up a seashell, or to wave and talk to a neighbor strolling from the other direction. Tonight, she had seemed filled with joy when she started out. He couldn't resist the sunset when he'd first noticed it from the kitchen window. He came out to the deck, wanting to share it with her—even if from afar. She'd run to the ocean and danced like a mermaid with newfound legs.

Then something happened. Her entire body had visibly sagged. Now she stood, her back to the sunset, her arms tight around her. He squinted, trying to see more clearly. Was that a shudder? He wanted to run to her, to grab her around the waist and twirl her in circles, to shake away whatever sudden doubt she'd had.

He hesitated. He should give her space. He knew about relapses. Hell, he'd had them several times for nearly a year. But she was different. Unlike him, she had been born into light. This dark patch in her life was expected, given what she'd gone through. But he'd watched the light slowly come back to her over the past few weeks.

Finally, he could stand it no longer. He bounded down the stairs and ran toward her still form.

Reed gathered her into his arms and held her tight as the sky darkened. "My love, what's wrong? You started out the door so happy. What happened?"

She clung to him, her face buried in his neck. Deep sobs racking her shoulders, pools of tears soaking into his T-shirt.

"I've killed it," she choked out.

He sat on the damp sand and rocked her as the tide lapped around them. Not again. Not back to the beginning. Back to her nightmares, her confusion over killing the guard—even if it was in self-defense.

"Come back to me, Jenna; you can get through this."

She shook her head and the cries started anew.

He held her head steady and looked into her eyes. "Listen to me. You had to do it—to save yourself, to save David."

"No," she wailed, pulling his hands away from her face. "Not that. Us! I've killed us!" She curled into him, her tears silent now, but just as continuous.

He was confused. *Is she hallucinating? Is this some new nightmare?*

"I'm right here, Jenna. Alive…holding you." He grazed her temple with his lips. He stroked her arm. "I'm alive. You're alive. You haven't killed us. We're fine. We're both fine."

She quieted and swallowed back hiccups.

He lifted her into his arms and moved her up the beach, away from the cold water. The tide was coming in. He found a blanket closer to the cabin, one he'd left earlier as he'd watched her dance in the moonlight. His arms wrapped the blanket around her, enveloping her small form as he sat, keeping her cuddled in his lap. He'd sit here all night if needed.

After what seemed like an hour, she scrubbed a hand across her face and looked up. Her eyes shone with yet more unshed tears in the moonlight.

"Then prove it to me…prove I haven't killed us."

He didn't understand. What more could she want than knowing they were both flesh and blood sitting here now.

"I don't know what you want," he finally said. "What kind of proof can I offer?"

"Touch me," she begged.

He pulled her close. "I am touching you, Jenna. Can't you feel this? Our bodies close together. Can't you hear my heart pounding next to yours? My breath in your ear?"

She pushed away, stood, and stripped off her clothes. "Prove I haven't killed us," she said again. "Touch me."

He took a deep breath as he looked at her perfect skin glowing in the moonlight. He'd wanted to touch her for so long. For five months, he'd been watching her, loving her, lusting after her but not daring to touch. Not daring to intrude on her healing—not even when she'd begged him to take her pain away with sex. So many nights he'd spent alone in the shower, thinking of her, taking care of his needs alone.

He closed his eyes and steeled himself to her beauty. "Jenna, you know I can't do that. You're confused. You don't know what you're asking."

She knelt in front of him, grabbed his hand and

held it to her breast. "I'm not confused. I'm just asking you to touch me. Is that so hard? Am I so repugnant to you that you can't even look at me?"

He opened his eyes and pulled her to him. His mouth rained kisses along her cheekbone, her brows, her shoulders. Then he crushed his lips to hers. All the waiting, all of his need poured into that kiss. Devouring her, he forced her mouth to open as his tongue pushed inside. Tasting her, his hands moved from her breast to her back. He cupped her firm bottom to bring her closer. He couldn't get enough. He couldn't stop.

Reed pulled hard on his mental reserves, he shut down his feelings, his lust, and pushed her away. She stared at him as he fought hard to catch his breath, to regulate his heart.

"That's why I can't touch you," he said. "I can't stop, Jenna. I can't stop."

"I don't want you to stop." She nibbled on his earlobe. "Even if you don't love me anymore, at last you can give me this." She reached for his shorts and pulled.

He stayed her hand. "What did you say?"

She plunged her hand into his shorts and folded her fingers around his erection. "I said, you could at least give me this." She moved her hand up and down. Up and down.

He groaned. It took all his energy to pull her wrist then her hand out of his shorts. "The part before that," he said between deep breaths. "The part about loving you."

She sat back on her heels and looked at him. Her shoulders sagged. "I said…" her voice was a whisper, low and sad. "Even if you don't love me, at least…"

He put a finger to her mouth. "Stop."

Her eyes opened wide. Her lip trembled.

"I love you. God, Jenna, I think I've loved you

since the day we met. I'll never stop loving you."

"But I thought...then why did you keep refusing to touch me? I begged you to make love to me many times since we've been here, but you never did. And now..."

He pulled her back into his arms. "I was giving you time. Time to decide who you were now. Who you wanted to be. How you wanted to be...and...if you wanted to be with me." He paused, his chest tightened as the pain of not knowing gripped him hard. "You weren't able to make those decisions before. It would have been just sex. Sex to make you forget. Not love. Sex. I couldn't do that to you—to me—and then have you walk away."

"I want to be with you," she whispered.

Reed wanted to believe her. He'd hoped all this time that, when she came back to herself, she would still want him. But he'd never been sure. He wasn't one hundred percent sure now.

"I want to be with you," she said again, her hands framing his face. "I love you more than I ever did before. I understand even better now. I understand how violence and tenderness can live in the same man."

He hesitated.

She lifted his shirt and pressed her lips to his chest. She moved up his breastbone, pushing his shirt higher. "Please," she said. He raised his arms and she pulled the shirt over his head. She pressed her body against him and took control of his mouth, pouring her feelings into the kiss. Tender, yet forceful. Confident.

"I love you, Reed Adler, with every breath I take." She pulled at his shorts, and he lifted his hips so she could remove them. Her fingers moved immediately to his full erection, and he groaned. "I refuse to spend even one more day without you inside me."

Her lips trapped his in a dance of seduction. At the same time, she rubbed her mound against him, stiffening him even further. His tongue gained entrance to her mouth and she opened wider, then closed her lips and sucked. At the same time, she slid herself to his tip and teased him at her slick opening. He thought he would explode.

Reed reached for her head and pulled her closer, deepening the kiss. He didn't want even a millimeter between their bodies. She alternately softened, then attacked, writhing against him. Then, without warning, she rose up and pushed hard against his chest. In one smooth movement, she lowered herself onto his shaft and he almost screamed with the pleasurable agony as he filled every part of her. Then she churned, and slithered. At first slowly. Up, down. Up, down. Torturing him with pleasure. He could feel the orgasm building, he could feel himself losing control.

"Jenna…I don't think I can wait."

She laughed and increased her speed, faster and faster. "We're alive; I want your life inside of me, now. Let it go…now."

And he did. He had no choice. He placed his hands on her hips and she lifted her hands to the sky, as if calling down the moon. His vision blurred and all he saw was her pale skin glowing above him, her breasts moving to the rhythm of her strokes, her pelvis gyrating to a tune only the two of them could hear. He gasped as it built inside him. His breath grew shorter and shorter, and in only a few moments, his muscles tensed, his heart clutched, his hips rose up to fill her, and he called out her name as he pumped his seed into her in three great bursts. Her inner muscles clamped around him, sucking every last bit from him in an almost painful torture of sensation.

Then she fell on him and the high tide came in,

washing over them, drenching them. Cooling them. Cleansing them. Taking away the pain of the past and leaving them renewed to start again.

She clung to him, their bodies the only warmth as the tide receded again. He rolled to his side and lifted her to his arms. She laughed with joy, licking salt water from his shoulders.

"Are you alive, Jenna Mosier?" he asked, carrying her back to the cabin. "Are you convinced now?"

"I'm not sure," she teased. "I think that was the movie trailer. I want to know the rest of the story."

He laughed. "I thought so. It may take a while though. It's a very long movie, with lots of complex twists and turns. I think there may be more than one climax in the story."

He put her down and gathered their wet clothes from the beach.

"Is that so?" she said, dancing in circles around him. "How long will it take you to make love to me properly, Mr. Adler? An hour? Two? Four? What's the record?"

She ran toward the cabin and he chased after her.

She got to the door first and opened it, running inside.

He followed her and found her in the shower, the water on warm. He stepped in and backed her against the wall. She wrapped her arms around his neck and he kissed her hard, putting an equal amount of lust and love into it.

"Longer than four hours," he said between breaths.

"Eight hours?" she asked. "A day? A weekend?"

He turned off the shower and pulled a towel off the rack. He kissed off water droplets and dried her at the same time, then quickly dried himself. He put his hands under her buttocks and she wrapped her legs around his waist, laughing.

"Are you ready yet?"

"Getting there," he said.

He carried her to the bed and laid her on her back, her knees pressed into his side. He eased into her slowly.

"Hmmm," she murmured. "That's nice."

He rocked against her and withdrew just as slowly, then did it again. He took a nipple into his mouth and she gasped as he suckled and nipped. Then he rocked into her again and her feminine muscles clenched and released several times, stiffening him further.

"How long?" she said, her voice breathy, her muscles working him up while bringing obvious pleasure to herself. "Jason said your record was seventy-two hours. How long will it be for us, Reed? How long?"

He pulled out, then rocked in again and she groaned, moving her hips in slow, sensuous circles.

He rocked out and in again. "Years," he said, his lips capturing hers, savoring.

He rocked into her again. "I'm thinking a lifetime."

A word about the author...

Growing up I had the reputation for being a "goody-two-shoes." Some people rebel against that reputation, but I reveled in it. I didn't have fantasies of being a "bad" girl, and I never dreamed of growing up to marry a rich man. My parents raised me with the belief I could be whoever I wanted and accomplish anything. I have tested that belief many times through careers in psychology, acting, computer programming, and now helping faculty to teach through distance education, and bringing 21st-century technology to a rural part of California. I've always been one who loved my life no matter where it took me.

Both triumph and tragedy have shaped me into who I am. Like most women, I've survived illness, heartache, and disappointment. Yet, somehow, I found real love and passion in the end. Yes, the kind you read about in romance novels really does exist! That is why I feel compelled to write about overcoming obstacles in our lives and healing old wounds. It is only then that we can be open to love.